Chris Mullin is the Labour Party Member of Parliament for Sunderland South. He is also the author of *A Very British Coup* and *Error of Judgement*, an investigation of the biggest murder in British history – the Birmingham pub bombings – for which he believes six innocent men were convicted. As a journalist he has travelled extensively in Asia, reporting from Vietnam both during and after the war. He lives in Sunderland.

D0809870

The Last Man Out of Saigon

Chris Mullin

CORGI BOOKS

THE LAST MAN OUT OF SAIGON

A CORGI BOOK 0 552 13259 4

Originally published in Great Britain by Victor Gollancz Ltd.

PRINTING HISTORY

Victor Gollancz edition published 1986
Corgi edition published 1988

Copyright © Chris Mullin 1986

Conditions of sale
1. This book is sold subject to the condition that it shall not, by
way of trade *or otherwise*, be lent, re-sold, hired out or otherwise
circulated in any form of binding or cover other than that in
which it is published *and without a similar condition including
this condition being imposed on the subsequent purchaser.*
2. This book is sold subject to the Standard Conditions of Sale
of Net Books and may not be re-sold in the UK below the net
price fixed by the publishers for the book.

This book is set in 10/11 pt Plantin
by Colset Private Limited, Singapore.

Corgi Books are published by Transworld Publishers Ltd.,
61–63 Uxbridge Road, Ealing, London W5 5SA, in Australia
by Transworld Publishers (Australia) Pty. Ltd., 15–23 Helles
Avenue, Moorebank, NSW 2170, and in New Zealand by
Transworld Publishers (N.Z.) Ltd., Cnr. Moselle and
Waipareira Avenues, Henderson, Auckland.

Made and printed in Great Britain by
Hazell Watson & Viney Limited
Member of BPCC plc
Aylesbury Bucks

*For Ngoc
and for Vietnam*

"And ye shall know the truth
 And the truth shall make ye free"

A quotation from The Gospel According to St John etched on
the entrance lobby of CIA headquarters at Langley, Virginia

The Last Man
Out of Saigon

Chapter One

MacShane was on a hiking tour in Colorado when the shit hit the fan in Saigon.

When he got back to Denver there was a cable waiting. It said: COME HOME SOONEST STOP MOM STOP. That was Lazarowitz's idea of deep cover. The cable was four days old and the girl at the front desk said a man had telephoned twice. From Washington, she thought. There was no message.

MacShane took the elevator to his room on the third floor. He shaved and showered. The hot water was his first in ten days, but there was no time to appreciate it. From his suitcase he took clean underwear and a shirt. From a hanger in the wardrobe he took a pair of grey flannels and a sports jacket. 'Welcome back to civilisation,' he said aloud as he knotted his tie in front of the mirror on the wardrobe.

There was no time to scrape the mud from his walking boots so he wrapped them in an old copy of the *Denver Post* and placed them in the bottom of the suitcase. Then he transferred ten days' worth of dirty laundry from his backpack to the suitcase.

There was also a Pentax and four capsules of exposed film, a Hemingway novel and a pack of vitamin pills. When the backpack was empty he dismantled the aluminium frame and placed the parts in the case, on top of the dirty laundry. After thirty minutes he was back in the lobby checking out. The girl at the desk said she hardly recognised him.

MacShane took a cab to the airport and went straight to the United Airlines counter. There was a flight to Chicago within the hour. From there he could pick up a connection.

At a payphone in the departure lounge he dialled a number in Washington.

'Curzon Brothers Exports,' said a woman's voice.

'I'd like to speak to the vice president.'

'Who shall I say is calling?'

'I'm ringing about a consignment of wheat for Saudi Arabia. The invoice number is One-Seven-Zero-Three.'

It was a charade they went through every time he phoned into Langley. Lazarowitz insisted on it, though God alone knew why. Lazarowitz's cover had been well and truly blown four years back, during the Phoenix hearings. His picture had even made the *New York Times*. He was supposed to have been giving evidence in closed session, but the East Coast press was no respecter of secrets any more. Not since the Pentagon Papers.

'Putting you through now, sir.'

There was a click and Lazarowitz came on. 'Where the hell have you been, MacShane?'

'On vacation.'

'Vacation? The whole world's coming to an end and you're on vacation. You're supposed to leave a contact number.'

'There aren't many telephones in the Rocky Mountains.'

'MacShane, you're an asshole.'

'I'll be in Washington in six hours. See you.'

MacShane replaced the receiver. At the news-stand he bought an evening paper. The headline over the main story was in letters two inches high. It said: REDS TAKE HUE.

Night was falling when MacShane landed at National. It was raining, as it often did in March, and the puddles were full of neon light. When he got to Langley it was dark, but Lazarowitz was still at his desk in the basement. Pale, fat and mean as ever. With him was another man with grey crewcut hair and cruel blue eyes.

'This is Steiner,' said Lazarowitz. 'He's from East Asia Division.'

12

Steiner did not shake hands, but bowed slightly. Another bloody German, thought MacShane. The secret parts of Washington were crawling with them.

'We have got a job for you,' growled Lazarowitz.

'In Saigon,' said Steiner.

'But I've never set foot in Vietnam.'

'That's why we're sending you,' said Lazarowitz. He was smoking as he always did. The smoke drifted upwards in the airless room. On the desk between them there was a framed picture of a leaner, fitter Lazarowitz with Robert MacNamara taken in Saigon ten years ago. They were standing in front of a wall chart which listed each province in Vietnam alongside a figure giving the percentage of the population alleged to have been pacified. It read like the election results in Albania – An Giang, 100 per cent; Thua Thien, 100 per cent; Gia Dinh, 99.9 per cent; and so on down to Pleiku which was only 74.9 per cent pacified. The picture showed Lazarowitz explaining the finer points of pacification to Defense Secretary MacNamara.

It had marked the high spot of Lazarowitz's career. Soon afterwards Congress started taking an interest in pacification and Lazarowitz had been called upon to give evidence at the hearings. Some Congressmen thought he had pacified a few Vietnamese too many, and Lazarowitz's replies only seemed to confirm that impression.

One old pinko from Wisconsin had asked Lazarowitz how many 'liberals' he thought had been pacified.

'Sir,' replied Lazarowitz, looking the senator straight in the eyes, 'what you call liberals, I call communists.'

Later, during the lunchtime recess, Lazarowitz was overheard to remark, 'They're all VC once they're dead.' That did it. When the hearing resumed the pinkos had a field day. Lazarowitz never set foot in Vietnam again. From then on he was confined to Langley, running agents in Bolivia and Brazil from a small, windowless office in the basement. That was how he came to be in charge of MacShane.

'Charlie's rolling up the map,' said Lazarowitz. 'The entire

13

central highlands have gone in ten days. Today they took Hue. Da Nang will be gone by Sunday.'

'After that,' said Steiner, 'the road is clear all the way to Saigon.'

'What do you want me to do? Traffic duty?'

Steiner's eyes were hollow. He had sat up all night charting the advance of the North Vietnamese Army as it closed in on Da Nang. The wires between Langley and the White House were humming. The National Security Advisor was demanding to know what would happen next. Would they stop at Da Nang? Could they be stopped further down the coast? Could Saigon and the Delta be held?

Steiner didn't know the answers. Nor did anyone else at Langley. And as for the Saigon station, it was a joke. Saigon hadn't picked up even a whiff of the attack on Ban Me Thuot, which had begun the offensive, until four hours after it started. For months Defense Intelligence had been reporting the movement of troops and supplies and yet no one in Washington had foreseen what was coming. ARVN intelligence had picked up nothing. Nor had a single CIA field agent. Now it appeared that the entire North Vietnamese High Command was in the South and nobody had picked that up either. It was another disaster, but Steiner did not panic. He had seen a lot of disasters in his time.

'MacShane, I am no longer concerned with the present. Thieu is finished. The Saigon regime is finished. It will last one or two months. A year at the most.'

The faster Steiner spoke the more the German surfaced in his voice.

'I am concerned with the future. With what comes afterwards. The Communists will enjoy a short honeymoon and then discover they have bitten off more than they can chew. We estimate that in the whole of Saigon they have not more than 2,000 cadres. Not enough to run a city of four million, mostly hostile people.'

They were interrupted by one of Lazarowitz's coughing fits. It erupted from deep inside, fuelled by regular intakes of nicotine. When it subsided, Steiner continued.

'Without our aid the Southern economy will collapse. In the last 12 months alone we've put in two billion dollars. We paid the army, the police, the civil service. We are flying in thousands of tons of rice and every drop of oil in the country. When that stops the whole pack of cards will come tumbling down.'

'With any luck,' added Lazarowitz, 'it will destabilise the North as well.'

You had to admire these guys. Here they were on the eve of the greatest disaster in the history of American foreign policy and they were already planning for the next victory.

'So, where do I fit in?'

'We have to be in a position to take advantage of the collapse when it comes.'

Collapse. What collapse? The only collapse in sight was already happening. Half Thieu's army were running down Highway One as fast as their little legs would carry them. The General himself was rumoured to be trying to persuade Swissair to evacuate South Vietnam's gold reserves under his name, and these guys were calmly discussing the collapse of communism in Vietnam. One of us has to be mad, thought MacShane.

'Carl,' said Lazarowitz, indicating Steiner, 'has asked me to make you available.'

'We want you to go into Saigon and stay put when the Communists hit town,' said Steiner.

'You're joking.'

But Steiner was not joking. His cold blue eyes showed not a spark of light.

'You will go under journalist cover, same as before. There are a lot of journalists in Saigon right now and many of them will stay on when the other side hits town. You will not be noticed.'

'Mr Steiner,' said MacShane, 'I spent two years in Bolivia and three in Brazil. I speak fluent Spanish and Portuguese and I have never been further East than Boston. Can you explain how this equips me to assist in the recapture of Vietnam?'

15

'Listen, asshole.' It was Lazarowitz who replied. 'All our networks in Saigon have been blown. The embassy is leaking like a sieve. The Russians and the DRV have between them the names of just about every CIA agent who has so much as stopped over at Tan Son Nhut airport. We need someone who is smart, who is clean and who has never set foot in Saigon before. And that someone is you.'

Chapter Two

'Bangkok,' intoned the man from UPI, 'is the biggest cess pit in the world.' They were in a traffic jam on Siam Square. It was noon and it was hot. The air was a haze of exhaust fumes. The taxi driver in the car behind leaned on his horn and soon everyone had joined in. It made no difference. Nothing moved.

'I pictured Thailand as a land of temples, canals and wooden houses on stilts,' said MacShane.

'That's what I thought until I came here.' Stevens edged forward five yards. On the kerb stood a policeman in skin-tight pants and dark glasses, his head shaved almost to the bone. 'Any illusions I had disappeared on my second day here when I saw a Buddhist monk in dark glasses, smoking a cigarette, leaning over a juke box.'

'Saigon will be worse.'

'No, funnily enough. Only explanation I can think of is that the French got there before Uncle Sam. Civilised by comparison to this place.'

They inched past the policeman, who observed the scene philosophically, thumbs lodged in his gun belt. The truck in front belched fumes. Stevens wound up the window. It was a choice between suffocating from the heat or being poisoned by carbon monoxide. They sat in silence for a moment and then Stevens spoke again. 'Let me get this straight. You are going to Vietnam, right?'

'Yup.'

'To cover a war which has been going on for thirty years.'

'Yup.'

17

'And which will be over before the rainy season.'
MacShane did not reply. At the roadside a group of girl labourers in straw hats and sarongs hacked away at the dry earth, their faces masked against the exhaust fumes.

'And you have never so much as set foot in Vietnam in your life?'

'Nope.'

'With all due respect, don't you think you have arrived a little late in the day?'

MacShane trotted out his story. It had been rehearsed at the safe house in Maryland. Forum World Features was a London-based agency. Small but respectable. He'd done some stringing for them in Brazil a few years back and they had taken a shine to him. Now they had signed him up for Saigon. Of course, it was a bit sudden. He had been on holiday in Colorado when the call came (that part, at least, was true). Apparently their main man had gone down with malaria. Their number two was in Angola. So they had sent out an SOS for MacShane. They didn't seem troubled by his lack of a track record in Vietnam, so why should he be?

They lunched on the terrace of the Oriental Hotel, watching small boats navigating the filth of the Chaophraya River. Stevens, it emerged, had not seen a lot of action either. Just two days in Saigon, filling in for the Bureau chief, who had a touch of dysentery. A day trip to Phnom Penh, courtesy of the American embassy. That was about the extent of his career as a war correspondent. Like most agency reporters, he never strayed far from his telex. He was a rewriter of handouts, a retailer of tit-bits from off-the-record briefings, an attender of press conferences given by Congressmen returning from fact-finding missions.

He was forty, balding and in a rut. And if there was one thing he resented it was special correspondents picking his brains as they stopped over in Bangkok on their way to a war that he would never see.

It was the story of Stevens's life. He had been based in Hong Kong in '71 when the special correspondents passed through with the American table-tennis team on their way to Peking. He had been minding shop in Buenos Aires in '73 when Allende was overthrown in Chile and instead of sending him in, head office parachuted in some creep from Washington who didn't even speak Spanish. Now here he was, dining on the terrace of the Oriental with an ignorant hick who was on his way to witness the fall of Saigon. Stevens was bitter and he didn't mind admitting it.

The breeze from the river relieved the heat but brought with it a smell of rotten garbage. A small girl with a garland of white lilies moved from table to table with wide, pleading eyes.

'You'll just get there in time to be evacuated,' said Stevens with a malicious grin.

'I wasn't planning to evacuate.'

'If you've got any sense you will. Some nasty stories coming out of Phnom Penh since the new boys took over.'

'Cambodia's not like Vietnam. The North Vietnamese Army is one of the most disciplined in the world.' Or so Lazarowitz had said.

The small girl with the lilies was being shooed away by a waiter. Stevens scooped out a last mouthful of papaya. 'We had a report this morning of crucifixions in Hue.'

'CIA propaganda,' said MacShane. Lazarowitz had said that too.

When it was dark Stevens took him on a tour of the night-life. They started in the coffee shop of the Grace Hotel, just off Sukhumvit. There were a lot of foreigners, mainly middle-aged Germans and a few Arabs, here and there a long-haired traveller with no money to spend.

'Place was going to pot after the GIs stopped coming. Hotels were empty. Prices tumbled. Then travel agents started bringing in customers by the plane load.' Stevens gestured towards a large Anglo-Saxon with greying crew-cut hair and a belly which overspilled his trousers. The man was fondling a slim Thai girl, half his size and half his age.

'They're like children who've gotten lose in a candy store,' said Stevens. 'Imagine. Twenty years on the production line in a Volkswagen factory. Wife is going to seed. Nearest thing to pleasure is a beer festival in Bavaria. Suddenly you discover an endless supply of pussy. Young. Beautiful. And all for the price of a ticket to the movies.'

The big Anglo-Saxon was nuzzling the girl's neck. One plump paw was planted firmly on her small breast. She gave the appearance of smiling. It was one of the fixed smiles that film stars and politicians put on for the cameras.

Stevens ordered two beers and they sat down at an empty table. A juke box played 'Let's go to San Francisco'. Stevens shouted to make himself heard above the din. 'Six months ago the Ministry of Tourism carried out a survey on what attracted tourists to Thailand. Was it the smiles? The temples? The golden beaches?'

The beers came. MacShane paid with a 50 baht note and waved away the change.

'Do you know what the survey concluded?' Stevens took a sip of his beer and almost at once beads of perspiration glistened on his forehead. 'It concluded that 75 per cent of all tourists came to Thailand for the fucking.' Stevens guffawed and took another sip of his beer. MacShane smiled weakly.

The girls stood around in groups of two or three, sipping orange juice and giggling. Those who were less good-looking made eyes at the customers. On the whole, they were modestly clothed in bright new dresses which came down to their knees. Sometimes there was one in tight trousers or a blouse that exaggerated her breasts or bottom, but most had an air of innocence. They might have been West Coast college girls had they not been whores.

There were Thai men too. Some were pimps. Some were the sons of generals. They all expected to marry virgins and they all hated foreigners who fucked their women.

The girls' room was brightly lit so that the customers could see them clearly, but they could not see the customers. On the wall was a small altar upon which sat a statue of the Buddha with joss sticks burning. 'Very religious people, the Thais,' said Stevens.

They were met at the door by the mamasan, a fat woman in a sarong. 'Take time,' she said. 'I have number one girls.'

They were young girls. Much younger than the freelance operators at the Grace. The youngest, MacShane guessed, was no more than fourteen. Their clothes were new but ill-fitting, suggesting that they had been purchased by someone else.

Around her neck each girl wore a piece of green cord to which was attached a number. 'Seven very good,' whispered fat mamasan. 'She give you number one good time.'

'Just looking,' said Stevens, but mamasan ignored him.

'You no like seven? Which you like? I give you good price. Short time 200 baht. If you want, you can have all night . . .'

'Shut up,' said MacShane, but mamasan affected not to understand.

'Maybe you like young girls.' She indicated number 13. A thin, shy girl who sat apart from the others. She wore a turquoise smock that was several sizes too large for her and in her hair she had a big red ribbon that had been put there by someone else. Her wide eyes seemed on the edge of tears and she gazed vacantly into the darkness beyond the sound-proof screen, remembering perhaps her brothers and sisters in a little wooden house of stilts on a river bank in northern Thailand.

'Number 13 very new,' said mamasan. 'Come last week from Cheng Mai. For her I charge extra 50 baht. Cheng Mai girl very good.'

MacShane had seen all this before in Bolivia and Brazil. He didn't like it then and he didn't like it now. 'Let's get out of here,' he said.

Fat mamasan followed them to the door. 'You no like my girls? I give you best price. Short time only 100 baht.' She was a woman without shame.

After a couple of beers in a bar on Patphong, Stevens said he had something special to show. A trick you wouldn't see anywhere else in the world. A speciality of Bangkok. He led the way out of the bar and down Patphong, brushing aside

21

pimps with offers of girls who did unmentionable things with cucumbers and table-tennis balls.

They crossed the street into an alley, at the entrance to which was a sign made up of light bulbs. Half the bulbs had fused, but it was still possible to make out the sign. It said BAR MONTMARTRE, and below it was an arrow pointing down the alley. At the end of the alley was a narrow staircase which creaked as they went up. At the top was a shifty-looking youth in an Ohio State University T-shirt. As they reached him, the youth banged twice on the door, which opened just wide enough to admit them.

The inside was a gloomy roof with a low ceiling. On one side was a makeshift bar at which sat a middle-aged European who was being attended to by two small girls in T-shirts and sarongs. Along the opposite wall sat four plump Thai men, sharing a bottle of Mekong whisky.

Stevens and MacShane took seats at the bar, beside the European, who did not give them so much as a glance. A girl behind the bar placed two beers in front of them and scribbled out a bill which she placed in a little plastic cup. A fat woman approached. She seemed to know Stevens and smiled broadly when he whispered a request.

One of the girls who had been attending the foreigner disappeared behind a screen and emerged clad only in a pair of thin black knickers. She was carrying a roll of bamboo mat, a box of tissues, a felt pen and a quarto-size drawing pad which she placed on the floor in the centre of the room.

The girl had large, firm breasts which belied her small body. MacShane guessed she was about 17. Someone put a record on the stereo. It was P.P. Arnold singing 'Angel of the Morning'. It reminded MacShane of his youth in Vermont. It brought back memories of dances in the scout hut on summer nights, and of Sally-Anne Clark, the first girl he ever kissed. It was a reminder of an age of innocence. Too good a song for a dump like this.

> *Just call me Angel of the Morning,*
> *Touch my cheek before you leave.*

The girl gyrated half-heartedly to the music, her face blank, her breasts scarcely moving.

> *Just call me Angel of the Morning,*
> *Then slowly turn and walk away.*

The music stopped. Still without expression, the girl stepped out of the black knickers and threw them in the direction of the Thai men. She then stooped and unrolled the bamboo mat, over which she squatted, legs apart. She placed the drawing pad on the mat between her feet. Then, taking the felt-tipped pen, she wrapped the end in tissue and proceeded to insert it, grimacing as it went in. The pen protruded about two inches, wedged tightly between her legs.

The European at the bar had not even turned round. The other girls watched, expressionless. The Thai men were mumbling encouragement. MacShane affected disinterest. Stevens was practically drooling.

Then, squatting over the drawing pad, the girl started to write, using only the movement of her hips. She wrote quickly in bold, clear strokes and when she had finished she gave a little smile of triumph and held up her work for everyone to admire. In letters two inches high she had written: WELCOME TO BAR MONTMARTRE. It was in English and the spelling was correct.

The girl did not wait for an encore. Turning her back on the audience, she removed the pen and tissue and stooped to recover the bamboo mat. Then, giggling nervously, she scampered out through a door at the back. The stereo was playing P.P. Arnold again:

> *You don't know what it's like,*
> *Baby, you don't know what it's like*
> *To love somebody . . .*

The European at the bar still sat with his back to the room, as he had done throughout the performance. The Thai men offered desultory applause and went back to their Mekong whisky.

Fat mamasan approached brandishing a plastic beaker containing what purported to be a bill for the beers. 'You like show?' she said. MacShane said nothing. He felt dirty. He was thinking of women he respected. His mother; his teenage sister; Josie, the last girl he had loved. What would they say if they could see him now? He had only had such thoughts once before: in an army barracks outside Recife watching a young man writhing on a wooden bed frame while two Brazilian sergeants dosed him with electricity.

Stevens took a bundle of notes from the breast pocket of his safari jacket and counted out 300 baht for the mamasan. She was reciting a range of other services which her girls could supply, but MacShane was already halfway to the door.

Outside the air seemed cool after the claustrophobia of the Bar Montmartre. They walked quickly away, brushing aside the pimps and the children selling peanuts. 'Don't say you didn't like the show,' said Stevens.

MacShane walked on without replying.

'Culture shock, that's what's the matter with you,' pronounced Stevens. It was always the same with first-timers, but it never lasted more than a fortnight.

When they reached Silom, MacShane said he'd be going. Stevens didn't argue. He had never taken to MacShane anyway. A taxi cruised to a halt beside them. Stevens opened the rear door and got inside. 'I'll drop you at the Oriental.'

'I'll walk,' said MacShane.

He woke up six hours later to the sound of a waiter clearing his throat on the terrace below his window. A long, gargling intake of breath, followed by a sudden expectoration.

MacShane's head ached. Half the night he had spent chasing mosquitoes. Eventually, he had gone in search of assistance and aroused a sullen youth who flatly declined to believe that there could be a single mosquito in the Oriental Hotel. Only when MacShane exhibited a 10 baht note was the youth persuaded to acknowledge the possibility by producing a box of matches and a mosquito coil.

After a breakfast of papaya and black coffee, MacShane

took a taxi to the airport. The headline on the *Bangkok Post* said THIEU FLEES. MacShane bought a copy at an airport news-stand. Apparently the General had been seen off the premises by the American ambassador. 'I just said "goodbye",' the ambassador was quoted as saying. 'Nothing historic, just "goodbye".'

Chapter Three

Apart from MacShane, there were just six passengers on the flight into Saigon – two journalists, three spooks and a worried-looking Vietnamese who sat chain-smoking throughout the flight. In heavily-accented English he told anyone who would listen that he had come from Paris to get his relatives out, but feared that he was too late.

The journalists were both Europeans in safari jackets. Each carried a typewriter festooned with airline labels. One, an Englishman, eyed MacShane with suspicion. The other, an Italian, told stories which he seemed to find extremely funny.

The spooks were clean-cut young men with close-cropped hair. They wore identical blazers and carried identiccal attache cases.

MacShane sat well away from everyone, wondering which he resembled more, the journalists or the spooks.

The Air Vietnam hostesses wore pale blue *ao dais* and smiled nervously at each of the passengers. The pilot was one of those Americans who make a speciality of understatement.

'Ladies and gentlemen,' he drawled, 'welcome aboard this Air Vietnam flight to Saigon. We shall be cruising at approximately 30,000 feet and, because Cambodia is under new management, we shall not be stopping over at Phnom Penh.'

A report in the *Bangkok Post* said that Cambodia's new management were emptying the cities and killing everyone connected with the old regime, down to the rank of corporal.

'Our flight time will be approximately two hours,' continued the pilot. 'On behalf of Air Vietnam I wish you a pleasant journey.' A hostess repeated the message, first in

26

French and then in Vietnamese, her voice on the edge of tears.

In a pocket on the back of every seat there was a glossy brochure published by the Ministry of Tourism. *Welcome to Vietnam*, it said. *We have many facilities for tourists.* It went on to extol such attractions as the beach at Da Nang and the Perfume River at Hue. MacShane could not suppress a smile. General Giap was probably running day trips on the Perfume River by now.

They were out over the Gulf of Siam when MacShane got to thinking that he must be mad. It had been so different when he had signed up in '64. That was in the days before Watergate, Chile and My Lai. Before Vietnam veterans started throwing away their medals on the steps of the Capitol.

In those days fighting communism had been an honourable profession. In those days, of course, America had been winning.

In Bolivia MacShane had it easy. He'd invested in a politician or two, a general and several colonels. Even a bishop. A man in the La Paz Central Post Office provided photostats of all mail to and from communist countries. A woman at Bolivian Airlines passed on copies of the passenger lists. He had a man inside the tin miners' union and there had been a couple of half-hearted attempts to set up Eastern Bloc diplomats. And there had been coups, of course. But coups were part of life in Bolivia. No one cared much about Bolivia. At least, not until Che Guevara showed up in '67, and by that time MacShane was in Brazil.

By then most of the dirty work was over in Brazil. In the early sixties the Company had pumped twenty million dollars into the elections. After it was over there had been an enquiry, but five of its nine members had been bank-rolled by the Company. That, together with the refusal of the American banks to reveal the source of funds deposited for their clients, had kept the lid on.

Not that it mattered. By '64 the CIA had had enough of playing politics and opted instead for a coup. By the time

MacShane arrived, Brazil was well and truly in friendly hands. There was even a modest economic boom underway.

After Brazil there had been a spell at Langley. Sifting, analysing, recommending from an office overlooking the Potomac. It had been easy work. There were no crises. The heat was in South-East Asia. At least, it was until Chile blew up.

At Langley, MacShane was promoted to GS 12. Not bad at thirty-three. They even asked him to do a little lecturing to the new recruits at Camp Peary. He spent a week showing them how to do dead drops and live drops, how to open diplomatic pouches and how to recruit agents. It was hard to think of the lady at Bolivian Airlines or the little man at the post office in La Paz as agents, but the kids at Camp Peary seemed impressed.

It was while he was at Langley that MacShane met Josie, the daughter of a professor at a West Coast university. Josie was different from the other girls he had been with. Usually MacShane went with Company girls. Secretaries, clerical assistants and even a GS 8. Going with Company girls meant that there was no need for elaborate cover stories.

In Brazil he had once had a six months' fling with the secretary to the military attaché, a Baptist minister's daughter from Pennsylvania. She had been a girl largely innocent in the ways of the world until MacShane enlightened her a little. It was not love, but it was fun.

In Bolivia he had set up home briefly with the daughter of a local businessman. She had done wonders for his Spanish, but left him after three months for a cocaine smuggler.

Josie was majoring in politics at George Washington University. MacShane found her one evening in the laundry room of his apartment block.

'Excuse me,' she said, 'can you loan me a quarter for the dryer?'

MacShane took a handful of change from his back pocket and handed her a quarter. 'As good an opening line as any,' he said.

'What makes you think it's an opening line?'

'Never know your luck.'

She smiled and said nothing, but by the time she had had a quarter's worth of drying time MacShane knew where she went to university, what she studied, that she shared an apartment two blocks away with two other girls, and that her father was a professor. By the time he had helped her fold her sheets he also knew that she had a brother who was about to be drafted for Vietnam.

Afterwards he gave her a lift home in his blue-and-white Ford Pinto.

'Come up for coffee.'

'How do you know I'm not a rapist?'

'Don't worry,' she said sweetly, 'I'm a black belt in karate.'

The apartment was up-market for students. There was a night-porter, an answer-phone and carpets in the corridors. The other girls were Jane and Marie. Jane was short, dark and Jewish. Marie was thin, blonde and shy.

There was a Bob Dylan record on the stereo. The bathroom door was half open and through it MacShane could see knickers drying on the towel rail. On the wall in the living room there was a large framed picture of Che Guevara. It occurred to MacShane that he was about to meet unpatriotic Americans.

Marie disappeared into a bedroom as soon as the introductions were over. Josie went to make coffee. He was alone with Jane.

'Where you from? she asked.

'Two blocks up the road.'

'I meant originally.'

'Vermont.'

'Nice place, Vermont.'

'Yes, nice place.' He ran his eye along the bookshelves. Novels mostly. Hemingway, D.H. Lawrence, Steinbeck. His eyes came to rest on a book by Noam Chomsky, *At War with Asia*. He picked it out and flicked through the pages.

'You read this?'

'No. It belongs to Josie. She's been into Vietnam since her brother got drafted.'

Josie reappeared carrying three mugs of coffee on a tray. She had blue eyes that sparkled and a complexion that had seen a lot of sunshine. MacShane noticed for the first time that she wore no make-up.

'Chomsky's speaking at the university on Wednesday evening. We're all going. You can come too, if you want.'

MacShane was about to reply that Chomsky was a traitor who shouldn't be allowed to poison young minds, but he just stopped himself.

'Unfortunately I have an engagement on Wednesday.'

Not until she slept with him did Josie manage to wring out of MacShane what he did for a living. It was the week Nixon mined Haiphong harbour. They were in bed at his apartment. The lights were out but the curtains were open and the darkness was broken intermittently by the headlights of passing cars.

'You lied to me.'

'I didn't.'

'You said you were in business.'

'I didn't say what business.'

She had gone limp in his arms. From two blocks away came the distant wail of a police siren. Untangling herself from him Josie shifted to the side of the bed. She lay facing away. They were not touching at any point.

The wailing police siren drew closer. It was a full minute before she spoke again. 'Have you ever killed anyone?'

He laughed. 'Of course not. Mostly I just shuffle paper. Reports, analysis, that sort of thing.'

'The CIA has killed a lot of people.'

'You shouldn't believe the nonsense peddled by people like Chomsky.' The wail of the police siren was receding into the distance. An image of the boy being dosed with electricity in the barracks at Recife flashed through MacShane's mind, but he did not allow it to temper his indignation. 'The CIA doesn't kill people. It's an intelligence organisation. We collect information.'

'What about Operation Phoenix? It's all been in the *Times*.'

'Lies and exaggeration. Typical of the East Coast press. Anything to slander America.' He paused and then added quietly, 'Anyway, Vietnam's not my department. I deal with South America.'

Later it occurred to MacShane that this was the first time in his career that he had been called upon to defend the Company to a girl-friend. Most girls he went with were only too happy to make it with a GS 12 from the Western Hemisphere Division.

MacShane had not expected to see Josie again, but she came back. She returned one evening in the fall bearing two tickets for a Bob Dylan concert. She said she had won them in a college lottery, but later admitted she had queued all night to buy them. He hadn't the heart to tell her that in his book Bob Dylan was a communist too.

They stayed together all that year and most of the next. She moved gradually. First she left a toothbrush in the bathroom. Then a change of clothes in the wardrobe. Then she left her Bob Dylan records. By the time the first snow fell her mail had started arriving at MacShane's apartment. He let her put her books on his shelves. She even found space for Chomsky between a couple of Robert Ludlums and an Ed McBain.

Only the picture of Che Guevara was left in Josie's trunk, hidden under MacShane's double bed. Chomsky was bad enough, but MacShane drew the line at Che Guevara. Lazarowitz would have had a fit, if he had known.

Of course Lazarowitz had to be told about Josie. It was an Agency rule that anyone mixing with a security risk had to own up at once. MacShane waited until she had moved in before sending a memorandum to Lazarowitz. He said no more than he had to. Just that she was a second-year student at George Washington University. He gave her parents' names and address, but said nothing about Che Guevara and Chomsky. Lazarowitz summoned him at once.

'A student. What kind of student?'

'Politics and urban studies.'

'What sort of politics?'

'How should I know?'

'Don't bullshit me, MacShane. Of course you know.'

'Theory. Just theory.'

'Marx, Mao, Ho Chi Minh? That's all kids seem to learn about these days. Treason, I call it.'

'We don't talk about it much.'

Lazarowitz lit a Stuyvesant. It was his twentieth since breakfast. The ashtray was overflowing with the remains of its predecessors. He opened his mouth to speak again, but the words dissolved into one of his coughing fits. MacShane passed the time looking at the picture of Lazarowitz with Robert MacNamara. In those days Lazarowitz had all his hair and only one chin. The Lazarowitz in the photograph bore almost no resemblance to the spluttering ruin MacShane now saw in front of him. If that was what five years in windowless rooms could do to a man, maybe he should take Josie's advice and quit while he was still ahead.

'If you know what's good for you, MacShane –' Lazarowitz had found his voice again – 'you'll dump her.'

'There's nothing in the regulations. . . .'

'Fuck the regulations.' Lazarowitz took a drag on his Stuyvesant, and when he resumed his voice was tinged with an uncharacteristic note of concern. 'Listen, MacShane. You're a GS 12. You're 34 and your record is clean. Why louse up a good career over some 20-year-old freak.' In Lazarowitz's world anybody who read books was a freak.

Josie stayed all through the winter and into the next summer. MacShane rearranged the spare bedroom so that she could use it to study and she came to treat it as her own. She put up her pictures – a poster from the Bob Dylan concert, a David Hockney reproduction from a magazine and once, just to annoy him, she got out the picture of Che Guevara and put that up too. When they were friends again she took it down and put it back in the trunk under the bed. Later they laughed about it.

They bought an old varnished dining table in a thrift store and Josie used it as a desk. On her desk she set up a small framed photograph of her family – Mum, Dad and a younger sister. Like Josie, they were lean, blond, sun-tanned West Coast people. Josie's father was a McGovern supporter and Josie said she was too. She told MacShane that all the kids at her college were McGovern supporters and two weeks before the election she brought home a large picture of McGovern and stuck it on the wall in her room next to the Bob Dylan poster. That was what caused their first big row.

'You'll get me fired, if anyone finds out about this,' he had shouted at her.

'In that case I'd be doing you a favour.' Josie looked magnificent when she was angry. She gritted her perfect teeth, her blue eyes gleamed, and a lock of hair fell across her forehead and bobbed back and forth with each sudden movement of her head. She never lost an opportunity to bug MacShane about his work. 'Anyway, I thought you were supposed to be defending freedom. Or isn't your idea of freedom large enough to cope with a picture of George McGovern?'

'It's my apartment and I'll decide what goes on the walls.' MacShane knew he'd lost once he reduced the argument to this level.

'I thought you were my lover, not my landlord.' And with that she disappeared into her room and slammed the door. After a few minutes he heard the sound of Rolling Stones music coming from Josie's stereo. And just to bug him she turned it up loud.

If it was a big row, he would not see her again until morning. She would sleep in the spare bed and not emerge until after he had left for Langley. A small row would be over in time for the late night news. The McGovern poster was a big row and it was two days before they made up.

In November McGovern was wiped out, just like MacShane had said he would be. Josie spent election night at her old apartment, with Jane and Maria. She said that, except for MacShane, she did not know anyone who supported Nixon. To which MacShane had retorted, that only went to show what limited circles she moved in.

By Christmas Nixon was bombing Hanoi again and even MacShane had trouble explaining that away. In the end he gave up trying and they agreed not to talk about it. They spent New Year with Josie's parents in Santa Barbara. Before they went Josie made him promise not to reveal where he worked. Josie had told her parents that MacShane worked in the PR department of an oil corporation (that was his Washington cover). The holiday passed uncomfortably. Josie's father, it turned out, was no more keen on oil companies than he was on CIA agents.

As for Lazarowitz, he raised the question of Josie from time to time, but did not press it. 'You still living with that young freak from California?' he would say. MacShane would nod and Lazarowitz would wander off, shaking his head and mumbling that MacShane could have had the pick of the girls at Langley.

Sometimes – usually when they lay together after making love – Josie would question him about his work. Usually he took refuge behind the regulations. When she pressed him, he resorted to generalities.

'What were you doing in Brazil?'

'Keeping out the Russians.'

'There aren't any Russians in Brazil.'

'No, but there would be, if we weren't there.'

'How do you know?'

'Look at Cuba. The place is crawling with Russians.'

When she didn't have an answer, Josie would go away and do some reading. Then she would bring the subject up again two or three days later.

'Cuba was a popular uprising. The Russians didn't have anything to do with it.'

'I told you, the Russians are all over Cuba.'

'But they came later. Only after Kennedy started trying to screw Castro.' She turned so that she was half on top of him. 'To be precise,' she said, 'it was the CIA who tried to bring down Castro.' She paused. He could feel her breath on his face in the darkness. 'Which is why I am so interested in what you do for a living, *Mr MacShane*.' She always used his surname when she was interrogating him.

'Bay of Pigs was in '61. Three years before I signed up.' Which was not the whole truth. Half the Western Hemisphere Division had worked on Cuba at one time or another.

Sometimes Josie would read something in a newspaper or learn at college a nugget of information which she would store up to ambush him with when she got home. 'Do you believe,' she said one evening while they were clearing away the supper dishes, 'that if the majority of people want a communist government, they should be allowed to have one?'

'Sure.'

'So that if the majority of people in Vietnam had wanted Ho Chi Minh, America would just have stood by and let him be elected?'

'Sure, but . . .' He was about to tell her that communists did not allow free elections.

'In that case, why didn't we allow the elections provided for in the 1954 Geneva Agreement to go ahead?'

He smiled and she swiped him with the dishcloth. 'Don't laugh at me. This is serious.'

'I give up.'

'Because the American government knew that if elections were held, Ho Chi Minh would win.'

'You've been reading Chomsky again.'

'Not Chomsky, Eisenhower. It's in his memoirs: *Mandate for Change*, page 372. I looked it up in the library.'

When he got to Langley next day, MacShane went straight to the library and dug out the Eisenhower memoirs. Josie was right. There it was in black and white. *'I have never talked or corresponded with a person knowledgeable in Indo-Chinese affairs,'* Eisenhower had written, *'who did not agree that, had elections been held at the time of fighting, possibly 80 per cent of the population would have voted for Ho Chi Minh.'*

They both knew that sooner or later it had to end. Either MacShane would get posted abroad or Josie would run across someone who shared her views on McGovern and Vietnam and who didn't object to her poster of Che Guevara.

Marriage never entered their heads. Josie wouldn't have made a good Company wife. In any case, she would never clear security. If he stayed with Josie, he'd end up pushing paper at Langley for the rest of his life. Lazarowitz had made that clear.

They had no friends in common. He couldn't introduce her to his friends and she didn't want to introduce him to hers. She had told Jane and Marie the same lie that she had told her parents – that MacShane worked for an oil company. On the rare occasions that his friends stopped by, Josie would shut herself in her room or take herself off to Jane and Marie's for the evening. At the end of the summer term, when the exams were over, she started going to college parties – without MacShane. He was welcome to come too, she said, but when he declined he sensed she was relieved.

The end came about two weeks after the coup in Chile. She had made him swear that he had nothing to do with it.

'I swear,' he said, raising his right hand, but she must have sensed that he was lying. He was up to his neck in Chile. So was everyone else in Western Hemisphere Division.

'So much for free elections,' she taunted.

He tried to argue. Allende only had 37 per cent of the votes, he said. But it only made matters worse.

She quizzed him about the reports of torture. At first he feigned ignorance. Then he said it was communist propaganda and that made her even madder. 'Don't give me that crap,' she shouted. 'People are being plugged into the electricity mains. You can read about it in *Time* and *Newsweek*. Or are they run by communists too?'

Later, when she had calmed down, she asked quietly whether he had ever heard of anybody being tortured with electricity when he was in Bolivia or Brazil. For a moment he glimpsed the face of a boy in the army barracks at Recife twisted in pain as the sergeant administered another 500 volts. He looked Josie straight in the eye. 'No,' he said, 'I never have.'

*   *   *

They were in bed one morning in late September when Josie announced that she was going. They had made love, as they often did before he went out to work. Or rather *he* had made love. Josie just lay still until he rolled off her. She let him catch his breath and then said, 'I've been thinking that it's about time we split.'

MacShane lay alongside her, his eyes fixed on the ceiling. Their bodies were not touching. 'I'm sorry,' he said.

'You don't sound very sorry.'

'What do you want me to say?' Maybe she had expected him to plead. Maybe even to cry. But his training had taught him not to show emotion.

'I thought you might at least ask why.'

'Why?'

'Can't you guess?'

'If I could, I wouldn't ask.'

'You are the most insensitive man I've ever met.'

'I'm sorry,' he said again. And with that he got up, showered, shaved, dressed and went to Langley.

When MacShane came home that evening she was gone. The bed was made. Her half of the wardrobe was empty. Her washbag was gone from the bathroom. The trunk was gone from under the bed. He looked in her room. The McGovern poster was gone. So were the Hockney print and the Dylan poster. Only the lighter patches on the wall showed where they had been.

On the living room table, opened out flat, was the picture of Che Guevara. Beside it, the Chomsky book. On the title page she had written: *To the most insensitive man I ever met, love Josie.* Beside her name there was a single kiss.

In the bottom right-hand corner of the poster she had written with a blue felt-tip pen, *A souvenir of Josie*.

MacShane looked at the poster and then at the inscription in the book. Then he did something he had never done before. He cried.

'Monsieur.' A hostess in a pale blue *ao dai* was offering a hot flannel. For a moment MacShane just blinked at her; then he reached across the two empty seats and took one. She smiled sadly.

Vietnam was now visible far below, a mass of palm trees dissected by mud-coloured rivers and canals. The houses were specks of brown thatch along the river banks.

MacShane pressed the steaming flannel to his face and then passed it back to the girl in the *ao dai*. She smiled sadly again and disappeared.

'Ladies and gentlemen,' said the pilot. 'In a few minutes we shall be landing at Saigon. The temperature on the ground is 37 degrees centigrade or 100 degrees fahrenheit, but that is the least of your problems.'

A hostess repeated the message, minus the embellishment, in French and then in Vietnamese.

The wheels came down with a dull crump. They were descending fast now. Below, the delta had given way to green fields of rice. Here and there were clustered houses with roofs of corrugated iron. There was a road too. Long, straight and treeless, its tarmac surface just wide enough for two cars to pass. Once or twice the gleam of the sun on a wing mirror gave away a vehicle, but by and large the road was empty.

Suddenly they were over Tan Son Nhut. The engines screamed as they were slammed into reverse. And there, stretched out along either side of the runway, were the remnants of General Thieu's airforce. The third largest in the world. Row after row of F5s and A-37s in pristine condition, separated by walls of sandbags. They were about to become a gift from the American taxpayer to the Vietnam People's Airforce.

By the time the plane taxied to a halt the other passengers were standing in the aisle, the three Americans holding their identical briefcases, the two Europeans clutching their typewriters. The worried-looking Vietnamese appeared to have no baggage.

The Air Vietnam hostesses stood in a line by the door. One of them was weeping openly. The tears trickled down her face and dripped on to her *ao dai*, making a small wet stain just above her breast. MacShane was thinking of Josie again. It was just as well she had left because she would never have forgiven him for this.

38

Chapter Four

'So,' said the immigration man, 'you have come to see my country die.'

MacShane said nothing. The man flicked carelessly through the passport and tossed it back across the counter. It was not clear whether he proposed to stamp it.

'For you Americans Vietnam just a game, like baseball. First you make us fight. Now you leave us to die. And all the time you take pictures.' He gestured at the Pentaxes slung round the neck of the men in safari jackets who stood uneasily behind MacShane.

'It's okay for the big men,' said the man from immigration. 'They go with you. The small men you leave behind. I am a small man . . .' His voice trailed off hopelessly.

MacShane picked up the passport and started walking away. The others followed. The immigration man did not call them back.

Someone had already dumped the luggage in the customs hall. There was no sign of anyone to inspect it and so they picked up their bags and started walking to the exit. MacShane's was a battered brown leather suitcase held shut with straps. It had been with him since Brazil.

Outside, the concourse was choked with Vietnamese. Trim little men in white sleeveless shirts: merchants, bankers, middle-rank police chiefs and army officers. People for whom the party was over, but who were not important enough to rate a ride out with the Americans.

Most of them brandished tickets bought with black market dollars for flights that no longer existed. The Pan Am desk

39

was closed. So was Singapore Airlines. And China Airways. That only left the Air Vietnam desk, to which the crowd laid seige in a jabbering mass. Behind it two more girls in pale blue *ao dais* pleaded for patience.

The centre of the concourse was piled high with luggage. Metal boxes, crates, suitcases, upon which perched bewildered grannies and young children. On the wall behind the Pan Am desk a framed picture of the General hung at 45 degrees. His forehead was marked by a single bullet hole. Someone had taken time off from the chaos to settle a personal score.

MacShane and the two journalists got outside just in time to see the three Americans disappearing into a black Chevrolet with diplomatic plates. It was moving even before the rear door was closed.

One of the journalists, the Italian, disappeared and came back with a man who was prepared to drive them into town for ten dollars.

'Only dollars,' he kept repeating. Last week one dollar was worth 750 piastres. Now it was worth 5,000.

The car was a spotless white Mercedes, so new that the upholstery was still covered in plastic. It had belonged to the director of the Hatien Cement Works – 'but he not need now,' said the driver with an eerie smile.

Overhead a C–141 transport roared into the sky. For a moment its huge belly eclipsed the sun and then it disappeared eastwards. Long after it was out of sight the engines could still be heard receding into the invisible distance.

'Evacuation,' said the Italian. 'The Americans are taking out the non-essentials.' He gestured towards a large warehouse. A crudely-painted sign with an arrow said that it was the office of the United States Defense Attaché.

A steady stream of non-essentials were making their way past the sign in the direction of the warehouse, all hoping for a place on the Great Freedom Bird. Families weighed down by great tin boxes labelled with the names of distant relatives in San Francisco, Seattle, Los Angeles, Paris, Lyons, Nanterre . . . anywhere but Saigon. Bar girls clutching Eurasian children and bits of paper with the misspelt addresses of long-forgotten GI boyfriends. Bank managers with briefcases bulging with stolen dollars. Secret policemen in civilian clothes, anxious to conceal their identity even from those with whom they were fleeing. Pimps, drug pushers, money changers and typists from the Bank of America. A girl who had once worked for a month for Associated Press. A steady stream of desperate people, all absolutely certain that their association with America, however tenuous, marked them out for terrible retribution under the new order. All making one last blind act of faith in Uncle Sam who had let them down so badly. All anxious to be anywhere but Saigon by the time the music stopped.

There were Americans too. Deserters, contractors, small-time racketeers. People who had disappeared from the official records years ago only to be smoked out by the impending disaster. Some were drunk, some stoned. Some herded along recently-acquired Vietnamese 'families' who had paid gold and dollars to Chinese middlemen to be adopted by an American, any American.

In those last crazy hours desperate fathers were approaching Americans in hotel lobbies and even in the street offering huge sums to anyone who would marry their beautiful daughters and save them from communism.

Weddings even took place at the Defense Attache's compound at the airport. In saner times a moment's thought would have been sufficient to realise that a young woman's virtue was far safer in the hands of a whole regiment of Communist soldiers than in those of some boozed-up contractor from Dallas, but these were not sane times.

The driver wove the white Mercedes out of the airport. No one tried to stop them leaving. There was a long queue of cars at the gate trying to gain admission. Soldiers were going from car to car, poking their M-16s through open windows and ransacking the luggage. The Italian was sitting in the front of the Mercedes, his typewriter on his lap. He turned and beamed at MacShane. He was glad to be back, he said. He had been expelled a month earlier for insulting the Chief of State and throwing mud at the Republic. Now the Chief of State had fled and no one cared any more who threw mud at the Republic. So the Italian had come back. And to make sure that he could not be expelled again he had come back on a plane that would not depart – the last one.

As they left Tan Son Nhut the Italian pointed out places of special interest. 'On our left – ' he indicated a run-down building with a roof of corrugated iron – 'the Magic Fingers Massage Parlour.' The doors were padlocked and the windows shuttered. Outside two girls were loading their meagre possessions on to a cyclo. They were dressed like peasants, but their permed hair and plucked eyebrows gave the game away. One still had traces of red varnish on her toenails. The Italian waved, but they ignored him. This was no time to be seen flirting with foreigners.

By the airport gate there was a stone inscribed in block letters. The inscription was in English and said: THE NOBLE SACRIFICE OF THE ALLIED SOLDIERS WILL NEVER BE FORGOTTEN.

They drove down a long tree-shaded avenue. Once or twice it was dissected by a railway line which no longer led anywhere. On either side there were villas behind high walls overhung with purple bougainvillaea and barbed wire. Some had empty sentry boxes reinforced with sandbags.

The Italian talked most of the way, sometimes to the driver in a mixture of French and English, sometimes to MacShane and the other journalist, a young Englishman who replied in monosyllables. The Italian talked about Vietnamese women, about the weather, about the French restaurants in Saigon and, of course, about the war.

Once they were stopped at a road block. A policeman ordered them out of the car and lined them up with their hands on the roof. For the first time the Italian stopped talking. The driver was white with fear. The policeman was shaking with anger. There was a terse exchange in Vietnamese, after which they were allowed back into the car and waved on. 'What did you tell him?' MacShane asked the driver, when the policemen were out of sight.

'I tell him you are not Americans.'

The white Mercedes took them into the centre of the city and dropped them outside the Continental Palace Hotel which, the Italian said, was where he always stayed. MacShane checked in at the Caravelle on the opposite side of the square. That was where Lazarowitz had told him to stay. 'On a clear day,' he had said, 'you can see the war from the roof.'

He was given a room on the fourth floor. Dinner was at seven. The curfew was at eight. From his window MacShane looked across the terrace of the Continental Palace. That was where Graham Greene had written *The Quiet American*, or so Lazarowitz had said. Although he never read books, Lazarowitz was not short on local colour. For good measure, he had added that Graham Greene was a son of a bitch and probably a communist too.

In the afternoon MacShane took a stroll to the post office. It was in the square by the cathedral, one of several places Lazarowitz had marked on a tattered map of the city with which he had presented MacShane on the day of his departure. Besides the post office Lazarowitz had marked the Reuter's office, a bar called Mimi's and the Café Givral which, he claimed, did the best breakfasts in Saigon.

At the post office MacShane produced his international cable card and persuaded a worried counter clerk to cable Forum World Features. The cable was marked for the attention of Jack Feinstein, whoever he was. It said: ARRIVED SAFELY STOP WILL FILE SOONEST STOP REGARDS MACSHANE. That was what he had agreed with Lazarowitz. Now it was just a matter of waiting.

On the way back to the hotel MacShane called at the Continental and found the Italian sipping a *citron pressé* at a table on the terrace. With him there was another, worried-looking Vietnamese with a wispy beard.

43

With a flourish of his hand, the Italian directed MacShane to an empty seat. With another flourish he summoned a waiter whom he made a point of calling by his first name in order to demonstrate that his contacts extended to the lowest in the land.

MacShane ordered a Budweiser.

'It seems they will not negotiate,' beamed the Italian. 'Not even with General Minh.' Outside the street was a tangle of Hondas and cycles, hooting horns and ringing bells. On the pavements small, pyjama-clad girls selling peanuts and cigarettes harassed pedestrians.

'My friend here – ' he indicated the anxious little Vietnamese with another wave of his manicured hand – 'has just come from the French embassy. Apparently Monsieur Merillon, the ambassador, has been out to the airport to talk to the PRG.' The Italian took a sip of his *citron pressé*. 'He found them digging bunkers.' For some reason he found this hilarious. *'Bunkers'*. He slapped the table with his hand. He was probably the only man in Saigon who found something to laugh about that day.

Overhead, there was a constant drone as the C–141s took off and landed at the airport. The Italian was giving his views on the French in general and on the Saigon French in particular. 'Their restaurants remain open. They are stocking up with camembert, salami and champagne ready to welcome the new order. They are confident they know how to deal with the Communists. A couple of free meals for the colonel in charge of relations with foreigners and life will go on.' He paused to stir his *citron pressé* with the end of a ball-point pen.

'They are in for a bad surprise, these French. Already they are hanging tricolours on their verandahs. They think that will make them safe, but they are so wrong. Many Viet Cong suffered their first taste of torture and imprisonment under the tricolour.' And with that he slapped the table again and embarked on a new round of guffaws. A nervous smile flashed across the face of the worried-looking Vietnamese and disappeared faster than the muzzle flash of a 130 mm cannon.

From the distance came the sound of a muffled explosion,

barely audible above the din of the traffic. The Italian stopped laughing abruptly and they listened. There it was again. Then again. 'Bien Hoa,' said the Vietnamese quietly. MacShane nodded. Bien Hoa was the airbase ten miles north-east of Saigon. Lazarowitz had said they would take that out first.

With evening came the curfew and the din on the streets subsided. The explosions at Bien Hoa could be heard clearly.

MacShane dined alone in the restaurant on the ninth floor of the Caravelle. He started with French onion soup, followed by steak in mushroom sauce, sauté potatoes and a glass of red wine. The waiter was one of the old school. He wore a white jacket, buttoned to the collar, and carried a serving cloth over his left arm. He apologised profusely for the lack of fresh vegetables. There would be no more until the war was over, he said. He seemed quite upset about it, as though the shortage of fresh vegetables reflected on him personally.

While dinner was served, an American journalist went from table to table making a note of everyone's name. 'For the evacuation,' he explained, when he reached MacShane's table.

'But I only just got here.'

'Look buddy, tonight they are shelling Bien Hoa. Tomorrow it will be the airport. After that the only way out is by helicopter. If you have any sense, you'll put your name down.'

'Suppose I don't?'

'In that case, buddy, you are on your own.'

'Thanks, but I'll pass.'

'Suit yourself.' The man shrugged and moved to the next table. He was what Lazarowitz sometimes referred to as a patriotic journalist. All week he had been writing bloodbath stories put out by the embassy. He didn't really believe them, but it irritated him to think that no one else did either.

After dinner MacShane took his coffee out on to the roof. It was nearly dark and there was a warm breeze. Someone was telling a story about a Vietnamese girl who was threatening suicide if he didn't help her get out. Someone else was saying that a CIA agent had been captured at Phan Rang.

45

MacShane's ears pricked up at that. 'Fellow by the name of Lewis. They've probably strung him up by the balls by now.'

An Englishman who had put his name down for the helicopter ride was justifying himself to someone who had not. 'It's not the Communists who scare me,' he was saying, 'it's what ARVN will do when they discover they've been betrayed.' Now that was one scenario Lazarowitz hadn't thought of. Or if he had, he sure hadn't mentioned it.

It was dark now. To the north the horizon was lit by orange flashes, each followed by a dull rumble. To begin with the flashes were evenly spaced at the rate of about one a minute. Gradually, however, the intervals narrowed until the sky was permanently alight and the rumble of the guns continuous. Bien Hoa would be gone by morning.

Chapter Five

MacShane went to bed around 22.00 hours. The guns at Bien Hoa were still rumbling. The flashes lit up the skyline. The journalists sat drinking among the potted palms on the roof of the Caravelle. Those who had decided to leave were still explaining why. Those who were staying were discussing the prospect of a bloodbath. Someone said there would be a new government in the morning, but no one thought it would make any difference.

It was 10.00 hours Washington time. By now Lazarowitz would be in his windowless room at Langley coughing his guts out. Poring over the night's cables from Saigon. Answering damn fool questions from the National Security Council and the State Department. Offering advice that was going to be ignored anyway.

Or maybe Lazarowitz was operating to a different time frame. Maybe he was working on his long-haul strategy. Perhaps he was already plotting the downfall of the next regime. Or the one after that. Perhaps he was not letting himself be distracted by a little matter like the fall of Saigon.

Outside Saigon was silent. In the square below, a lone policeman sat motionless on the steps of the National Assembly building, his head in his hands, his M–16 across his knees. From the shops and houses across the street light filtered from between the cracks in the shutters. Behind such shutters all over Saigon a thousand small deals were being done, a thousand small betrayals were taking place. A thousand little acts of despair.

*　　*　　*

Sometime in the night, around four in the morning, MacShane was awakened by a huge explosion which shook the windows and rattled the glass cup on the wash-basin. Before he hit the floor there was another. Then another, and another, the last two further away. Then silence.

He lay waiting for more, but none came. Outside in the corridor someone ran by screaming, 'They're here.' The street below started coming to life. A siren wailed. Lights came on. Shutters opened. The policeman on the steps of the National Assembly was pointing his gun uncertainly at the sky.

MacShane dressed hurriedly and went down to the lobby. Outside it was still dark. A dozen other foreigners were already there, still in pyjamas and dressing gowns. Someone had tuned an FM radio into the security circuit of the embassy. A marine at the airport was trying to rouse the embassy duty officer.

'Whiskey Joe, Whiskey Joe, do you hear me?' The voice at the airport was shaking with fear, but Whiskey Joe was not answering. The airport voice tried again.

'For Christ's sake, Whiskey Joe, everything here is in flames. Do you hear me, Whiskey Joe?'

At last Whiskey Joe answered. His voice was deep and calm. 'Okay Big Mac, we hear you. Go ahead. Over.'

'They've hit the runways and the ammo dumps. About 30 rockets. They look like 122s. Do you hear me, Whiskey Joe? Over.'

'I hear you, Big Mac. Just take it easy and we'll find out what's going on.'

There was a click and the line went dead. Outside it was getting light at last. Upstairs in the restaurant the waiters were laying the tables for breakfast. One of the Americans from the CBS suite on the third floor disappeared and came back ten minutes later brandishing a telex. 'The evacuation's on,' he said. 'My office heard it from the Pentagon.' With that most of the Americans went off to pack.

Suddenly the radio crackled back to life. It was Big Mac at the airport again. He sounded more worried than ever.

48

'We've lost two marines on Gate Four. Do you hear me, Whiskey Joe? Two of our guys dead. What do we do with the bodies?'

But there was no answer from Whiskey Joe. He had more important things on his mind. Ten minutes later a new voice came on the line from Tan Son Nhut. 'Whiskey Joe, this is Jacobson. Do you hear me? Over.'

Silence.

'Whiskey Joe, this is Jacobson. Where the hell are you?'

'Right here, Jacobson. Over.' Whiskey Joe was back again as unruffled as ever.

'The situation here is serious. Repeat, serious, Whiskey Joe.'

'I read you, Jacobson.'

'The evacuation plan will have to be changed. Options one, two, three no longer valid.' And with that the line went dead.

The news was received in silence in the lobby of the Caravelle. Everyone knew what it meant. There was now only one way out of Saigon – by helicopter.

By dawn the shelling at Bien Hoa had stopped. What sound there was came from closer at hand. Thick columns of smoke were rising from the direction of the airport as MacShane went up to the ninth floor for breakfast. From the north came the rattle of machine-gun fire punctuated by louder explosions. Someone said: 'They're on the Newport Bridge.'

'How far's that?'

'Five miles.'

'Jesus Christ.'

From the dining room they could see the helicopter gunships ducking and weaving over distant rooftops, guns blazing. MacShane stood watching as he munched a croissant. The waiters in their white jackets and bow ties commuted between the tables without looking up. It was not their war. It belonged to the foreigners.

Most American journalists seemed to have cables from their head offices ordering them home. The Pentagon was leaning on editors to pull their men out. The next few days were not going to be a very creditable episode in American history and the powers-that-be wanted as few eye-witnesses as possible.

Those who were going seemed glad to have the responsibility for leaving taken from them. They showed their telexes to anyone who was interested and implied that they were reluctantly obeying orders.

The French grew more insufferable with every rocket that fell on Tan Son Nhut. They feigned amazement at any suggestion that they should consider leaving, let alone stoop to asking for a ride out on an American helicopter.

'Us evacuate?' they exclaimed, whenever confronted by a fleeing American. 'This is your war, not ours. What have we to fear?'

And when anyone was indelicate enough to mention the 80-year French occupation of Vietnam, they snorted with contempt. 'That is in the past. Today our cultures are inextricably linked. We have spilled each other's blood. Besides, half the North Vietnamese Politburo were educated in Paris. They understand us, and we understand them.'

An English journalist offered a less lofty interpretation. 'The war is ending and, as usual, the French wish to end up on the winning side.'

By mid-morning the news that the Americans were going had spread, and all around the city little groups of Americans and high-risk Vietnamese were assembling at pre-arranged venues. But there was no word from the embassy about the evacuation.

The radio in the lobby was still tuned to the embassy circuit and Whiskey Joe was still fielding calls. About every fifteen minutes a voice could be heard saying: 'I'm Father Devlin from Yen Do. When is the evacuation?' To which the gravel voice of Whiskey Joe would reply: 'I have no instructions. Call back.'

Someone said they had heard on the BBC that the President had called an emergency meeting of the National Security Council. It had started at nine o'clock Saigon time, which meant that any moment now Whiskey Joe should get his instructions.

Chapter Six

At the Caravelle, something approaching calm had descended. Those who were going had gone and those who were staying settled down to watch the last hours of the war from their vantage point on the roof.

The journalists were like guests at a film premier watching from a safe distance events being acted out on a big screen: events in which most of them had no direct part to play and had no influence over the outcome. Their role would be to write up the events after it was over and give the actors good or bad reviews.

To complete the analogy, every effort was made to assure the comfort of the guests. To the end, waiters served iced tea and soft drinks. The bar remained open, enabling the guests to sip a cool lager or a *citron pressé* while watching the show. Not once did any of the waiters give vent to his true feelings. They were models of self-control, calling everyone 'sir' and sometimes bowing slightly in return for a tip. If asked about the war they would reply only with polite generalities.

Occasionally, one of the guests standing by the rail looking down at the street would call his colleagues over and draw their attention to a little tableau being enacted in the real world nine storeys below. Once a Ford Pinto driven by what appeared to be a drunken American careered off the street and ploughed into a line of noodle stands, bowling over the stands and their owners like nine-pins before coming to a halt against the trunk of a willow tree. Another time they stood watching as a crowd of youths casually stove in the plate-glass window of a jeweller's shop on Tu Do and made off with the contents.

Two small worries nagged at the journalists as they stood sipping their beers on the roof of the Caravelle. One was that the North Vietnamese would shell the city and that their 130 mm shells would not be able to distinguish between the spectators and the actors.

The other was that some of the actors would forget their scripts and turn their rage on the specially-invited audience.

MacShane observed with detachment. Vietnam was not his war. It was not his fault that the country was going down the pan. His wars had been in Bolivia, Brazil and Chile. In those wars America was winning.

Had he served a couple of years in Vietnam he might have felt able to share responsibility for the disaster unfolding before his eyes. But he had not and he did not. He just cursed that son of a bitch Lazarotitz for dumping him on the losing side with three days to go after twenty years of bad policy.

From the direction of the embassy a pall of thin grey smoke rose and drifted over the city. A piece of charred paper floated down from the sky. The boys on the top floor were feeding the classified files into the incinerators. MacShane pictured the scene inside. The controlled panic. The humming of air-conditioners. The haze of cigarette smoke. The empty beer cans. The non-stop ringing of scrambled telephones. The chatter of the telex with IMMEDIATE cables from Washington. That was his world. That was where he belonged. Not up here, on the roof of the Caravelle, with these vultures.

There was a moment, just a moment, when MacShane considered making a run for the embassy. He could easily have made it. Once inside, of course, there would be some explaining to do. If there was time, they would cable Langley and ask what to do with him. But they couldn't refuse to take him out. Anyway, if he waited another few hours, there would be no time to contact Langley. At least, not until he reached the Seventh Fleet, and by then it would be too late.

Of course, there would be trouble when he got back. He'd be accused of running out on the job; but in Vietnam everybody

52

was running out on the job. In any case, he had half a mind to tell Lazarowitz what he could do with the job.

As he watched the thin grey smoke rising from the embassy, MacShane envied the unseen men stuffing the incinerators. By this time tomorrow they would be relaxing on the deck of the USS *Denver*, sipping cokes and watching the coast of Vietnam disappear over the horizon. Their war would be over. MacShane's was just beginning.

After the departure of the American journalists – or most of them – MacShane began to feel conspicuous. Most of those who had gone were journalists whose dispatches reflected the national interest.

Lately, MacShane reflected sombrely, the patriotic school of journalism was seriously in decline, what with Watergate, Chile – and now Vietnam. Now there was a new breed of journalist, always searching out information with which to run down his country, always willing to believe the worst. Lazarowitz was forever going on about the unpatriotic attitude of the East Coast press. 'It's bad enough having foreigners run down our country,' he used to say, 'without Americans getting in on the act.' Lazarowitz had been sore at newspaper-men ever since Operation Phoenix had such a bad press.

On the roof of the Caravelle on Saigon's last full day as a paid-up member of the Free World, there was a distinct shortage of patriotic journalists. The French were the worst. MacShane got the impression that they were rather enjoying seeing America humiliated. One of them expressed the view that America was urgently in need of a defeat. Lucky Lazarowitz wasn't there. He'd have tossed the bastard over the side.

The evacuation from the embassy began around three in the afternoon. The helicopters came in up the Saigon River and swung low over the city centre before disappearing into the embassy compound. They were big jobs, Chinook 53s. MacShane guessed they could take about 70 people apiece. At that rate the evacuation would last all night. No sooner had one chopper taken off than another appeared. They could be heard coming long before they came into view: specks in a grey sky, gradually growing bigger until they were hovering over the embassy. The drone of the engines and the whirr of the rotor blades went on for the rest of the day and long into the night.

Downstairs in the lobby the radio was still tuned in to the embassy circuit and Whiskey Joe was fielding ever more frantic pleas for help.

All afternoon, there were calls coming in from the Duc Hotel, a CIA residence four blocks behind the embassy, where a group of Vietnamese employees and their families had gathered.

'I am Mr Hai, the cook,' said one.

There was silence at the other end, and then an angry exchange between Whiskey Joe and a colleague in the background. 'Where in hell's name did they get that radio?' The colleague mumbled something about 'the fucking gooks.'

'I am Mr Hai,' said the voice again. 'Here my family. Where to go? Please tell us.'

At last Whiskey Joe condescended to reply. 'Go home, Mr Hai. Buses and helicopters will come and pick you up.'

'Please, when? We wait many hours.'

Whiskey Joe took a deep breath. 'Mr Hai, I must ask you to get off the line. You are impeding urgent transmissions.'

There was a click and Mr Hai disappeared. Ten minutes later the Duc Hotel was back on the line. 'Hello, hello. I am Mr Anh, the chauffeur. You must know me. I am working . . .'

'Will you get off the line.' Whiskey Joe was losing his cool. Then, doing his best to sound reassuring, he said: 'Mr Anh, I have already told you that you will be picked up.'

'Yes, you have already told us.'

'Please go home and wait.'

'How you know where to come, if we go home?'

'We will know.'

'How?'

'Get off the goddamn line.'

There was a click and Mr Anh was gone.

Half an hour passed and Mr Hai came back on again. This time he sounded desperate. 'Please, come quickly. They are breaking in.' In the background was the sound of gunfire. 'They are breaking in . . .'

'Who's breaking in? The Communists?'

More gunfire and a woman screaming.

'No, not Communists. ARVN.'

More screaming. Then the sound of Mr Hai sobbing. Then silence. That was the last contact with the Duc Hotel.

MacShane sat in the lobby of the Caravelle, listening. A switchboard operator, the receptionist and assorted Vietnamese were listening too. Not all of them spoke English and the receptionist translated each exchange between Whiskey Joe and the Duc. They listened impassively, and during the intervals between each exchange talked quietly among themselves in Vietnamese. In the middle of it all someone rang for room service and the receptionist dispatched one of the boys with a flask of hot water.

When he couldn't stand it any longer, MacShane decided to risk a walk outside. He had gone about 50 yards when he was accosted by a group of hard-faced young men. They were dressed in jeans and sweatshirts and had military-style haircuts. One of them had the words LOVE and HATE tattooed on his forearm. The one with the tattoo did the talking.

'We look for an American.'

'Which American?'

'Any American.'

He held out a crumpled letter with a United States Defense Department letterhead. It was addressed 'To Whom It May Concern' and said: '*The bearer of this letter has served and fought under my command. He is a person who believes firmly in the values of democracy and the Free World. If he should fall into Communist hands his life would be in serious danger because of the services he has performed. You are urged to give him all possible help and assistance.*' There followed the illegible signatures of a couple of American colonels.

55

MacShane read the letter and returned it to the young man. 'I am sorry,' he said. 'I am not an American.' He walked away across the square. The young men watched him go. He expected them to come after him, but they didn't. They just stood and stared blankly.

MacShane could see the Italian holding court on the terrace of the Continental Palace. Waiters served tea. The Italian did not see him and MacShane walked on, up Tu Do in the direction of the cathedral.

Most of the shops were still open. Street vendors were still selling American cigarettes and chewing-gum from makeshift stalls on the sidewalk. A little peanut-seller chased after MacShane. 'Mister, mister,' she called, 'you give me money, I go America.'

The proprietor of the looted jeweller's shop was sweeping glass into the gutter. The Air Vietnam office had a sign in the window saying it was closed until further notice.

In front of the cathedral an old woman was sweeping the road with a broom made of long twigs. She swept with unhurried, graceful strokes, oblivious to the pandemonium around her. She had nothing at stake. Whichever side won she would still be a road-sweeper in the morning.

There were crowds around the central post office. The queue for the cable desk spilled out of the doors and down the steps. It was an unruly queue of small men, arguing, haggling, bribing, pushing. Sending desperate telegrams to long-lost aunts and uncles in Paris or San Francisco. 'Most Urgent You Send One Thousand Rpt One Thousand Dollars Care Of National Bank Of Vietnam Stop Your Loving Nephew.' But it was already too late. The only way out now was by helicopter and for that many were called, but few would be chosen.

MacShane moved cautiously into Thong Nhat Avenue in the direction of the embassy. The pavement was littered with ARVN uniforms: shirts, trousers, boots, helmets, holsters. They were scattered over a distance of about twenty yards, as though their owners had undressed while running.

A Chinook passed low overhead and disappeared behind a

56

row of tamarind trees into the embassy compound. It passed so low that MacShane caught a glimpse of the pilot, a young Negro, his face strained with concentration and glistening with sweat. The downdraught from the double rotors was so strong that it disturbed the grey film of ash from the embassy incinerators which covered the streets around the embassy. Ash was everywhere, on trees and on the bodywork of abandoned cars. Even the grass was grey.

MacShane stopped well short of the embassy. People streamed past without giving him a second glance. The embassy looked the sort of place that architects win awards for: an oblong of whitewashed cement protected by a rocket shield of reinforced concrete and punctuated by hundreds of small rectangular holes through which seeped the only daylight that the inhabitants were permitted. The roof was a forest of antennae save for an elevated section in the centre which was a landing pad for the smaller helicopters.

A Huey was already on the pad, its engine running, rotor whirring. By the door an American with an M-16 hanging from a shoulder strap was half-crouching. With one hand he held the gun and with the other he counted in people from a queue which stretched in single file down a ladder to the lower part of the roof. When the Huey was full, the man made a sweeping gesture with his arm and the people retreated to the foot of the ladder. The man then followed, retreating a few rungs down the ladder and waiting while the chopper took off. Inside an unseen hand slid the door shut. The rotor accelerated and the machine lifted off into the clear blue sky, causing the trees to sway as it passed overhead. Within less than a minute another helicopter appeared, and the man with the M-16 was waving aboard the next batch of passengers. There was no panic. No one pushed or tried to overtake. There was no need. Those who had got as far as the embassy roof knew that their turn would come. On the streets below it was a different story.

A wall ran around the embassy. It was about eight feet high and made of reinforced white concrete to match the facade of the embassy building. The wall might easily have been climbed except that it was decked out in barbed wire and along the top, at intervals of about ten yards, stood gum-chewing marines who had been specially flown in for the occasion from the Seventh Fleet.

A crowd laid siege to the wall. Elegant women struggling with Samsonite suitcases, men in sport shirts and flannel trousers, carrying executive briefcases: people who twenty-four hours before had sat at desks in air-conditioned offices, whose telephones were answered by secretaries or maids, who had learned impeccable English at universities in California and Hawaii.

They were people who in better times had attended receptions and cocktail parties in the very building to which they now laid siege. Who had sat round the swimming pool at the Cercle Sportif discussing whether to send their children to universities in California or Paris. Who had everything the Free World had to offer except an American passport. Who had grown used to dealing with Americans on equal terms and to whom it had come as a profound shock to discover that in the last analysis they were just gooks.

Sometimes a new arrival would march boldly up to the gate and announce with as much self-confidence as he could muster that he was a personal friend of the ambassador. The marines would look at him stone-faced, expressionless except for the rhythmic chewing of gum. Once a lone Caucasian fought his way to the wall and was plucked out of the crowd on the strong arms of a marine. Sometimes a white face would appear in the crowd and edge his way towards the gate, which would open just wide enough to admit him and one or two Vietnamese who squeezed in behind. Each time this happened the fury of the crowd would rise to fever pitch. They would hammer on the gate and scream at the marines; some even tried to scramble over the wall, only to be repelled with a boot in the chest or the butt of an M-16 in the face. It was a dirty end to a dirty war.

Towards evening the dead heat of the day started to give way to a warm breeze. The blue sky turned grey. MacShane walked slowly back down Thong Nhat towards the cathedral. From two blocks away there was a crackle of gunfire and from the direction of the airport the muffled sound of an explosion. Then another and another. It was too far away to tell if it was mortars or artillery, but MacShane quickened his pace.

On the steps of the post office a girl sat weeping, her face buried in her hands, her small shoulders heaving. At another time in another country, MacShane might have offered help. But not in Saigon on the last night of the war.

The last night was the longest. The electricity went off around nine in the evening and did not come on again. In the restaurant on the top floor of the Caravelle the journalists ate by candle-light. Outside the city was in darkness, punctuated only by huge explosions from the direction of the airport followed by immense orange balls of flame soaring far into the sky. Now and then the flame briefly revealed silhouettes of people on rooftops. Some said they were the Viet Cong. Those who knew better said they were the families of high government officials and secret policemen awaiting rescue by helicopters.

No one knew what terrors the darkness held. The only clues were provided by unexplained bursts of small-arms fire. Once or twice the streets around the Caravelle were suddenly illuminated by bright purple or green flares fired in a fit of pique by a fleeing ARVN soldier. Each time a flare exploded some journalists would throw themselves to the floor, covering their heads with their hands. Others would race to the window, peering into the empty streets. Once they glimpsed a drunken soldier riding a bicycle in a ragged circle around the square in front of the National Assembly building. Once a flare surprised a gang of looters laden with beer and whisky from the PX store on the corner of Nguyen Hue street. They scurried away down back-alleys, like rats caught in the beam of a torch.

At around midnight the explosions from the airport ceased. From then on the darkness was interrupted only by small-arms fire or the sound of breaking glass. Overhead, helicopters commuted between the Seventh Fleet and the roof of the embassy. They were invisible now except for the red lights flashing on their underbellies. They came in at five-minute intervals, rotors whirring, red lights flashing, taking care to avoid the radio antennae on the roof of the embassy and the twin spires of the cathedral.

MacShane went to bed around 02:00. His room on the fourth floor was about level with the tin roof of the National Assembly building. The bed was in a direct line of fire from the window, so he took off the mattress and dragged it to the bathroom, where it just fitted between the toilet and the shower. He lay down, still clothed, and placed the pillow over his head. His last thought, as he closed his eyes, was of Josie. If he had listened to her, he might by now have been selling real estate in Florida.

Chapter Seven

The last Huey took off from the embassy as breakfast was being served at the Caravelle. MacShane stood on the roof and watched it go. The pilot went high to avoid ground fire and then accelerated away to the east. MacShane stared after the helicopter until it was a tiny speck in a grey sky. A Frenchman raised his glass of orange juice in the direction of the disappearing helicopter. '*Vive Saigon libre,*' he said. No one else spoke.

Below, the streets were empty save for a blind beggar feeling his way past the shuttered shops, a single coin rattling in his tin can, unaware (or perhaps not caring) that the earth was about to change places with the sky.

Now and then a cyclist on urgent business hurried past, head down, looking neither left nor right. Abandoned ARVN uniforms and debris from the previous night's looting clogged the gutters. Occasionally a gust of wind would catch the waste paper, carrying it in small whirlpools before depositing it back upon the pavement.

By and by a lone army officer appeared. He walked with determined strides along the centre of the street. His uniform was neatly pressed and on his chest he wore campaign ribbons pinned there by the President himself. The officer marched up to the statue of the unknown soldier – a huge concrete monstrosity in the centre of Lam Son square, facing the now deserted National Assembly building. He stood rigidly to attention and saluted briskly with his right hand. With the left hand he reached for the pistol on his belt. Then he placed the barrel against his temple and squeezed the trigger. For a few seconds he remained standing to attention, his right arm still raised in salute. The blood spurting from the side of his head stained his spotless uniform and trickled down over his campaign ribbons. He was still saluting as he fell.

The sound of the shot ricocheted around the square. Faces appeared at windows and quickly disappeared again. A youth on a Honda appeared and parked his bike against the kerb. He walked up to the still-twitching body and prised open the hand that held the pistol. Pulling a handkerchief from his pocket the youth wiped the specks of blood from the barrel of the gun and placed it in his satchel. Then he remounted his Honda and sped away in the direction of the river.

No sooner was the youth out of sight than a small girl appeared, one of the little peanut-sellers who haunted the sidewalks. She hovered just long enough to relieve the dead man of his watch and disappeared into the shadows. As she turned from the corpse she accidentally stepped in a pool of blood and she went away leaving small red footprints across the white paving stones.

The end came just before noon. They were on the roof of the Caravelle: MacShane, the Italian and an English journalist whose name he didn't catch. The Englishman was one of those cocky bastards who had been everywhere and done everything. He had a scar on his neck which, he claimed, was caused by a bullet wound in Korea, but the Italian said was probably a love bite from a Bangkok whorehouse. The Italian drifted over to the rail and was looking down at the street. As soon as he had gone, the Englishman started asking questions. 'Who did you say you worked for?'

'I didn't.'

His eyes narrowed. 'Perhaps it's a secret.'

'It's a small syndication agency you won't have heard of.'

'Try me.'

So MacShane explained about Forum World Features. It was London-based, serviced 150 newspapers worldwide and dealt mainly in feature material.

'I see,' said the Englishman, but plainly he did not. Who

ran it, he wanted to know. And what was its address in London? MacShane gave him a couple of names, but the man said he had never heard of them in his twenty years in journalism. MacShane said that was hardly surprising, since most of Forum's business was overseas. Head office was at somewhere called Lincoln's Inn Fields. MacShane said it meant nothing to him since he did not know London. The man conceded that he had heard of Lincoln's Inn Fields. That was something to be grateful for. He also said he would look up Forum next time he was passing. 'Be sure to mention my name,' said MacShane.

The Englishman looked him straight in the eye. It was a look that said, *You're a lying bastard.* What, he demanded, had MacShane done for a living before taking up with this syndication agency? He stressed the word *agency* as though he knew something he ought not to have known. MacShane did not bat an eyelid. Instead he talked about his seven years with Hearst in Bolivia and Brazil. That was straightforward enough and the Englishman listened without interrupting.

MacShane omitted to mention how his contract with Hearst had been abruptly terminated after seven years the day old man Hearst found out who was pulling his strings. Old man Hearst had hit the roof. It was not the discovery that one of his journalists was a spook that upset him. What really bugged him was that it had been done behind his back. At first he had threatened to make a big production out of it, and was only dissuaded from doing so by a written assurance from the Director that such a thing would never happen again. That was when they took MacShane back to Washington and put him on the desk. He was lucky. Three years later, when the *Village Voice* started naming journalists with Company connections, his name never surfaced. There must have been a dozen people at Hearst who knew about MacShane but no one had breathed a word. His cover was intact. So far, at least.

The Englishman sat stroking the scar on his neck. There were many more questions he might have asked had this been anywhere but Saigon on the last morning of the war. Questions such as, how could a two-bit agency like Forum afford to have its own man in Saigon? And why, in heaven's name, should Forum send MacShane halfway across the world when Saigon was crawling with distinguished journalists? And who the hell ran Forum anyway?

MacShane was spared further embarrassment by a cry from the Italian. 'They're here, look.' He was pointing up Tu Do in the direction of the cathedral. A tank had nosed out of a side street. At first just the nose of the tank was visible. The driver seemed uncertain of the direction. He swung the tank left, then right. Someone said. 'It's only ARVN.'

'Since when did ARVN drive Russian tanks?'

They raced downstairs, the Italian in front, followed by the Englishman and then MacShane. A waiter on the way up had to pin himself against the wall to avoid being swept away. Others fell in behind until, by the time they reached the lobby, just about everyone in the hotel seemed to know what was going on.

Out on the street the Italian flagged down a youth on a motorcycle. He climbed on the pillion and they rode off in the direction of the palace.

By the time MacShane reached the palace the first tanks were already chewing up General Minh's front lawn. The General and his ministers had been meeting in the cabinet room on the ground floor. Hearing the commotion outside they filed out on to the steps of the palace. MacShane arrived just in time to find them confronting a group of young soldiers in green pith helmets and armed with AK–47s. One of the soldiers carried a red and blue flag with a gold star. There was fear on the face of Minh and his ministers.

MacShane crept as close as he dared. There were three tanks on the lawn and behind him a fourth rumbled through the shattered gates. The Italian was in the thick of it. His head of thick black hair and his white shirt stood out clearly above the soldiers in their pith helmets and green battledress. He was taking photographs with a Pentax, commuting between the two groups as though they were guests at a wedding. He stood waving his arms, directing people this way and that. Nobody questioned his right to be there.

General Minh eyed the new arrivals uneasily. They stood there in their green uniforms, their baggy trousers flecked with mud, guns pointed upwards. Mostly they were just boys, peasants from the Red River delta. Some had never seen a city before and none had ever seen a palace, let alone a president. Later, MacShane reflected that if the General had ordered them off the premises, they might have left without a murmur.

But the moment passed. The soldiers stood their ground and Minh and his ministers stood theirs. Then, from among the soldiers, an older man stepped forward. He wore the same olive-green battledress and the same pith helmet as the other soldiers. His only distinguishing feature was a breast pocket from which a pen protruded. He was completely calm and spoke only a few words. MacShane was too far away to hear what was being said, and anyway he didn't speak the language; but whatever it was, it did the trick. When he had finished speaking the man stepped forward and embraced General Minh. The ice broke. Soldiers and ministers shook hands and embraced. Some were in tears. The young soldier with the flag disappeared inside the palace to find a place from which to fly it. And all the while the Italian was there taking photographs.

'What did that little guy say?' MacShane asked the Italian that evening as they took supper at the Caravelle. The Italian pulled a notebook out of his shirt pocket and flicked back through the pages until he turned up the words. 'Here,' he said, 'translated for me by General Minh himself: "Do not be alarmed. Today the war has ended. All Vietnamese are victors. If you have any feelings for the people of Vietnam, consider today a happy day." ' The Italian folded the notebook and returned it to his pocket. 'Or as your General Westmoreland would say, "Come out with your hands up or I'll blow your balls off." '

After the tanks came the North Vietnamese infantry. They came in trucks thick with dust and red mud, down the Avenue Thong Nhat and past the now-deserted American Embassy. They came also along the roads from the airport and from

Bien Hoa, waving cheerfully at the little knots of Saigon citizens who turned out to watch them pass. MacShane saw the first arrivals set up camp under the shade of the trees between the cathedral and the palace. They went about their business efficiently. Guards were stationed around the perimeter. Machine-guns were assembled, tents erected, latrines dug.

Before long, however, their defences had been overwhelmed by curious citizens. At first they watched from a distance, uncertain as to how to cope with the strangers. Gradually, however, they crept closer. Children went first. Then the older women. Then a priest from the cathedral. Then long-haired youths on Hondas appeared and began to circle cautiously. Someone offered an American cigarette. When they saw their commander smoking, the soldiers also began accepting cigarettes. Others took chewing gum offered by the long-haired youths on Hondas. An old lady was handing out mangoes.

MacShane watched from a discreet distance. It was incredible. People who only hours ago had confidently expected to be murdered in their beds now stood under the shade of tamarind trees, calmly exchanging gossip with their conquerors. What would Lazarowitz have said? That it was all part of the script. That it wouldn't last. That for every citizen of Saigon who welcomed the Communists, there were another thousand who didn't. Anyway, it didn't matter a tinker's curse what Lazarowitz would have said. He wasn't there.

Chapter Eight

But Lazarowitz was there, in spirit at least. In Washington it was nearly dawn but Lazarowitz was still hard at work in his windowless room at Langley, poring over satellite photographs taken over Saigon four hours earlier. In one hand he held a half-smoked Stuyvesant, in the other a magnifying glass. On the edge of the desk, next to the picture of Lazarowitz with MacNamara, there was a half-eaten sandwich: salami in white bread glued together with mustard and ketchup. Beside the sandwich stood a plastic beaker two-thirds full of cold coffee polluted with cigarette ash.

The photographs were spread out across the centre of the desk. Some of them were still wet and curling at the edges. Through his magnifying glass Lazarowitz could make out the T-54 tanks drawn up in a neat semi-circle on the palace lawn. He could see the trucks loaded with troops and supplies, advancing bumper to bumper along the roads from Tay Ninh and Bien Hoa. He could see clusters of citizens emerging from their homes to welcome the victorious army. Had he called for blow-ups, he might even have been able to make out agent MacShane entering into the spirit of the occcasion by hitching a ride on a North Vietnamese tank on its way to take over the Ministry of Defence.

Lazarowitz leaned back on his swivel chair and took a drag on his Stuyvesant. The smoke spiralled upwards. Flakes of ash showered down his tieless shirt. He made a half-hearted effort to brush away the ash, but it clung to him like dandruff. There was nothing in the satellite pictures to give him cause for alarm. He, after all, was operating on a different time frame from the rest of the Administration, one in which the fall of Saigon had long been taken for granted.

The plain fact was that the Reds had bitten off more than they could chew. They did not have enough good cadres to run the North, let alone the South. They had Operation Phoenix to thank for that. That and the Tet offensive.

History would be kind to Phoenix. Of that Lazarowitz was certain. Phoenix had eliminated some of Charlie's best agents. Men and women who commanded respect in the villages. Who had experience gained in a lifetime of struggle: against the Japs, against the French and against the Americans. Men and women who knew how to organise and how to lead, who could never be replaced. Not everyone at Langley would agree, but as far as Lazarowitz was concerned, Phoenix was one of the Company's biggest successes and he was proud to have been associated with it.

Too bad about the publicity. The Senate hearings. All that whining about innocent civilians in the East Coast press. Sure, innocent people died. That happened all the time in war. The Company top brass should have had the guts to stand up to the defeat-minded liberals. In the end, of course, there had to be a scapegoat and Lazarowitz was number one candidate.

Phoenix had put an end to his career above ground. From then, his career was played out in windowless rooms in Washington. Even now, after five years, there was a lot of foot-shuffling whenever Phoenix was mentioned. Still, no one except Lazarowitz had the guts to say out loud that Phoenix was a rip-roaring success. In private, of course, it was a different matter.

'Listen, Laz, *I* know that Phoenix worked,' the Director had said at the final interview. 'And *you* know that Phoenix worked. The trouble is that the media and the politicians don't see it that way. In ten years' time it will be different, but right now we've got problems.'

The Director had been pleasant enough. 'It's nothing personal, Laz. We just want you to lie low for a while. There will be no cut in salary. We may even be able to arrange a small increment. It's just that someone has got to take the rap and right now you are in an exposed position.'

So Lazarowitz had been sent down to the basement. They'd found him an office and a secretary, or at least half of one. He shared her with another refugee from an unpopular programme. They switched him out of East Asia Division. Put him on Bolivia. Even gave him an agent or two to run. That was how he picked up MacShane.

'It won't be forever,' they said. 'Just until the heat's off. Memories are short in Washington.'

But not that short. Lazarowitz had remained below ground for five long years. Once in a while he was called on to lecture the new recruits at Camp Peary, but by and large he was forgotten. His memoranda were noted but never acted upon. When he ran into people in the cafeteria with whom he used to work they never gave him much more than the time of day. Sometimes he'd stroll up to the third floor to look up old colleagues. Nowadays, though, there weren't many faces he recognised and some of those he knew seemed embarrassed to see him. But Lazarowitz knew more about Vietnam than anyone in East Asia Division. One day, he knew, they would be back for him. But it wasn't until that day in February, when Steiner appeared in his basement office, that Lazarowitz knew he was back in business.

It was good to be back in the big time again. All those conferences on the top floor where he was introduced as 'one of our oldest Vietnam hands'. Not a word about Phoenix. No more footshuffling or embarrassed silences. His memoranda were read and promptly replied to. They even found him a full-time secretary.

And it was good to be working with someone like Steiner who thought big. The project on which they were engaged was one of the most important on the Agency's books. The aim was to achieve what two-and-a-half million soldiers and 236 billion dollars of hardware had failed to achieve: to roll back communism in Vietnam. Not just the South but the North as well. To snatch victory from the jaws of defeat. That was how Lazarowitz and Steiner saw it, anyway. And as for Congress, they would have been horrified. If only they had known. Like all grand designs it started small. First, they set up a stay-behind network to run messages, organise some basic intelligence and indulge in a little sabotage when the situation allowed. That was where MacShane came in.

But MacShane was only a small part of the big plan. If the worst came to the worst he was expendable. Part two was refugees. Life was going to get hard in South Vietnam without all that American aid, particularly for the middle classes. When they got over their relief at not being butchered, many of them were going to want out. Lazarowitz and Steiner would be there to lend a helping hand.

After every revolution all kinds of riff-raff came tumbling out, claiming the hospitality of the Free World. It had happened in Eastern Europe in '45. In China in '49. Then there was Cuba. Castro had managed to off-load half of Havana's underworld on to Uncle Sam. Most of them were running the rackets in Florida to this day.

This time it had to be different. America had enough gangsters and dope peddlers of its own without taking in Vietnam's as well. This time America wanted only the best – doctors, engineers, managers. The people Vietnam most needed, if it was to rebuild. Get them out and the whole structure would start to crumble. In East Germany it had got so bad, they had to build a wall to keep the middle classes in.

Lazarowitz and Steiner had their own little refugee programme. The money to fund it was carefully hidden in the USAID budget and the armed services estimates. There was even a million dollars buried in the military aid estimates for Thailand to fund a clandestine radio station broadcasting in Vietnamese. Voice of America would run programmes about refugees who had successfully resettled in the United States. Refugees already settled would be encouraged to write to relatives in Vietnam advising them of openings for doctors, engineers, managers, nurses . . . anyone with a marketable skill in the Free World.

AID officers would be sent to comb the refugee camps that

would soon be set up in Thailand and Malaysia, in search of people who would fit into the American way of life. They in turn would be encouraged to write to relatives back home – especially those still holding down good jobs – advising them of the advantages of life in the Free World. In due course, there would also be openings for former South Vietnam Army men with certain types of specialised military skills. But that was a programme for which Lazarowitz had yet to obtain clearance.

Then there were what Henry Kissinger would call geo-political factors. Steiner and Lazarowitz had plans to exploit these, too. First Cambodia. All that stuff the Company pumped out in the early seventies about the Khmer Rouge being puppets of Vietnam was hogwash. All the signs were that the Cambodians and the Vietnamese hated each other's guts. So now the line would have to change. Discreetly, of course. Right now, if Cambodians hated anyone more than the Vietnamese, it was the Americans. That would pass. Time was a great healer.

As of this moment, Lazarowitz had no authorisation for a Cambodian operation, but when the time came he would be ready.

In due course contact would have to be made with the Khmer Rouge. That could be done through China. Who, five years ago, would have guessed that Chairman Mao could have been persuaded to shake hands with Richard Nixon? And at the very moment when Nixon was bombing the shit out of Vietnam. It was no secret that the Chinese didn't like the Vietnamese any more than the Americans did. Where Vietnam was concerned America and China had a common interest. If the Americans could do a deal with the Chinese, then no one in Washington need get his hands dirty. It was a long shot but worth a try. Lazarowitz already had a man in Peking working on the problem.

For all his grand schemes, Lazarowitz did not kid himself that he was in control of events. Unlike some in his profession, he was not a world conspiracy man. He simply believed in giving events a helping hand.

Lazarowitz was always going on about what he called *exploitable weaknesses*. These, he used to tell the new recruits at Camp Peary, were the key to a successful operation. 'Don't waste the Company's time and money trying to undermine the enemy where he is strongest.' He would take a long drag on his Stuyvesant. 'Our job is to identify the enemy's weak spots and exploit them to hell.' At this point he was usually overcome by a fit of coughing. If Lazarowitz had an exploitable weakness it was Stuyvesant cigarettes.

Lazarowitz was that rare phenomenon in Washington – a man who thought long-term. In Hanoi and Peking, where governments presided over ancient civilisations, it was nothing to plan ten or twenty years ahead. But in Washington the next Presidential election was the nearest anyone came to long-term thinking. And as for the politicians, most of them could not see beyond the next opinion poll: a point starkly underlined by the appearance in Lazarowitz's in-tray of a terse little memorandum dated April 29, 1975. It read:

From: *The Director*
To: *All Departments*
Subject: *American Nationals in Vietnam*
Classification: *Secret*

As you will be aware the final evacuation of American nationals in Vietnam commenced today at 15:15 Saigon time. The Secretary of State has instructed that all, repeat *all*, American nationals are to be out of Vietnam by 23:00 Saigon time. CIA personnel, overt or covert, still in Saigon must be instructed to comply forthwith.

William E. Colby

When he saw the memorandum Lazarowitz nearly blew a gasket. 'What do these pissheads think they're playing at? We spend weeks setting up a cover for MacShane. The operation has been cleared at the highest level. And no sooner do we get him in than they want him out again.' With that he subsided into one of his coughing fits.

Lazarowitz's first instinct was to go charging into Colby's office and demand to know what the hell was going on, but Steiner counselled caution. 'Colby's only covering his ass, so that if questions are asked he can tell Kissinger that his hands are clean.'

'And we end up the fall guys?'

Steiner said nothing. They sat in the twilight of Lazarowitz's basement office. Somewhere in the distance a telephone was ringing. Lazarowitz was chain-smoking, as he always did. He was being set up again and he did not like it. They had stitched him up over Phoenix and he was not going to let it happen again. Covering asses was a game that anyone could play and this time Lazarowitz's ass would be covered.

After Steiner had gone, Lazarowitz drafted a little cable of his own. It was addressed to Tom Polgar, CIA station chief, Saigon, who was at that very moment on the top floor of the embassy supervising the destruction of the telex link with Washington.

Lazarowitz translated his cable into code, took it up to the telex room and personally put it on the wire. It was timed 15:19 Washington time, April 29, which corresponded to 03:19, April 30, Saigon time. With luck it would arrive too late to be acted upon, but if anything went wrong, no one would ever pin the rap on Lazarowitz. This time he played it by the book.

Mission accomplished, Lazarowitz went back to the basement. He carried with him two copies of the telex: one for the file and one for his personal records, in case of emergencies. Never trust those bastards on the top floor not to doctor the files.

Later, much later, it was established that the telex link with Saigon had been broken at 03:20 – one minute after Lazarowitz's telex was transmitted. For some months it was unclear whether the telex had been received in Saigon. Certainly Polgar claimed never to have seen it.

An internal enquiry later established that, seven hours after he sent his telex, Lazarowitz put a call through to the office of

Admiral Donald Whitmire, who was supervising the evacuation from the USS *Blue Ridge*, 15 miles off the coast of Vietnam. The call was logged by Admiral Whitmire's office at 10:01 Saigon time – 22:01 in Washington. Lazarowitz had wanted to know whether an agent by the name of MacShane had been evacuated. After some delay he was told that no one of that name was on anyone's list, but it was possible that in the confusion he had not been recorded. He was told to ring back later. The log in Admiral Whitmire's office showed that Lazarowitz had rung at around noon Saigon time and again at around 14:30. On both occasions he was told there was no record of anyone by the name of MacShane.

The enquiry found that Lazarowitz had acted at all times in accordance with his orders and was in no way to blame for MacShane's disappearance. It even went so far as to praise his diligence for having stayed on duty so late into the night to check on MacShane's whereabouts. On being informed of the enquiry's findings, Lazarowitz caused his bloated features to become contorted by a rare smile. His ass was well and truly covered. Unhappily, the same could not be said for MacShane's.

Chapter Nine

For the first week MacShane kept his head down. He trailed around with a camera and notebook, doing his best to look like a journalist. To begin with it was not difficult. There was too much going on for anyone to notice him. The Italian was having the time of his life sucking up to the big shots. The French were unbearable. One French photographer produced a Communist Party card which he used to ingratiate himself with the new regime.

A handful of American correspondents had stayed. The guys from CBS; Matt Franjola and George Esper of Associated Press; Al Dawson of United Press International. MacShane avoided them like the plague. Likewise the Englishman who had proved so interested in Forum World Features.

After three days he had had enough of playing hide-and-seek and transferred from the Caravelle to the Majestic, on the river front. The top floor of the Majestic had been taken out by a rocket in the last week of the war, but the hotel stayed open. Its only concessions to the new order were a portrait of Ho Chi Minh which appeared over the reception desk and the red and blue flag of the Provisional Revolutionary Government which now adorned the main entrance.

Saigon adapted as swiftly to the new order as it had to all previous occupations. The traders soon realised there was money to be made out of the revolution. On the pavement outside the Café Givral a man and his son began turning out Ho Chi Minh sandals made from old truck tyres. Before long he had been joined by competitors from all over the city.

Ho Chi Minh was big business. His picture began to appear everywhere: in shops, offices, houses; on the windscreens of the little Fiat taxis which plied for business outside the Rex Hotel. Pictures of Uncle Ho were even to be found in the bars on Tu Do, which had discreetly resumed business. The new authorities took a dim view of the fortunes that were being made out of Ho Chi Minh pictures and soldiers soon began touring the shops saying that 'Uncle Ho was not for sale', but market forces prevailed and Uncle Ho went on selling.

The northern soldiers were quite unlike any that Saigon had ever seen. They soon became a familiar sight in their green pith helmets, rubber sandals and baggy uniforms. They called themselves *bo doi*, soldiers of the people, and before long the expression was to be heard in conversations all over the city. The *bo doi* were mainly young men from the northern delta and they gazed in awe at the opulence of Saigon. The cynics said it would not be long before Saigon corrupted them, just as it had absorbed and corrupted all previous conquerors. However, any illusions that the *bo doi* were a soft touch were swiftly dispelled. On the second day they caught a youth snatching an old woman's purse in the central market. The *bo doi* delivered a short lecture on law and order and then shot the youth on the spot. Another was saved from a similar fate after the girl whose wallet he had stolen begged for his life. Word soon spread. The *bo doi* were not to be messed with.

MacShane witnessed only one piece of aggravation. A young officer in charge of an army film crew had stormed into the third-floor suite of the Canadian Broadcasting Corporation at the Caravelle and demanded that the CBS correspondent hand over his film. Evidently the officer and his crew had hit town too late to record the final act and were anxious to lay their hands on some live coverage.

When he failed to get satisfaction, the officer, a handsome young man in mudspattered trousers, brandished a pistol. For ten minutes there was deadlock. The CBS correspondent refused to oblige and the officer made gestures progressively more threatening. Eventually, help arrived in the shape of a colonel. He directed a few well-chosen words of Vietnamese to the young man, who went pale, put away his pistol and disappeared without another word.

When it was over, someone produced a bottle of scotch and offered the colonel a drink. He replied in English, 'Now, no. Much work.' And as he reached the door he added, with a smile that revealed a mouthful of blackened teeth, 'Later we will have much merry times.'

Not everyone foresaw merry times. 'Soon Saigon will be as poor as Hanoi,' remarked an elegant man with whom MacShane found himself sharing a table at breakfast in the Café Givral one morning.

The old man claimed to have been a finance minister for a few months in one of the many governments that came and went in Saigon in the early sixties. He said he had a Master's degree from Yale and spoke perfect American.

'Your government will want revenge for this.'

'I'm sorry?'

'You are an American?'

'Yes.'

'Then you will know.'

'Know what?'

'That your government will want revenge. For the defeat. The humiliation. They will try to isolate us. To break our economy, organise uprisings as they did in Eastern Europe and China. And what will be the result? An increase in repression and absolute dependence upon the Soviet Union. Perhaps your government is run by Soviet agents?' He smiled bitterly at the thought. There was no anger in his voice, only resignation. 'Your leaders never learn, do they? They have forced half the world into communism and still they do not learn.'

MacShane munched his croissant in silence.

'Forgive me,' said the old man. 'I am sure you have no more influence than I upon your government.'

77

MacShane said he quite understood. These were hard times.

The old man shook his head. 'Dear sir,' he said, 'hard times do not worry me. In many ways I admire the Communists. They are patriots. They have suffered for their country while we drank champagne and grew rich on foreign money. If it is our turn to be poor, we have no right to complain.'

He spoke impartially. He was seventy-five and beyond the reach of events. Too old to run away. 'No,' he said, 'it is not the poverty I fear. It is the lies. From now on we must tell lies, even to live a simple life.'

Outside a crowd had gathered in front of the monument to the unknown soldier. A young man in a white shirt with a red arm-band was making a speech. Several times he was interrupted by applause. A youth with a sledgehammer had scrambled on to the shoulders of the monstrosity and was battering the head.

'What's happening?'

The old man brushed the crumbs from the front of his shirt. 'Students,' he said. 'They are destroying all vestiges of the puppet regime. Yesterday they were burning books and magazines. Today statues. Tomorrow, who knows what they will destroy?'

A waiter came with more coffee. The old man resumed. 'These people,' he said, waving a freckled hand towards a couple of passing *bo doi*, 'they are very good at war, but they cannot organise the sale of rice or vegetables. Most of their economists have been educated in Moscow and do not understand that the Soviet economy is a disaster. The Communists want to control how everyone eats, thinks and breathes and they will end up controlling nothing.'

From outside there came the sound of a sledgehammer pounding on granite. 'They will break up the Chinese rice monopolies. That is sensible. But they will not stop there. They will then attempt to fix the price of rice. They will fix it so low that the farmers will stop selling and so rice must be rationed.

'Then they will fix the price of meat and vegetables and the farmers will sell only on the black market.'

He paused and took a sip of his coffee. Outside there was a cheer, and they looked up to see the head of the unknown soldier topple to the ground in a cloud of dust. 'But it won't end there. To stop the black market, they will set up road blocks to search the buses and stop the farmers smuggling.'

Outside, youths with pickaxes were hacking away at the base of the headless statue. 'So the farmers will bribe the officials to let them take their meat and vegetables into the city. The result will be a big increase in black-market prices, corrupt officials and people who have to tell lies in order to live.'

The crowd outside was several hundred strong. The students clapped and cheered each time a piece of the monument fell away. The old man finished his coffee. A waiter appeared with the bill. He paid in the currency of the old regime, leaving a generous tip. 'The worst part,' he said when the waiter was out of earshot, 'is that every week we shall be summoned to meetings where the man to whom we must pay bribes and tell lies will explain to us that the system is working perfectly. And everyone will agree with him.'

He was on his feet now. The waiter appeared with a bamboo walking stick. The old man took it in his left hand and shuffled toward the door. MacShane followed. Outside on the pavement they shook hands and stood for a moment surveying the chaos of hooting cars and Hondas that clogged Tu Do. The old man shook his head. 'Poor Saigon,' he said. 'It is going to be very hard. We are a ginger-ale economy that likes to drink champagne.'

At the end of the first week, the new rulers held a victory celebration at the Doc Lap, the presidential palace lately vacated by General 'Big' Minh. It was the first time the new rulers had appeared in public and people went along as much out of curiosity as out of a desire to celebrate their liberation.

The palace was decked out with a portrait of Ho Chi Minh which spanned three floors and was hung on each side with red streamers reaching to the ground. The picture was framed with blue neon lights which looked as though they had been requisitioned from one of the bars on Tu Do. Underneath was the slogan, in large gold letters: NOTHING IS MORE PRECIOUS THAN INDEPENDENCE AND FREEDOM.

MacShane stood in the crowd and watched the new rulers file on to the steps of the Doc Lap. Mostly they were small men in ill-fitting olive-green uniforms. There was a handful of middle-aged women in plain white *ao dais* which looked as though they had not been worn for years, and half-a-dozen elderly citizens in white sleeveless shirts. They were men and women who had lived for decades in the shadows and they stood smiling and waving on the steps of the Doc Lap, blinking rapidly as though unaccustomed to daylight. Not quite believing that it was over and that they had won.

Later, MacShane gatecrashed a reception in the Doc Lap. Most of the journalists were there, mostly uninvited. MacShane even managed a quick handshake with General Tran Van Tra. The victory celebration was, he reflected later, the only time in the entire war that a CIA agent had come close enough to kill the NLF chief of staff. Even Lazarowitz might have raised a smile for that one.

Chapter Ten

On the eighth day of Liberation MacShane made his first contact. Wait at least a week, Lazarowitz had said, then play it by ear.

Lazarowitz had given him two names. The first was a Chinese by the name of Le Chan who ran a coffee shop on Nguyen Hue, a wide boulevard that ran down to the Saigon River, parallel to Tu Do.

'This guy's a one-man intelligence service,' Lazarowitz drawled. 'He's got five brothers and eleven children and they are *everywhere*. There's not a government office north or south of the 17th Parallel where Mr Chan does not have a relative.'

Lazarowitz had gone on to enumerate. There was awe in his voice – and it took a lot to impress Lazarowitz. A daughter at the National Bank. In the foreign exchange department, no less. Another in the Air Vietnam ticket office. Two sons and a nephew in the Saigon police department – one a senior customs official at Tan Son Nhut airport. A daughter in the US Army PX store at Cam Ranh Bay. A son who, when last heard of, was commanding a Viet Cong unit in the Delta.

'Mr Chan claims the son was killed at Tet in '68, but we have reason to believe he is still alive. He's a cunning old bastard. Every year at Tet he makes a trip to the temple at Cholon and lights a few joss sticks in memory of his son. Wouldn't surprise me if the guy didn't show up as soon as the new management arrives.'

North of the Parallel, Mr Chan had a brother who was Bishop of Vinh. A nephew in the DRV embassy in Paris.

Three brothers in the North Vietnamese Army – a major, a colonel and a general – and a half-brother on the central committee of the Vietnam Workers' Party.

'And they still all keep in touch with each other through an uncle who runs an antique shop in Vientiane. Beautiful, isn't it?'

'Just one problem.'

'Yeah?' Lazarowitz was lighting a new Stuyvesant even as the remains of the previous one were still glowing in the ashtray.

'How do we know this guy is still on our side?'

'Our side? Of course he's not on our side.' Lazarowitz was stunned by the stupidity of the question. 'Mr Chan is not on anyone's side. He's got a side all of his own. His family. And – ' Lazarowitz was having trouble with his cigarette lighter and he cursed loudly – 'in 35 years of war, in a country that's seen half-a-dozen violent changes of government, lost one-and-a-half million dead and maybe three million injured, Mr Chan's family has not suffered a single fatality. Unless you believe that bullshit about the son killed in the Delta – which I don't.'

Lazarowitz had abandoned the lighter and was now striking matches on the side of a metal filing cabinet. At the third attempt he was rewarded with a flame. 'I call that quite something.'

MacShane had staked out Chan's coffee house for three days before he made an approach. Mr Chan did not appear to sell many cups of coffee, but there was a great deal of coming and going. On the second day MacShane had witnessed the arrival of a grey-haired man in the uniform of the North Vietnamese army. He came on a bicycle, which he parked against a lamp-post three doors away, taking care to padlock it. He was inside for over an hour and when he left there was a great deal of backslapping and embracing. He returned the next day accompanied by a gaunt young man in his late twenties who was dressed in a loose white shirt, baggy trousers and rubber sandals. Was this the missing son?

There was more backslapping and embracing. A young woman, presumably a daughter, went out with a shopping basket and returned an hour later laden with vegetables and spices. It was dark before they emerged and MacShane, watching from the shadows, just caught sight of a wafer-thin man with grey hair which had receded halfway across his head, but which was long enough at the sides to cover his ears. Except when he smiled, his lips were concealed behind a luxuriant Zapata moustache, also grey. Mr Chan was easily recognisable from the photograph on file at Langley. 'Looks like an ageing hippie,' Lazarowitz had said. 'And thin, very thin on account of the opium.'

MacShane made his approach under cover of twilight. He had sat for an hour toying with a bowl of noodles at a stall on the wide island that ran down the centre of Nguyen Hue. It was almost opposite Chan's coffee shop and afforded a clear view of the comings and goings. He sat there three evenings running, watching and waiting until he was sick of noodle soup. The woman who ran the stall smiled at him sympathetically. She had seen a lot of noodles in her time, too.

It was a day when he was sure that none of Mr Chan's northern relatives were visiting. MacShane crossed the road, taking care to avoid the bicycles and the puddles – for it was now the season of monsoons and the rain came every afternoon.

The coffee shop was empty except for a youth and a girl who held hands discreetly at a table in the corner. The juke-box was playing an old GI favourite, 'Billy, Don't Be a Hero' turned down low so that it could not be heard on the street outside. The youth in the corner was lightly tapping his fingers on the table in time with the music. From the wall above the jukebox a picture of Ho Chi Minh smiled down. The faded area behind the picture indicated that a slightly larger picture of General Thieu had until recently occupied the same space.

A curtain of beads separated the cafe from the family living quarters. The beads parted and a young girl appeared. It was the girl he had seen go out shopping after Northern uncle had showed up. She looked about sixteen but was probably older. She wore a Chinese silk jacket and around her neck a small gold crucifix. She seemed surprised to see MacShane.

'*Puis-je vous aider, Monsieur?*'

'A coffee please.'

'*Au lait?*'

'No, black.'

The girl disappeared into the back room. She was gone a long time. She came back with a black coffee in a cup and saucer embossed with the legend: *Continental Palace Hotel*. The wrapping on the sugar indicated that it had once been the property of Air Vietnam.

This time, instead of leaving, the girl sat at a table near MacShane and stared at him. Each time he looked up she turned quickly away. Once when he caught her looking at him, she smiled. Her features were as delicate as a painted egg-shell: a high forehead, plucked eyebrows and indented nose; a hint of lipstick and a touch of eyeshadow.

They sat for five minutes without speaking. The jukebox stopped and the girl started it again without putting any money in. This time it was 'Bahama Mama' by Boney M.

Bahama, Bahama Mama
Got the biggest house in town
Bahama Mama
She has six daughters and not one is married yet
And she's looking high and low . . .

After the first verse the girl spoke. '*Vous êtes Français, Monsieur?*'

'No.'

'*Anglais?*'

'No.'

The record had finished. The youth and the girl in the corner got up and left.

'I am American.'

'*Américain?*' The girl's eyes widened.

'Please tell your father I wish to speak with him.'

She disappeared behind the beads. MacShane heard her light footfalls on a stairway. A minute later she was back. At first she did not speak. She went to the window and closed the shutter. Then she closed and bolted the door. *'Allons, Monsieur.'* She held back the beads and ushered MacShane towards a narrow staircase at the back of the building.

The girl showed him into a room at the top of the first flight of stairs. It was a large room that ran from front to back of the building. There was a table with family photographs. On one wall was an ivory crucifix and on the other an altar to the ancestors on which scented joss sticks burned. Above the altar there was a picture of Ho Chi Minh. Mr Chan sure liked to have a foot in every camp.

At the far end of the room, two small children were watching a Donald Duck cartoon on television, a colour television. There, also, was Mr Chan, clad incongruously in Levi jeans and a very loud shirt that would not have looked out of place in Bermuda. MacShane approached, hand outstretched. Mr Chan was seated in an armchair piled high with cushions. He did not get up, but gestured to a chair.

'They said they would send somebody.' He was very thin and had a glazed expression, due probably to opium. 'But I did not expect you so soon.'

The girl switched off the television and shooed the two small children out of the room. 'Have you met my daughter?'

'Yes.'

'She is very beautiful, don't you agree?'

'Yes.' The girl blushed.

'Daughter Number Six. Altogether I have eleven children. Six daughters, five sons. I expect they told you.'

'Yes, they told me.'

There was a noise behind them. A young man had entered. MacShane's heart skipped a beat. It was the gaunt young man he had seen arriving the day before with the Northern army officer. The son who had fought with the Viet Cong.

Mr Chan saw MacShane's discomfort and smiled. It was the gentle smile of a man completely at ease. Perhaps it was the opium. 'This is Son Number Two.'

MacShane half stood as the young man came towards him. 'I thought he was dead.'

'He was dead but now he is alive again.' Mr Chan beamed. The young man was also smiling. He held out his hand and MacShane took it. The young man sat between them, cross-legged on the floor.

'Don't worry, Mr . . . what did you say your name was?'

'Jones.'

'Ah, Mr Jones.' The man smiled as though he saw straight through the lie. 'Mr Jones, my son speaks no English. He is also deaf. Deaf from the bombs. The bombs in the forest.'

The girl reappeared, this time with tea, Chinese tea in small bowls. Mr Chan took his and placed it on a table beside his chair.

'You speak good English,' said MacShane, one eye fixed on Number Two Son.

'You are too kind.' Mr Chan beamed again. 'My father was a very wise man. He was a rice merchant in Hanoi. He knew there were bad times coming and he wanted his family to survive. I had four brothers and one step-brother and he arranged for four of us to be educated in a different language. One he sent to Paris to learn French. One to Moscow to learn Russian. One to Peking to learn Mandarin and one to the British Concession in Shanghai to learn English. I was the Shanghai son.'

'And the fifth son?'

'He stayed in Hanoi to learn business.' Mr Chan took a sip of tea. 'He was a failure at business so he became a Communist.'

He smiled serenely. It was an infectious smile and MacShane smiled, too. You had to admire the old rogue. There was a long silence interrupted only by the sipping of tea. At length Mr Chan spoke again. 'So, Mr Jones, why have they sent you?'

'They said you would help us.'

'Help you? How?'

'Information. Contacts. Same as before. They will pay, of course. They have given me money for you.' MacShane tapped the wallet in the breast pocket of his shirt.

'Mr, er, Jones. All that is past. Over. Finished.'

'I don't understand.'

'I am 62 years old. My country has been at war for as long as I am able to remember and for most of that time my family has been divided. Now my family is together again for the first time in more than 20 years.' He indicated Number Two Son who, despite his alleged deafness, showed every sign of under-standing. 'This week my son came home from the forest. He has been gone for ten years. During that time his mother has died, three of his sisters have married.'

He took another sip of tea. The girl refilled his cup. 'Mr Jones, I do not like the Communists any more than you, but above all I love my family. The war is over. We have survived. It is a miracle.' He looked at MacShane and the smile returned to his eyes. 'Also, it is due to a certain amount of, how do you say, skilful diplomacy.'

Mr Chan stood up, or rather unfolded. His limbs creaked and he was very thin. Number Two Son stood up. Chan took MacShane's arm and led him to the doorway. 'You must go. It is not good for you to come here. You should leave Vietnam quickly. Before they find you.'

He took MacShane's hand and patted him on the shoulders as if to say, I am sorry we are unable to provide you with another war but please do not be too upset. It is nothing personal.

Daughter Number Six led him down the stairs and he waited while she unbolted the door.

'*Bonne nuit, Monsieur*,' she whispered as he stepped out into the cool night air. As he walked away he heard the bolts slide shut behind him.

Chapter Eleven

The other contact was a Catholic priest who, according to Lazarowitz, had the distinction of having been jailed in both the North and the South.

'Walks with a limp. Came from Phat Diem, about 50 miles south of Hanoi. Lot of Catholics around there. The Bishop staged a bit of an uprising and boyo here got picked up.' Lazarowitz had pushed the file across to MacShane. There wasn't much to go on. A couple of pages of computer print-out and a hazy picture shot with a telephoto lens on a street in Saigon ten years before.

'Best we can do. I asked Saigon to send an update but I guess they've got other things on their minds.'

According to the file, the priest had spent four years digging ditches in a labour camp near the Chinese border. Then one day they had put him on a plane to Laos and washed their hands of him.

'He makes his way down to Saigon, gets himself a parish at My Tho in the Delta. Minds his own business for ten years or so, then along come Thieu's police and drag him off to Chi Hoa jail. They said he was a spy. Roughed him up pretty badly. He was in a bad way when we got him out.'

'Was he a spy?'

'Was he hell! He just got fingered because he fell out with the local police chief. We sprung him because we thought he could be useful. And he was.'

They'd been at the safe house in Maryland when Lazarowitz turned up with the file on the priest. It was strange to see Lazarowitz in daylight. Somehow, he didn't seem half as mean, but appearances can be deceptive.

'What did you use him for?'

'Phoenix. It's in the file.' It was, too. The priest's spell in prison had given him credibility with the local NLF. The Phoenix operatives had used him to finger half-a-dozen Front cadres, each of whom had ended up at the bottom of a wet paddy field with his throat slit.

'Did the priest know what you used him for?'

'He didn't then, but we soon let him in on the secret. Boy, was he sick.' Lazarowitz slapped his side with something approaching mirth. 'Yessir, he was sick.' Then, seeing that MacShane did not share his sense of triumph, Lazarowitz went briefly on to the defensive. 'Listen, MacShane, it was a war. If we hadn't got them they'd have got us. You should have seen what they did to our guys.'

'I was thinking about the priest.'

'We had a word with the Archbishop and he was shipped up country, out of harm's way. He had a lot of praying to do.'

'What makes you think he'll co-operate with us again?'

'He's got no choice, has he?' The daylight did wonders for Lazarowitz's cough. He'd been up in Maryland for three days with hardly a splutter.

'What do you mean, "no choice"?'

'If he doesn't co-operate, we shop him.'

'Would we?'

'What do you think, MacShane?'

A few days after his visit to Mr Chan, MacShane decided to pay the priest a visit. He waited until evening and then took a cyclo from outside the Caravelle and headed west along Tran Hung Dao. According to Lazarowitz, the priest now lived under an assumed name and helped out in a parish which took in the maze of alleyways along the Ben Nghe canal. Lazarowitz had indicated the approximate location on a map published by the Ministry of Tourism, but it showed only the main streets. 'You can't miss the church,' Lazarowitz had said. 'Big white place with a statue of the Virgin outside. Still got a few bullet holes from the Tet offensive.'

89

They passed three churches. Each was white and each had bullet holes and statue of the Virgin. No doubt the cyclo driver could have helped, but MacShane wasn't about to share his secrets with anyone, let alone a cyclo driver.

'VC number ten,' the cyclo man kept saying. Apparently he had been a chauffeur at the British Embassy, but they had pissed off home and left him to it. 'They go England,' said the cyclo man. 'Have place on plane for car, but no place for me. I work ten years for English.' Remarkably the cyclo man seemed to bear the British no malice. He blamed his misfortune entirely on the Communists. 'VC no like me,' he said. 'VC no like American. No like English. No like Catholic. No like Buddha man. VC number ten.'

They had gone about two miles down Tran Hung Dao. The road was empty except for bicycles, and once or twice a taxi passed, one of those ancient blue-and-white Fiats, held together by string and chewing gum, that had been around since the French. There would be no more where those came from.

MacShane paid the cyclo driver off at a crossroads which, if the map was to be believed, was about half-a-mile from the church. The cyclo man pedalled off into the night murmuring imprecations against the Communists. Maybe it was just a show for MacShane's benefit. Or maybe it was for real. If they couldn't take the cyclo drivers with them, the VC had problems. On the other hand, it wasn't every cyclo driver who started life driving the British ambassador's Rolls Royce.

MacShane found the church in twenty minutes. It was where Lazarowitz had said, give or take a block or two. The bullet holes were still there and so was the statue of the Virgin, minus four fingers on her left hand.

There was a mass going on. The church was crowded. There were people in the aisles, on the steps and even outside in the yard. They were young and old, mainly well-heeled folk. You could tell by the western-style suits and silk *ao dais* and the Hondas parked four-deep alongside the outside wall.

There were cars, too. A couple of black limos, an MG (*circa* 1965) and a few old Citroens, but mostly people had come by bike or on foot. It wasn't wise to be seen doing too much conspicuous consuming ten days after a revolution.

MacShane waited in the shadows until the mass was over. It ended with a couple of verses of *Ave Maria*. It was in Vietnamese, but the tune was recognisable. It reminded MacShane of his childhood. His family had lived across the street from a Catholic church. It wasn't so much a church, more a sort of barn made of planks painted white with a bell tower at the front, also made of wood. On summer evenings you could hear the choir practising. *Ave Maria* had been one of their tunes. You could hear them at it two blocks away. It was a tune that had stayed with MacShane all his life.

It took the best part of an hour for everyone to go home. People stayed gossiping and smoking in the dim light of the street lamps. The conversation seemed serious. Who was likely to be re-educated. Whose long-lost relatives had turned up from the North. Who had taken to the boats. Eventually a couple of *bo doi* strolled round and told people to break it up, and gradually they drifted away into the night.

The lights in the church went out one by one. Then a man appeared on the steps. A minute later he was joined by another. They were both priests in black cassocks. Together they heaved the main doors shut and locked them. Then they split up. One, a younger man, disappeared into the darkness behind the church. The other crossed the yard and came out into the road. He passed within ten feet of MacShane. He walked with a limp, just as Lazarowitz had said he would, and the crown of his head was bald.

'Father Thach.'

The priest jumped about two miles into the air. Then he stood quite still. He did not turn round.

'Who are you?'

'I have come from Washington.'

Still the priest did not turn. He crossed the road and MacShane followed. When they were in the shadows the priest stopped and half-turned, staring at the ground. He did not want to see who he was talking to.

'Did anyone follow you here?'

'No.'

'How did you come?'

'By cyclo.'

'The cyclo driver?'

'I paid him off half-a-mile up the road.'

The priest started walking again, still without looking round. They were on what appeared to be an asphalt school playground. It was marked out with white lines for basketball. They came to a row of prefabricated classrooms. The priest took out a ring of keys and fumbled with them until he had opened the door. He locked the door behind them. He was shaking and the keys jangled in his hands. They walked along a few yards of corridor and then the priest turned into a classroom. He did not switch on the light but sat down at a desk. MacShane did likewise. There was about four feet between them. The outline of the priest was just visible against the window.

'Why have you come?'

'To help you.' Lazarowitz had insisted on this lie. 'That's the only way we'll ever squeeze any more out of this guy,' he had said.

'They promised they would take us with them.'

'I know.'

'We waited all day for the helicopter. We kept ringing the embassy. "Be patient," they said. "Be patient," that's all they would say. All day we waited and all night, but no one came.'

'It was very difficult.'

'All day and all night.' The priest was almost in tears. They sat for a moment in the dead silence. When MacShane's eyes had adjusted to the darkness, he could make out writing chalked on the blackboard, in French. It said. '*Rien n'est plus précieux que l'indépendance et la liberté.*'

The priest spoke first. 'You know about me?'

'Yes.'

'About the killings at My Tho?'

'Yes.'

'I was tricked. They asked me to help them. Just give us the names, they said. I thought they would be arrested, not killed. If I'd known, I . . .' He broke off and they sat again in silence.

'You know what they will do when they find me?' It was the priest again.

'I have come to help you.'

'How? It is too late. It is only a question of time until they find me. Maybe only days.'

'How can they know? It was seven years ago. Your name is changed. The records are destroyed.'

'No.' The priest almost shouted. 'The records are not destroyed. The Communists have captured everything. *Everything*. Do you understand? The secret police files at Bach Dan street. The CIA files from the embassy. The Phoenix files. Computer tapes. They were all captured intact.'

Surely not. The Agency must have destroyed its files weeks ago. What was all that smoke coming out of the embassy chimney? All that grey ash?

'There were duplicates. Duplicates of almost everything. The CIA helped Thieu's police set up their own file. It had all the same names on it – and many more. They were captured intact.'

'How do you know?'

'I know. That is all.'

The priest lit a cigarette. He did not offer MacShane one. MacShane caught a glimpse of his face in the flare of the match. He was deathly pale. At length, he spoke again.

'So, Mr CIA man, how can you help me?'

'First you must help us.'

'No. Never. I have been tricked once. I will not be tricked again. Why should I trust you?'

'Because you have no choice.'

The priest considered this for a moment. MacShane watched the glow of the cigarette go up and down and he smelled the tobacco. It was an American cigarette.

'What do you want from me?'

93

'Information. Contacts.'

'That is what I gave you before.'

'This time it is different. We want to save people. Not kill them. We must know who needs to leave and who wants to stay and fight.'

The priest puffed at his cigarette. His voice was calm now. 'In this area, there are many officers of the Thieu army. Also many big policemen. They have not yet been called for re-education but it is only a question of time. I can give you names.'

'And addresses?'

'Yes, but no more.'

'That is all we are asking.'

'And in return?'

'We will help you resettle in America.'

'How?'

'There are boats leaving.'

'Yes, from Vung Tao and the Delta, but it is very expensive – one tael of gold for the papers and another for a place on a boat.'

MacShane took a roll of hundred-dollar bills from his pocket. He counted off ten and passed them across to the priest. The priest lit another match and examined the dollars. Then he counted them. 'That is enough for documents but not for a place on the boat.'

'The rest you can have in exchange for names.'

'And if I get to Hong Kong or Thailand?'

'We will take care of you.'

'How can I be sure?'

'You must take my word. There is no other way.'

The priest came up with the names there and then. He had most of the addresses in his head, too. Macshane scribbled them into his notebook. It was slow going in the dark but he managed. The priest said he would arrange for the other names to be slipped under the door of MacShane's hotel room. What made the priest think he was staying in a hotel? asked MacShane.

In that case, said the priest, he would get someone to hand

over the information. In the post office maybe. By the Post Restante counter. Either way, he did not think another meeting would be necessary, if MacShane would kindly hand over the rest of the money here and now.

No way, said MacShane. Another meeting was essential. He didn't wish to be taken for a ride either. He would make contact again next week, at a time and place of his choosing. In the meantime he planned to go knocking on a few doors.

Chapter Twelve

It was a rainy day in May when they came for him. The rain had been falling since dawn. It came down in sheets and ran in rivulets along the gutters and pavements, washing away the flotsam of the old regime. In the side roads and alleyways people rolled up their trousers and went about their business knee-deep in flood water. The *bo doi* took shelter in doorways or huddled together under pieces of black plastic, rain dripping from the rims of their pith helmets.

MacShane sat in his room on the third floor of the Majestic and wondered how long it would be before they rumbled him. Already they were asking journalists how long they intended to stay. Tan Son Nhut was open again, but so far there were no international flights. There was talk of an Air France flight to Paris. Some said the Red Cross were sending a plane from Hong Kong to collect the stragglers, but the truth was that nobody knew.

Telex links with the outside world had been restored on the eighth day. MacShane waited for the rush to subside, then filed a thousand words on life after Liberation. It was a life-goes-on piece, not at all what they wanted to read at Langley. No bloodbath. No lynchings. Rather less violence than on a Saturday night in Brooklyn. He even put in a good word for the *bo doi*. Disciplined, friendly, a damn sight more popular than ARVN – or the New York City police, come to that. Of course, he said, it was a honeymoon. Only time will tell. That sort of crap. He led off with the victory celebration outside the Doc Lap palace. He described the neon lights around the picture of Ho Chi Minh, the crowds, the banners, the cheering. He re-typed the intro four or five times before he was satisfied. After that the story told itself.

When he was done he took the copy to the post office, where there were forms to be filled in triplicate and much activity with rubber stamps. MacShane's copy was inspected by a man with three pens in his shirt pocket who handed it back with a smile, pausing only to correct the spelling of Tan Son Nhut. The clerk at the telex counter refused to acknowledge MacShane's international cable card and insisted on payment in dollars. That apart, it went as smooth as clockwork. The copy was filed to FWF London and in due course a message came back. It said: NICE WORK MACSHANE STOP WE'RE PUTTING YOU DOWN FOR A PULITZER STOP. No doubt that was Lazarowitz's idea of a joke.

Liberation euphoria took about a week to wear off. The first sources of strain were the loudspeakers. The old regime had rigged up speakers on every street corner, but they had fallen into disuse. The *bo doi* had them working again within 48 hours and from then on Saigon was awakened at first light to the sound of revolutionary music interspersed with exhortations and official announcements. Before long the wires were being cut under cover of darkness. That was the first sign of resistance.

Then the petrol began to run out and there wasn't any more, at least not for public consumption. What limited supplies remained were strictly rationed and for official use only. Gradually cars began to disappear from the streets. There was also a flourishing black market in stolen petrol.

At the beginning of the second week all soldiers of the 'puppet' army were ordered to register with the new authorities in preparation for re-education. They were given until the end of the month to present themselves, but before long there were rumours of house-to-house searches.

One day an official appeared at the Majestic with a pile of poorly-duplicated questionnaires on paper which had been much recycled. Every foreigner was required to fill in not one, but four.

Most journalists sat around in groups completing their questionnaires, making fun of the quaint English and the absurdity of the questions. MacShane took his seriously. He went with the document to his room and pored over it. Who did he work for? When had he arrived? Had he been in Vietnam before? If so, please give details of previous visits. With which Vietnamese citizens had he met? Give names and addresses. Had he relatives in Vietnam? Did he have any moveable estates, whatever that meant, in Vietnam?

In MacShane's case the answers were short and simple. Too short and too simple, some might say. His hand trembled as he gave the completed forms to the receptionist. He hoped they would not be too carefully scrutinised.

It was almost dark when they came. The knock on the door was no more than a furtive tap. He opened it cautiously. There were two men. Vietnamese. Both aged about 30, MacShane guessed, but it was impossible to be sure. They had sunken cheeks and prominent cheekbones. They were dressed identically, in white sleeveless shirts and battledress trousers. Neither man smiled.

'Mr MacShane?' said the taller of the two.

'Yes.'

'Come with us, please.'

'Where to?'

'Please come.' The man gestured in the direction of the lift. The third finger of his right hand was missing.

The two men waited while MacShane put on his jacket and locked the door. He followed them along the corridor to the lift. They travelled down in silence.

MacShane handed in his room key at reception while the two men waited at a discreet distance. Outside it was still raining heavily. One of the men, the one who had not spoken, produced an umbrella and indicated a jeep parked by the kerb about fifty yards up Tu Do. The driver was wearing an olive-green pith helmet and the uniform of a *bo doi*. It was not until

MacShane caught sight of the driver that he knew for certain who they were. Until then he had half-hoped they might have been sent by the priest or Mr Chan.

The man with the umbrella held open the canvas flap at the rear of the jeep while MacShane climbed in. The man climbed in behind, his umbrella dripping rainwater on to the floor. The other man seated himself beside the driver.

'Where are we going?'

'You will see.'

They did not go far. Up Tu Do, past the cathedral and the palace. It was difficult to see where they were going because of the rain. After less than ten minutes they pulled up outside one of the fortified villas that MacShane remembered passing on the way in from the airport.

There was a *bo doi* on guard at the gate, sheltering from the rain in a little makeshift sentry box of sandbags covered by a sheet of black plastic. When the jeep approached the sentry emerged into the rain and opened the gate.

The gate closed behind them. The drive was fringed with palm trees. On the lawn at the left there was a fountain, empty except for rainwater and leaves. On the right, set back from the house, there was what appeared to be a landing pad for helicopters. Two more jeeps were parked in the drive.

The house itself was an elegant concoction of glass and concrete smothered with green creepers and jasmine. The entrance hall was marble and, in urns by the door, there were two large ferns. Half-a-dozen *bo doi* were lounging in the hallway, laughing and smoking. They stopped talking as MacShane entered.

'This way.'

The taller of the two men opened a door and MacShane found himself in a large room at the back of the house. One side was entirely glass, looking out on to a green lawn. The floor was polished mahogany, covered at the far end by a Chinese rug decorated with dragons.

In the opposite corner there was a large desk with a polished surface, like the floor. Behind the desk sat a small man in army fatigues with a row of pens in the breast pocket of his shirt.

'Ah,' he said, 'you are Mr MacShane.' He spoke as though MacShane's arrival had been long expected.

There were two wicker chairs opposite the desk. MacShane sat in one without waiting to be asked. The taller of his two escorts sat in the other, resting his hands palm downwards on his legs exposing the stub of his missing finger.

'I am Colonel Anh,' said the man behind the desk. 'I have responsibility for foreign guests.' He was smiling broadly as he spoke.

The colonel gave an order in Vietnamese and the second of MacShane's two escorts, who had not yet spoken a word, left the room. There was a moment or two of silence broken only by the patter of the rain on the window. Colonel Anh pondered MacShane, stroking his chin as he did so. In due course, but not before the elapse of a full minute he said just one word, 'Bulgaria.'

'Pardon me, Colonel?'

'Bulgaria. That is where I learn to speak English.'

'Your English is excellent.'

'No, Mr MacShane, I speak lousy English. Lousy. That is the right word?'

'Your English seems okay to me.'

'You think so?'

What was this creep on about?

'You have ever been to Bulgaria, Mr MacShane?'

'No.'

'You are fortunate. No good place. Cold winter and very fat women. Fat like so.' He used his hands to indicate what he alleged was the average girth of a Bulgarian woman.

The second escort came back carrying a tray with a teapot and four porcelain cups with saucers. He placed the tray on the desk.

'You like fat women, Mr MacShane?' The colonel was pouring the tea.

'Never really thought about it.'

The colonel was taken aback. 'Never thought about fat women. Never thought about . . .' Colonel Anh was giggling hysterically.

100

MacShane was thinking that it was a month to the day since he had returned from his hike in the Rockies and found the telegram from Lazarowitz. If anyone had told him then, that in four weeks he would be sitting in Saigon, drinking tea with a colonel in the North Vietnamese army, discussing the vital statistics of Bulgarian women, he would have advised the guy to go and see a shrink.

They drank their tea. The man with the missing finger stared blankly out into the garden. He, too, had no opinion about Bulgarian women. Colonel Anh had recovered from his fit of giggles. 'I expect you are wondering why I have invited you here,' he said eventually.

'Yes.'

'There are one or two, er, problems with your papers.' MacShane could see now that the forms he had filled in two days earlier were on the colonel's desk.

'You came to our country only three days before Liberation?'

'Yes.'

'That is very late.'

'I was not the only one. Two other journalists came in on the same plane.'

'We know that, Mr MacShane. But they are known to us. They have been here many times before. Your case is different because you appear to be coming to Vietnam for the first time in your life.'

So MacShane explained why Forum had sent him. That he had not been their first choice. South America was his beat, but this was an emergency. Saigon was falling and their main man had been down with malaria. Their number two was in Angola. They had sent for him, out of the blue . . . How many times had he told Lazarowitz that they would never swallow this bullshit? But Lazarowitz would have none of it. 'What's the matter, MacShane,' he had snarled, 'losing your nerve?'

'This agency,' said Colonel Anh. 'We never hear of it. Reuter we know; UPI, AP, AFP we also know; but not Forum World Features. That is new for us. Completely new.' The

101

man with the missing finger was taking notes. His partner hovered by the door.

MacShane explained that Forum wasn't like the other agencies. They dealt in hard news. Forum dealt in features – background, analysis, that sort of thing.

'And what happens to this, er, analysis?'

'It gets syndicated.'

'Syn-dic-ated? How do you spell?' MacShane spelled it out. The colonel wrote it down letter by letter.

'My articles are sent to maybe one hundred and fifty newspapers all over the world. Papers that subscribe to Forum's feature service.'

'And they publish them?'

'If they like them, yes.'

'I see.'

Colonel Anh considered the concept in silence. Syndication was a new one on him, but the ways of foreigners were mysterious. For the time being he would give MacShane the benefit of the doubt.

'Mr MacShane, I am afraid you must stay here with us for a few days while we, er, clarify your situation.'

The colonel looked very serious now. All thoughts of Bulgarian women had been banished. 'And I must ask you to write us a short history of your life. Paper and a pen will be provided. If there is anything else you need, Mr Ky – ' he indicated the man with the missing finger – 'will assist you.'

'You can't arrest me. I'm a journalist.' MacShane had risen half to his feet. Mr Ky had put away his notebook and made ready to restrain MacShane. Colonel Anh waved him back into his seat.

'Please be calm Mr MacShane. We are not arresting you. You are our guest.'

'I am a journalist and I demand to be treated like one.'

Colonel Anh didn't want to know. 'In time, Mr MacShane, we will check everything. Please be patient. In our country everything takes time. Now please go with Mr Ky.' He waved towards the door which the other man was holding open. Mr Ky was on his feet beside MacShane.

'Can I collect my luggage?'

'It will be done. Now go, please.'

The interview was at an end. Colonel Anh swivelled round in his chair and was looking out into the garden. It was still raining.

Mr Ky led MacShane down a passageway to a bedroom at the side of the house. It was a large room and the bed was big enough for three people. It had a writing desk and there was another door leading to a bathroom. The window looked out into a walled courtyard. On the rear wall, overlooking the bed, was a two-way mirror. This was a house that had known better times.

'I am next door,' said Ky, indicating in the direction of the mirror. With that he was gone.

MacShane removed his shoes and lay on the bed, looking up at the ceiling. He remembered Lazarowitz's parting words. 'If you get blown, MacShane, Uncle Sam's never heard of you.' He wished he had never heard of Lazarowitz. He wished he had told him where he could stuff his damn fool schemes for recapturing Vietnam.

MacShane was still lying on the bed when Ky came back with his suitcase and typewriter. The case had been searched, but nothing was missing. They must have seen the clippings with his by-line; that at least might help to stand up his story. There was also the Chomsky book. That might help too.

Another couple of hours passed. Ky appeared with food: a bowl of soup with noodles and cabbage, and two pieces of dry bread.

Outside the rain had stopped. He tried the window and found that it opened. The air was fresh and cool.

He sat at the desk and started writing. It was pretty much the version of his life they had agreed at the safe house in Maryland. Parents killed in a car crash ten years ago (Lazarowitz had even gone to the trouble of forging death certificates). Three years at Notre Dame, two in the Air Force at San Antonio. Seven years with Hearst in South America. There was still a guy at Hearst who would vouch for

103

MacShane. Lazarowitz had lined him up without telling old man Hearst. 'Only use him in emergencies,' Lazarowitz had said. This was an emergency. MacShane wrote down the guy's name and telephone numbers at home and work. Then there was Forum World Features. He had told Lazarowitz that they'd see through that in ten minutes. The whole outfit stank to high heaven. But Lazarowitz wouldn't have it. If there had been more time, he said, he would have fixed MacShane up with one of the networks, or even the BBC. But that sort of operation took time. It wasn't like the old days when a word in the right ear could secure a staff job with any newspaper or network you cared to name. These days there was always some half-assed Congressman waiting to finger anyone who so much as accepted a hamburger from the CIA. That was how it was since Watergate. Lazarowitz didn't like it any more than MacShane did. He was the first to admit that Forum World Features wasn't ideal cover, but so far no one had tumbled to it and MacShane would have to make do with it because it was all there was. Lazarowitz had given him the name of a man at Forum who rejoiced under the title of Managing Editor. MacShane put him down as a reference and kept his fingers crossed. He also gave the name of an oil corporation executive in Washington who, if contacted, would confirm that MacShane had worked in his corporation in the PR department for the last three years.

When he had drafted it out in longhand, MacShane typed a clear copy. To avoid being caught out he typed two versions of the final statement. One he pocketed and the other he left on the desk to give to Ky in the morning. It was around 03:00 when he finished. Outside he could hear the frogs croaking.

Ky reappeared around 09:00 with another bowl of noodle soup, more bread, and a cup of black coffee. He picked up MacShane's statement and took it away without comment.

At 14:00 hours the other man came with lunch – rice, vegetables and a banana. He also left a thermos flask of hot water, a tin of tea and a cup. Half-an-hour later he came back with

104

some magazines. They were in French and consisted mainly of pictures of revolutionary forces entering Saigon and of the victory celebrations. Next day there was still no sign of Ky. The second man came with the food and more magazines, this time in English, but three months out of date. He was polite, but said nothing.

Down the corridor MacShane could hear the *bo doi* laughing. From the road beyond the high wall he could hear the sound of traffic.

MacShane guessed they were checking out his references. That could take weeks. They didn't even have an embassy in Washington.

Ky came back around noon on the third day. 'Come with me,' he said.

They walked up the corridor to the entrance hall. Colonel Anh was there, holding his pith helmet.

'Ah, Mr MacShane,' he said, 'we make a short journey.'

'Where to?'

'Not far.'

And with that he led the way out of the front porch. The jeep was waiting, its engine already running, a *bo doi* at the wheel. Colonel Anh went to the front passenger seat and MacShane climbed in the back with Ky.

They drove out of the villa, turned right into the city, and were soon alongside the cathedral. Here they turned left and after a few hundred yards turned left again and stopped outside some high gates. Colonel Anh said something to the *bo doi* on guard and the gates opened.

'You will recognise this place,' said the colonel, looking over his shoulder at MacShane.

He did indeed. It was the American Embassy.

The oak door at the front of the embassy showed signs of having been battered open. The lobby was empty save for a plaque commemorating the marines who died recapturing the embassy from the NLF in the Tet offensive. Where the picture of the President once hung there was now a portrait of Ho Chi Minh.

The door which sealed the lobby from the rest of the embassy was hanging by one hinge; its combination lock appeared to have been shot open, and the door was studded with bullet holes.

'We take stairs,' said Colonel Anh. 'Lift not safe.'

They walked up the stairway, the colonel in front, Ky behind, MacShane in the middle. From about the second floor up, the stairs were strewn with debris. They passed a woman sweeping.

At the sixth floor the colonel said: 'We arrive.' MacShane was breathing heavily. He was out of condition. They went down a corridor and through a door labelled COUNTER INTELLIGENCE.

'CIA section,' said Colonel Anh.

There were about fifteen people in the room: men and women seated at desks sifting through paper and arranging it in bundles. There were piles of beige files with the CIA crest on the front. MacShane had seen plenty of these at Langley.

Colonel Anh paused in front of a young woman who was examining a card index and making notes. There were several hundred laminated cards, each about the size of a cigarette packet, arranged alphabetically. Every card contained a colour photograph, a name and a computer reference.

'They leave for us to find,' said the colonel. 'They don't even take care for their friends.' There was contempt in his voice.

In a corner at the far end of the room was a telex machine. Beside it a young man sat at a desk examining a pile of telexes. Most were in code, but the young man had a code book beside him and was laboriously translating each one into longhand. The Colonel said something to him in Vietnamese. The young man produced a key, unlocked the top drawer of his desk and took out a folder. Inside was a single sheet of telex which came out as a meaningless series of letters and numerals. To it the young man had clipped a translation in longhand. It read as follows:

PRIORITY FLASH:
  EX LAZAROWITZ
  PRO POLGAR
  AGENT MACSHANE STAYING CARAVELLE HOTEL UNDER
  JOURNALIST COVER STOP OPERATION TERMINATED
  STOP PLEASE EVACUATE SOONEST STOP REGARDS
  LAZAROWITZ.

The message was timed 03:19 hrs April 30. It had arrived
one minute before the telex link with Washington had been
disconnected – and some jerk had forgotten to put it in the
shredder.

Chapter Thirteen

Colonel Anh could not conceal his delight. It was not every day he uncovered a CIA agent. There was a spring in his step as they walked back to the jeep.

'You have not been entirely straightforward with us, Mr MacShane,' he said quietly, but without a hint of malice.

He had instructed the young man to make photocopies of the telex and its translation. They had waited while the copies were run off on a brand new Xerox. The young man had made two copies. The colonel took them both. One he kept for himself and the other he gave to MacShane.

'For you,' he said, grinning mischievously. 'Souvenir.'

MacShane had taken the paper without looking at it again. He folded it twice and put it in his back pocket. He looked neither at the colonel nor at Ky. He was thinking that if he ever saw Lazarowitz again he would ram that telex down his throat.

They drove back to the villa in silence. MacShane wondered what they would do with him. First, no doubt, they would interrogate him. They would want to know why he had been sent, and who his contacts were.

Then, he supposed, they would lock him up and throw away the key. Or maybe they would do a deal. Trade him for a war criminal or two. Or maybe a ransom. In which case the US government would have to decide whether to pay up or not. Lazarowitz's last words kept coming back: 'If you get blown, MacShane, Uncle Sam's never heard of you.'

He wondered why the operation had been aborted. Maybe

Lazarowitz had been overruled. That was the problem with fanatics like Lazarowitz. You could never be sure how high the authorisation went. Maybe it was just some crackpot scheme that he and Steiner had dreamed up on their own. MacShane kicked himself for not insisting on knowing the authorisation.

There was one other possibility. They might take him up in a helicopter and drop him out at five thousand feet into the China sea. It wouldn't be the first time it had happened. He had once met a guy in the cafeteria at Langley who had just come back from a spell in Saigon. The guy told him about a high-level North Vietnamese prisoner who they had kept in solitary confinement for four years, but who never cracked. And when they gave up on him they had just put him out in a helicopter and dumped him in the sea. MacShane looked at Colonel Anh sitting silently in the front of the jeep as they pulled up in front of the villa. He looked at Mr Ky sitting beside him. They had no reason to be merciful.

They kept him in the bedroom with the two-way mirror for the best part of a week. At least he guessed it was a week. After they got back to the villa, Ky took away MacShane's watch, his money and his luggage. He went through the suitcase item by item and noted down the contents. Then he made MacShane sign the inventory.

'Everything will be returned,' he said. When, he did not say.

Each time MacShane asked how long he would be kept at the villa they were evasive. Colonel Anh said that his case would now be decided by a higher authority. Ky said only that there were many worse places to be detained.

They came for him early one morning, shortly after dawn. They gave him back the suitcase, and the typewriter, but not the money or the watch, and told him to put on clean clothes. He was going on a journey, they said. A journey in an aeroplane. For a moment MacShane froze. Maybe they were going to dump him. But then he relaxed. If they were, they would

109

hardly tell him to dress up for the occasion. And in any case, they would still want to know his secrets.

Colonel Anh and Ky came with him to the airport. Ky was carrying an Air Vietnam bag with his clothes and personal effects, so MacShane guessed that they were travelling together.

'Where are we going?'

'To Hanoi,' said the colonel. 'You are very lucky,' he added. 'Hanoi is a beautiful city.'

MacShane could not bring himself to share the colonel's view of his good fortune. He was not going to Hanoi for the sightseeing.

They drove down the same tree-lined avenue that MacShane had come in on a month earlier. Past the same fortified villas with their sandbags and their walls topped with barbed wire and glass. Some of the gates were open and through them MacShane glimpsed groups of *bo doi*. Some sat talking and smoking. Once he saw soldiers kicking a football around in the driveway of a big house. Several of the houses were flying red and blue flags. On a grass verge near the airport they saw soldiers planting vegetable seed.

The stone at the entrance to the airport commemorating the 'noble sacrifice of the allied soldiers' had been whitewashed over. Instead there were the familiar words of wisdom from Uncle Ho: NOTHING IS MORE PRECIOUS THAN INDEPENDENCE AND FREEDOM.

They stopped at the gate while a *bo doi* checked papers presented by Colonel Anh. The *bo doi* looked long and hard at MacShane before waving them through.

The airport was a darn sight quieter than it had been when MacShane arrived. There had also been some changes in the decor. A wrecked helicopter lay on its side in front of the passenger terminal, its blades crumpled. The sign behind the Air Vietnam desk now said: HANG KONG VIETNAM. The picture of General Thieu with the bullet hole in the forehead had been replaced by a picture of Ho Chi Minh without a bullet hole.

The Hang Kong Vietnam desk was the only one functioning. A long, orderly queue had formed in front of it – mainly *bo doi* in baggy uniform and sandals. There were also civilian officials in white shirts. They had little plastic briefcases and pens in their breast pockets. Everyone had a pith helmet except for a handful of women in conical straw hats and baggy black trousers. Of the Air Vietnam hostesses in their blue *ao dais*, there was no sign.

There were foreigners too. Half-a-dozen overweight men with pink skins and damp armpits. Several had cameras slung sideways across their large frames. One addressed a few words to MacShane in what sounded like an Iron Curtain language. MacShane stared blankly and the man shrugged and walked away.

'This way, please.' Colonel Anh led MacShane to a room marked DEPARTURES in English. Mr Ky had produced two tickets and went off to join the queue at the Hang Kong Vietnam desk. He took MacShane's suitcase and typewriter with him.

Most of the windows of the departure lounge were broken. The wall of the lounge was bare except for a framed scroll hanging precariously from a nail which contained more thoughts of Uncle Ho. It read:

> The Vietnamese people are one,
> The rivers can be dried,
> The mountains can be eroded,
> But this truth can never change.

Ky returned with two boarding passes. His airline bag was still across his shoulder. They sat in silence for a while. Occasionally Ky and the colonel would exchange a few words in Vietnamese. The departure room filled up with other passengers; most were laden with hand luggage. Several carried television sets tied round with raffia. One had a gleaming new portable tape deck and radio – big and brash like you sometimes saw blacks with on the street back home. About half the passengers had cartons of American cigarettes. A woman carried two live chickens in a wicker basket. 'Saigon prices much more low than Hanoi,' explained Colonel Anh.

There was an inaudible announcement from an invisible loudspeaker and the passengers stirred. The colonel got up. 'Now I go,' he said. Then, to MacShane's amazement, he held out his hand.

'Mr MacShane, I give you one piece of advice. It is our policy to be lenient with those who confess their crimes. You must be straightforward with us, otherwise . . .' He did not finish the sentence.

With that he released MacShane's hand and walked away. MacShane watched him go with a tinge of regret. Colonel Anh wasn't a bad old stick, as secret policemen go.

The plane was an old Ilyushin. The hostesses were young girls with plaits and big smiles. They looked too innocent even to have travelled beyond the village post office.

MacShane took a seat by the window. The remains of General Thieu's airforce was still displayed along both sides of the runway, most of the planes still in their sandbagged blastproof bays. Some had bits of wings missing and shattered cockpits.

There was only one other civilian airliner. It bore the markings of Royal Air Lao. And in the middle distance there was a large passenger helicopter, with rotor blades at both ends. MacShane couldn't tell whether it was American or Soviet made, but on its side he could just make out the gold star of North Vietnam.

Hanoi lay beneath a thick blanket of cloud. The Ilyushin descended with caution. 'No radar,' said Ky. It was all he said during the two-hour flight.

For twenty minutes the plane nosed gently downward through the swirling cloud. Just as MacShane was beginning to wonder whether something had gone wrong, the ground suddenly appeared, a thousand feet below.

It was a land of flooded rice paddies, freshly rained upon and pock-marked by bomb craters. Small off-white stone houses in clumps of bamboo and banana trees. Every square inch cultivated, even the soil between the runways. Many of the bomb craters appeared to have been converted into fish ponds, and some had ducks on them.

As they came in to land the plane passed a bomb crater deeper than the others, so deep that little steps had been cut into the side. Around the rim, written in stones, were the words DAI THANG.

'What does *Dai Thang* mean?' asked MacShane, as the plane hit the runway with a bump.

'It means Great Victory.'

They trooped out on to the concrete apron. The Vietnamese passengers were laden with their television sets, radios and 555 cigarettes. The woman with her chickens. There were no other planes in sight and the airport buildings consisted mostly of prefabricated sheds with whitewashed windows. Inside the desks were manned by small, serious men in olive-green pith helmets. And there were forms to be filled in. Enough for every member of the Politburo to have a copy. The paper had been recycled so much it was a glossy brown.

Purpose of visit?

'What do I put here?'

'Just write "for consultation".'

Length of stay?

'Just write "not known".'

At the desk one of the small, serious men took the forms and examined MacShane's passport. He did not appear to realise that MacShane was a prisoner.

'You have been in the South,' he said, looking at the now expired visa of the old regime.

'Yes.'

'Then you have seen how we beat them.'

'Yes.'

'I should say, how we liberated them.'

'Yes.'

He closed MacShane's passport with a snap and passed it back to him. 'Then welcome, please, to the Great Victory.'

*   *   *

Outside there was another jeep, this one was Soviet made. And a man in a sky-blue shirt, frayed at the collar. It had recently rained and there were puddles everywhere.

'My name is Minh,' said the new man. He was short: only a little over five feet. When he walked, MacShane saw that he had a limp.

Ky took MacShane's case and put it in the back of the jeep. He put the typewriter in beside it. Then he spoke quickly to Minh in Vietnamese and walked away without looking at MacShane.

'He has gone,' said Minh. 'Now you are with me.'

MacShane climbed in the back of the jeep. There was no seat so he sat on the suitcase. The driver was a *bo doi*. On his belt he had a holster with a pistol.

'Please promise that you will not try to escape,' said Minh.

'I promise,' said MacShane. Minh seemed relieved.

They bumped for about an hour along dirt roads. Peasants bent double in waterlogged paddy fields were planting young green rice shoots. The fields were separated by small dykes along which walked girls in conical hats, each with a hoe over her shoulder.

There was no machinery, not even a water pump. Once they saw water being transferred from one field to another by girls holding a bucket on two long strings which they revolved in a circular motion.

Here and there a stately water buffalo walked along a dyke, sometimes guided by a child, sometimes alone. Young men with bamboo poles across their shoulders carried mud or manure in baskets strung from each end. They moved almost at a run, the baskets springing up and down in time with each pace.

Once or twice, when their jeep had to wait to cross a narrow bridge, children would gather and peer in the back of the vehicle. The sight of MacShane caused great excitement. *'Lien Xo, Lien Xo,'* they shouted.

Minh would attempt to shoo them away, but his efforts were ignored. Instead the children ran behind the jeep for as long as they could keep up with it, waving frantically and shouting: 'Lien Xo.'

'What does *Lien Xo* mean?'

'It means Soviet. They think you are a Soviet.' Unlike Ky, Minh seemed happy to talk.

'Where did you learn English?'

'In Cuba – and from the BBC.'

'What were you doing in Cuba?'

'I was sent by the Party. To repair my leg.' He tapped with his hand on his bad leg.

'What happened to your leg?'

'One of your mortar bombs,' Minh grinned. 'Hue in '68. Bad time.' He shook his head at the memory. 'Very bad time.'

They drove on in silence. The sky was grey, the air hot and damp. MacShane could feel his shirt grow wet where he leaned against the canvas wall of the vehicle.

They were passing through a small town now. More like a big village. Half the houses were made of stone and the rest of wood and thatch. Chickens scratched in the gutter. A child was leading a pig on a tether. They passed a little shop with a few poor vegetables set out in front, potatoes, cabbages, and a watermelon or two.

They had been driving for about an hour. MacShane guessed they had covered about twenty miles. During that time they had seen no more than half-a-dozen other vehicles, mostly army trucks. Once there had been another jeep and once a bus, a very old bus with people hanging out of the doors and windows. A youth was using the petrol cap as a foothold.

Minh had taken a packet of cigarettes from his trouser pocket. According to the pack, they were *Giai Phong* cigarettes. Minh offered one to the driver and then, after a moment's hesitation, turned and offered one to MacShane.

MacShane took a cigarette. 'What does *Giai Phong* mean?' he asked, indicating the name on the pack.

'It means "Liberation".'

In this country even the cigarettes were part of the war effort.

*　　*　　*

They passed through the town and headed back into the countryside.

'I thought we were going to Hanoi.'

'Not exactly, no.'

'Where are we going?'

'Son Tay.' Minh took a drag of his Liberation cigarette. 'Surely you have heard of Son Tay?'

Of course he had. Son Tay was the prison camp raided by the Green Berets five years back. They found it was empty when they arrived. The prisoners had been moved out four months earlier.

Another screw-up for which everyone involved got a Purple Heart and a handshake from the President.

Chapter Fourteen

At Son Tay they again took away his suitcase and typewriter. Minh first went through the case and made another inventory of the contents which MacShane signed. He asked if he could keep the Chomsky book since there was nothing else to read. Minh said he would ask, but it was not returned.

Before he took the book Minh looked at the inscription on the inside cover.

'Who is Josie?'

'A friend – at least she was.'

'What does "insensitive" mean?'

'It means "without feeling".'

'Are you without feeling?'

'Maybe I am.'

They put MacShane in a room about twelve feet by twenty. Once it had been divided into four cells. He could tell by the marks on the floor where the dividing walls had been.

The windows had bars and the door had sliding peepholes. They did not lock the door during the day and he was free to wander round the compound.

The bed was two wide planks placed across saw horses. There was a mosquito net and a clean sheet with many patches. After two nights Minh produced a mattress and later on the same day he turned up with an old table, one leg of which was shorter than the others. Minh put the table next to the bed.

They made MacShane wear prison clothes: a light cotton tunic with red and white vertical stripes, and trousers that were several sizes too big for him. He protested vigorously, and eventually they gave him back a pair of his own.

Son Tay was an island among flooded rice paddies and vegetable gardens. The prison compound consisted of three rectangular one-storey brick buildings with sloping tiled roofs and whitewashed walls. A six-foot brick wall ran around three sides of the compound, and on the fourth side, overlooking the homes of camp officials, it had tumbled down. In each corner there were guard posts, but there was no sign of any guards. When he looked at the walls, MacShane found bullet holes which, he guessed, must date from the Green Beret fiasco.

A small river ran along the back of the compound and beyond that were more paddy fields and a village partly hidden by trees. Sometimes, as he sat in the compound, MacShane could hear the laughter of children drifting across the trees from the direction of the village. Some evenings alone in the big room he could hear a girl singing.

After he had been in Son Tay for two days some men came to see him. Officers, to judge by the red stars on their collars. They did not give their names and they did not speak English. Minh interpreted.

'Mr MacShane,' said the taller of the two, 'your situation is very serious. It is the policy of our government to take a lenient view of all crimes committed during the war, but your case is different. You came to make trouble for us *after* the war.'

They were sitting in a sort of interview room just beyond the prison compound, where the camp officials lived. On the wall there was a picture of Ho Chi Minh surrounded by children. Between MacShane and the two men there was a wooden table. It had nothing on it except an unopened packet of Liberation cigarettes and an ashtray. Minh sat beside MacShane, interpreting in a neutral voice.

'Your only hope,' the man went on, 'is to be completely honest with us and then to ask forgiveness of the People's Government.'

He reached into his briefcase – it was made of black plastic and identical to the ones carried by important-looking *bo doi* in Saigon – and withdrew a sheaf of off-brown recycled paper. He counted out twenty sheets, marked each one with a number in the top left-hand corner, and then passed the paper to MacShane together with a ballpoint pen.

'You must write down every detail of your career from the time you left school. When you joined the CIA, where you were trained, where you were stationed. Why you came to Vietnam. You must be completely open with us.'

He closed the briefcase and the two men stood up. MacShane said it would be better if he had the typewriter. The men conferred for a moment and then instructed Minh to return the typewriter. 'We will come back in two days,' said the spokesman, 'and then we will ask many questions.'

MacShane set up the typewriter on the table in his room and sat on the edge of the bed. It was not easy to type because the bed was higher than the table and the short leg caused the table to wobble. He had been about to abandon the typewriter in favour of a pen when Minh appeared with an empty cigarette packet which he folded and wedged under one corner.

MacShane started typing in the late afternoon when the day was already fading. He continued by the light of the 40 watt bulb until the strain on his eyes forced him to stop. He made only one draft since he was planning to tell the truth. In any case the man had numbered the pages and would presumably want them all back.

At Camp Peary they ran a two-week course on how to resist interrogation. They even circulated a little booklet entitled: *Guidelines For Agency Personnel Apprehended on Hostile Terrain.* It opened with a preface by the Director saying how much the Agency loved its agents. How, in the unhappy event that an agent was apprehended on hostile terrain, Uncle Sam would do everything in his power to secure his safe return. Regrettably, however, it was necessary to make plans for such a contingency.

'*Admit nothing until you are absolutely certain that your cover has been blown.*' That was guideline number one. There followed a paragraph headed, '*Suggested ways of determining if your cover is blown.*' The possibility that the agent's immediate superior might send a telegram to the enemy informing them of his agent's precise whereabouts did not seem to have occurred to the anonymous author of the document.

Guideline number two said: '*In the event that his/her cover is blown an agent is authorised to reveal only such information as will not endanger the security of current operations or of other personnel employed directly or indirectly by the Agency.*' There then followed several pages of advice on how to stall for time to give other agents a chance to get clear and how to keep the interrogators happy with snippets of information the low value of which would not be immediately obvious.

The guidelines then went on to address a range of increasingly desperate scenarios. Guideline six was the bottom line. It was entitled: '*Advice for personnel subject to physical or mental duress beyond the limits of endurance.*' The author reminded his readers that as agents trained in the art of counter-interrogation, they were expected to have a pain threshold well beyond the limit of ordinary mortals. Grudgingly, however, he was prepared to concede that there were pressures that could break even the strongest will. He then went on to discuss, in the same antiseptic tones, the categories of information which could or could not be released under such dire circumstances.

As one of the trainees in MacShane's year had remarked, the author was clearly someone who had never had electrodes clipped to his balls.

Another place, another time and MacShane might have played it by the book. Had he been captured in Brazil or Bolivia, he might have stalled for time or fed his interrogators a few false leads. Those were his wars and he understood them. In Brazil and Bolivia he had always known that he had the Agency behind him – all the way up to the seventh floor at Langley.

Vietnam was different. It was not his war. It wasn't even America's war any longer. And as for the authorisation, there was no evidence that it went any higher than Lazarowitz's basement office. By the time he reached Son Tay, MacShane's mind was made up. He would tell them everything. Almost.

He started with the name of the tutor at Notre Dame who had first recommended him to the Company. It couldn't do any harm. The guy had been dead five years. He told them about the Officer candidate school at San Antonio, where Company recruits were distinguished by a triple X after their names on the school roll. He told them about the transfer to Air Intelligence at Bolling Airbase, Washington. About the three months' para-military training at Camp Peary. About the day the training officer, Jim Ferguson, assigned him to the Western Hemisphere Division and how they put him on the Bolivia desk in Branch Three. He told them about the orientation course on Bolivia at the Foreign Service Institute. About the intensive Spanish lessons in the language lab at Arlington. And how, at the end of it all, Ferguson called and said they had something special lined up. How would he like to be a newspaper reporter? MacShane had not liked the idea one little bit. What, he had demanded, was the point of all that training, if he now had to start all over again? Ferguson had assured him that the training would not be wasted, and that if he wanted a foreign posting this was the quickest route.

Reluctantly, MacShane had accepted. He had no option. Langley did not look kindly on junior officer trainees who turned down their first assignment. They had sent him to see a man at Hearst newspapers who said he had just the job for MacShane. But first there was more training. A crash course in journalism at Northwestern. Then they started him off on traffic accidents and muggings on the *Chicago Tribune*.

'There are two basic rules for a good reporter,' the editor had told him on the first morning. 'Keep your paragraphs short and never screw a colleague.'

The six months in Chicago had been the lowest point in MacShane's career. He had considered dropping out and joining his uncle's real estate business in Florida. Just when his mind was made up, the man at Hearst headquarters called to say they were sending him to Bolivia. That was how it had started.

MacShane wrote it all down. Even the name of the man at Hearst. He told them about Bolivia and Brazil and about every operation in which he had ever been involved.

When he got to Vietnam he told them about Steiner and Lazarowitz. How they had chosen him because they thought he would be unknown to the Vietnamese. He told them he had been sent to organise a stay-behind network. That he had been told to wait a week after Liberation – that was the word he used – and that he would be contacted. That he had waited, but there had been no word from anyone . . . Until the knock on the door from Colonel Anh's men. MacShane made no mention of Mr Chan or the priest. They were the only secrets he kept.

By about noon on the second day he was done. The statement came to eighteen pages of double-spaced type. Lazarowitz would have gone bananas to think that an agent of his would give away so much without even a turn of the thumbscrews. But MacShane no longer gave a damn what Lazarowitz thought.

Minh came in the afternoon and took the statement away. He returned later and gave MacShane a pack of Liberation cigarettes. That, at least, was a good sign.

It rained a lot that night. The rain came in through a leak in the roof and he had to move the bed. For a while he lay awake smoking and listening to the rain on the tiles. He wondered if they would torture him. He had once read in *Reader's Digest* that the POWs had been beaten with rubber hoses and strung up with their arms behind their backs until their shoulders dislocated. Was that worse than electricity? Since that boy in Brazil, MacShane had often wondered whether he could stand up to torture.

There was a new man with them when they came back next day, a white man who spoke English with an American accent. He did not introduce himself, but MacShane guessed that he was Cuban. The Cuban did most of the talking. To begin with anyway. He asked questions in English and Minh translated for the benefit of the two Vietnamese.

The Cuban was a professional. Hard and cold. He did not raise or lower his voice. He made no threats, but there was hatred in his voice and violence in his eyes. He was built like a T–54 tank and smoked continuously. He was also methodical.

He started with Camp Peary. Where was it? What was the lay-out? What courses were taught? Who taught them? The names of the other trainees in MacShane's year? When it came to names MacShane hesitated. For some reason it hadn't dawned on him that they would want everything.

'I can't remember.'

'Of course you can.'

'It was a long time ago.'

He started with the name of a guy who had dropped out of the course. Then he gave the name of a guy who was killed in Argentina.

'That is two. You said there were nine.'

'Maybe there were only eight.'

'You said there were nine.'

Then he gave them Streicher, who'd been in Panama. Then Colvin, who was in Madrid. Then Berger, goodness knows where he was. Then Calvert, who he had last run into at Langley two years ago. He told himself they probably had most of these guys on their files already.

'That's six.'

'I can't remember any more.'

'We will come back to the others.'

And so it went on. The Cuban asked questions. Minh translated. One of the Vietnamese took notes. There was also a tape recorder, a little Japanese machine that the Cuban had brought with him. It sat on the table between them and every 45 minutes the Cuban changed the tape.

They came to Bolivia. They wanted details on every operation. MacShane told them about the man in the post office who looked out for mail addressed to communist countries.

He thought the man's name was Guzman, but he must have retired years ago. In any case there were a lot of Guzmans in La Paz. He told them about the woman in the airlines office who provided the passenger lists. No, he couldn't remember her name. They would come back to her, said the Cuban.

They came to Brazil. He told them about the bribes to senators. Which senators, the man wanted to know. The bribes to the army men. Which army men? The bribed journalists, the subsidies to newspapers. Which journalists? Which newspapers? He told them about the attempts to set up Eastern Bloc diplomats. The buying up of a chauffeur at the Cuban embassy. An attempt to buy up a cypher clerk.

They came to Langley. How was Western Hemisphere Division organised? Who were the chief officers? What did he know about Chile? What operations were they running in Chile? Who were they bankrolling? Who were the field agents?

The Cuban made MacShane draw a diagram of the Western Hemisphere floor at Langley, marking out every office. Who worked there? He even wanted the names of the secretaries.

The routine was the same each day. Starting at 7:30 in the morning; breaking for lunch and a siesta around noon; beginning again at three and continuing until six. The Cuban asked questions, never raising or lowering his voice. Minh translated. And the Vietnamese officers listened and made notes. Occasionally the taller of the two intervened with a question of his own, but mostly they seemed content to let the Cuban ask the questions.

Always the Cuban smoked. He was the only one smoking and he stared with dead eyes at MacShane through a blue haze. He did not smile. He never made a joke. He just asked questions.

When they got to Vietnam, MacShane told them about Lazarowitz and Steiner. The Vietnamese officer asked about Lazarowitz's role in Operation Phoenix. Telling them was no big deal. It had all come out in the Senate hearings. In any case, ratting on Lazarowitz was the only pleasant part.

Over and over again, they asked about his contacts in Saigon. Over and over, he said he had none.

'We know you are lying,' they said, and nothing MacShane could say would convince them otherwise. They made him describe his days in Saigon in detail. They went through his time there, day by day, hour by hour, starting on the day of his arrival and through to the day of his arrest.

They recorded his movements on ten large sheets of paper: one for each day he had been at liberty. Each sheet was divided into three columns. In the first, they marked each hour of the day; in the second, they filled in MacShane's movements; and in the third, the name or description of every person he had spoken to. They wanted to know about everyone. Even the waiters and the cyclo drivers.

By the end of the fifth day they had identified two periods for which MacShane could not to their satisfaction account. One was the evening he had visited Mr Chan and the other was the Sunday he had visited the priest. They homed in with such confidence that it began to occur to MacShane that there was no point in holding out on them any longer because they already knew.

The interrogation lasted six days. And when it was over MacShane had betrayed everyone with whom he had ever worked.

Chapter Fifteen

When they were through questioning MacShane, a man came to take his picture. He was an old man, with a few wisps of white hair where there should have been a beard. His camera was also old. He set it up on a tripod in the centre of the compound and fussed about for the best part of an hour before he was ready to take pictures.

He was a courteous old man and took his job extremely seriously. Would Monsieur mind moving a little to the left? Head up a little. Perfect. And now, if Monsieur didn't mind, could we just try a shot from over here where the light was better. Yes, that's right. *Très bien.* He might have been photographing a model in a Paris studio rather than a CIA agent in Son Tay prison.

When the old man and his camera had gone, Minh came back and returned the Chomsky book. He seemed to have been reading it.

'This Chomsky. He is all right?'

'Depends on your point of view.'

'A strange book for a CIA agent to have.'

'It was a present.'

'From Josie?' Minh turned again to the inscription on the title page.

'Yes.'

'This Josie. She was all right too?'

'Yeah, Josie was all right, too.'

Not a day passed when he did not think of Josie. Of the night they first met in the laundry room of his apartment block. The

Che Guevara picture in the trunk under the bed. That awful New Year with her parents when he had to pretend he was working for an oil company. The row over the McGovern poster. How beautiful she looked when she was mad at him.

It was getting on for two years since Josie left. She had sent a card at Christmas, but that was all. He wondered where she was now and whether she ever thought of him. And he wondered what she would say if she knew he was in prison in Vietnam. Probably, she'd say it served him right. And she'd be right about that, too.

Now his interrogation was over, MacShane was allowed a ration of Liberation cigarettes. Six a day. The cigarettes came with the rice gruel at breakfast. Since he had come north there had been a decline in the quality of the food. Lunch was usually potatoes or noodles with a handful of cabbage and sometimes a few pieces of fatty pork, and the evening meal was much the same. Sometimes they threw in a piece of bread, and every two to three days a cup of coffee.

They had given him a razor, a bar of soap and an old piece of mirror, but he only shaved every three or four days. When he looked at himself in the mirror he could see that he was losing weight.

Minh stopped by most afternoons for a chat. He seemed glad of a chance to practise his English and MacShane was glad of the company. When they compared birthdates they discovered that Minh was almost the same age as MacShane – there were just twenty days between them.

Minh had been born in Long An, near Saigon. His family had fled north in the '50s to escape the Diem terror.

'We thought it would be for only one or two years, until the election was held to re-unify our country.'

But the election had not been held and Minh's family had never gone home. They had stayed with relatives in Hanoi until his father found a job teaching mathematics at a junior school, and later they had rented two rooms in a house near the main railway station. Minh had gone south with the NLF at about the time MacShane was taking up his first overseas assignment in Bolivia.

'At first, we thought it would not take long to liberate our country. One year, maybe two. Then we could go home and live in peace. We never dreamed the war would last so long.'

Minh had lost a brother and a sister in the war. His brother had gone south in '68 – a month after Minh had been wounded at Hue.

'My brother was a painter. He made pictures in water-colours. He used to go to the central market in Hanoi and make sketches. For five dong he would make a portrait. He could make his living this way. He was very talented.

'When he went south he took his paints and pencils with him, and sent my parents some small sketches made in the villages in the Delta. Then one day we got a message to say that he had been killed. Not how or why. Just killed. Six months later we received a small package. It contained his paint box and brushes. His comrades in the South had sent them back. My mother put them beside his picture next to the altar for our ancestors in her bedroom.' Minh smiled sadly at the memory. 'She is very, how you say, superstitious, my mother.'

They were sitting out in the compound, smoking. The air was hot and damp. MacShane had soaked a flannel in water and pressed it to his face, but it afforded almost no relief. Minh had no words of comfort. 'It will be worse yet, much worse,' he said cheerfully.

Later, Minh talked about his sister. 'She was in the militia. On the anti-aircraft gun at the end of the Long Bien bridge. If we go to Hanoi you will see the bridge.' A fly hovered, and he waved it away with his hand. 'One night, it will be three years ago on the last day of December–' the New Year MacShane spent with Josie's parents – 'that night the bombers came. They missed the bridge, but they wiped out my sister and her friends.'

From his pocket Minh took out a small polythene bag. It contained his identity pass, a wad of moth-eaten dong notes, and a worn photograph of three giggling girls. They were standing with their arms around each other, wearing uniforms slightly too big and helmets camouflaged with a sprig of foliage. They might have been dressed up for a school play.

'That's her,' said Minh. He was pointing to the girl in the middle of the trio. Slightly shorter than the others. Her helmet cocked at an angle so that one eye was covered. Wisps of black hair falling over her forehead.

'They were only sixteen,' said Minh. 'All in the same class at school. Volunteered together for the militia. All on the same gun. All gone in one night. So young. So beautiful.' He stared for a long time at the picture before carefully sliding it back into the polythene. A full minute passed before he spoke again. 'Mr MacShane,' he said, 'don't let anyone tell you it was a glorious war. We paid a high price for our freedom.'

They talked of many things. Of Minh's wife, who was a payroll clerk in the Yen Phu power station. Of MacShane's brother, who was a doctor in Baltimore. Of Minh's two children – a boy and girl aged seven and eight. Of baseball, of hamburgers and of Ho Chi Minh.

'Why does everybody call him Uncle Ho?'

'Because he was the Uncle of the nation.'

'American people don't call Nixon "Uncle Richard".'

'American people do not love their President like we love Uncle Ho.'

Minh talked of Ho as though he were one of the family. 'We had hoped to take Uncle Ho to see Saigon before he died, but unfortunately we were unable to liberate Saigon in time. We feel bad about that.' He spoke as if the fault were partly his. For a moment he sat in silence and then, realising he had not offered an adequate explanation, added: 'Uncle Ho was loved because, although he was President of our country for twenty-four years, he remained humble to the end of his life.'

With that Minh fell silent again and MacShane, sensing that the matter was too delicate for further enquiry, changed the subject.

*   *   *

'How much do you earn?' Minh asked out of the blue one evening, as they sat in MacShane's room watching a lizard chasing flies.

MacShane thought for a minute. It had been a while since he received his last pay cheque.

'About 450 dollars,' he said.

'A year?'

'No, a week.'

Minh took out his pen and made a calculation on the back of a cigarette pack. Then he put down his pen and looked up from the cigarette pack.

'At that rate,' he said, 'it would take me one hundred years to earn what you earn in one year.' He smiled at MacShane. 'Maybe I should have been a CIA agent.'

MacShane heard nothing for about a week. The interrogators had left. He had seen their car, an ancient Citroën, disappearing down the road that led to Hanoi. Then one morning, soon after breakfast, Minh appeared. He seemed happy.

'We are leaving,' he said.

'Where are we going?'

'To Hanoi.'

'That's what they told me last time.'

'This time definitely to Hanoi. You are going to be re-educated.' He beamed.

'Why are you looking so happy?'

'Because I was afraid they might shoot you.'

Chapter Sixteen

They set out for Hanoi soon after dawn. It was raining when they left. The rain was warm, and when it stopped the humidity was as bad as ever. At Minh's request the driver had tied open the back flap of the jeep to let the warm air flow through. But for that the humidity would have been unbearable.

The view from the back of the jeep was much as before: peasants bent double planting fields of young green rice; old ladies laden with baskets of cabbage and lettuce; children shouting, '*Lien Xo, Lien Xo*', every time they caught a glimpse of MacShane.

His clothes had been returned before they left Son Tay. They had even laundered his shirts and he changed out of the prison tunic into a clean shirt. Colonel Anh's souvenir, the telex from Lazarowitz, was still in the back pocket of his trousers. His wallet, complete with American Express traveller's cheques and a roll of dollar bills, was also returned.

They entered Hanoi by way of the Long Bien bridge – eighty years old and stretching one-and-a-half miles across the Red River. It was a patchwork of steel girders held together miraculously through years of continuous bombardment. Discarded sections of the bridge were visible in the mud below.

The crossing of the bridge took twenty minutes. 'That is where my sister died,' said Minh, as they came down into the city. He was pointing to a place on the dyke about 30 yards from the end of the bridge. 'There, by that tree. It was planted as a memory.' A young acacia tree had been planted in a slight indent. In front of the tree was a stone on to which three

131

names had been crudely engraved. And in front of the stone a beer bottle, from the neck of which protruded a single dead rose.

'They found her hat over there.' Minh pointed to a place at the foot of the dyke. 'My mother placed that beside the ancestors' altar, too. Next to my brother's paint box.'

Hanoi was a city of narrow lanes lined on each side by toy-town shops and houses, none more than two storeys, painted with flaking white emulsion. The doors and wooden shutters over the windows were green.

It was a city of bicycles. The driver threaded his way through wave upon wave of bicycles, all the time hooting furiously and cursing under his breath. The cyclists moved at a lazy, stately pace, meandering only to avoid pedestrians. Some had passengers seated side-saddle across the rear mudguards. Girls, their conical straw hats held in place by coloured ribbons beneath their chins, rode together in chattering groups, oblivious to the hooting. 'In Hanoi,' said Minh, 'the bicycle is king.'

Hanoi was unlike any capital city MacShane had ever seen. No Coca-Cola advertisements. No neon lights. Almost no cars. Only the occasional truck or jeep hooting its way through the bicycles. At crossroads and on public buildings there were huge hoardings depicting the heroic deeds of the People's Army, painted with bold brush strokes in red, yellow and blue.

They had reached what appeared to be the centre of the city: a road which ran around a lake in which there was an island. The island was linked to the shore by a narrow wooden bridge and on the island stood a pagoda.

A tram rattled by. MacShane glimpsed the passengers, their pinched faces, their string shopping bags and little bundles. Hanoi was a tired city. The tiredness showed in the flaking paint, in the rusting tram cars and in the pinched faces of the people. There were no fat people in Hanoi. None at all.

'We arrive,' said Minh.

They had come to a halt before two gates in a brick wall about six feet high. The wall enclosed a compound shaded by trees.

The driver hooted and at first nothing happened. He hooted again and after a while the gates were dragged open by a yawning *bo doi*.

'Plantation Gardens,' said Minh. 'At one time there were many Americans here. Now you are the only one.'

A man came to meet them. He appeared to have been disturbed from sleep, because he was pulling on an army jacket over his vest. 'My name is Major Mau,' said the man. His jacket was still undone. There were red stars on the collar. 'I am the commander of Plantation Gardens.' The major spoke in English. He shook hands with Minh, but not with MacShane.

Long, barrack-like buildings ran down either side of the compound. They had red tiles and white walls. Each was divided into about fifteen rooms and each room had a heavy door. The windows, which looked out on to the compound, were barred.

Major Mau spoke briefly in Vietnamese to Minh and then gestured to MacShane to follow him. Other soldiers had turned out to watch the new arrival. They stood around the edge of the compound as the commander led MacShane to one of the cells. It was a large clean room. There were two beds, both with mattresses and mosquito nets. On one there were two folded sheets and a pillow.

'For you,' said Mau.

MacShane put the suitcase on the bed. Minh followed with the typewriter. In the centre of the room there was a table and on it a flask of boiled water, an enamel cup and a tin of tea-leaves. There was also a pack of Liberation cigarettes and an ashtray which, upon examination, turned out to have been made from the wing of a shot-down B–52. Plantation Gardens looked like a step up from Son Tay.

'Today, eat, sleep, take exercise,' said Major Mau. 'Tomorrow we re-educate you.' He spoke English with a slightly sinister accent, like a German soldier in a B-movie.

In appearance, however, Major Mau was anything but sinister. His unbuttoned jacket and uncombed hair gave him a slightly dishevelled look and his round features were easily given to smiling.

'How long will re-education take?'

'Up to you,' beamed the Major. With that he was gone. Minh went too, saying that he would be back in a few days. He was glad to be in Hanoi because now he could be with his wife and children.

Later they brought food. Stewed pumpkin with bits of chicken, green peppers and a piece of bread. MacShane sat outside in the compound eating. Nearby a group of *bo doi* sat around playing cards for cigarettes. Afterwards a couple of them came over and tried out a few words of English.

'American?'

'Yes.'

'How many years have you?'

When they did not understand his reply, MacShane used his finger to draw 36 in the dust.

'You marry?' The *bo doi* indicated the third finger of his right hand.

'No.'

'No marry?'

'No.'

And with that the *bo doi* went away shaking their heads in amazement that anyone could reach the age of thirty-six without being married.

It grew dark very quickly, in the space of maybe thirty minutes. There are no evenings in North Vietnam, and darkness brings no relief from the humidity.

MacShane sat outside, leaning against the stone wall of his cell, smoking a Liberation cigarette. Around 20:00 hours a *bo doi* came to lock him in for the night. There was no fan in the cell, only two small barred windows. One opened on to the compound, and the other, set high in the rear wall, opened on to a street outside. By standing on the bed he could see out into the street. There were houses along the opposite side, each illuminated by a dim bulb. Neighbours sat talking on doorsteps. An old granny walked back and forth with a baby in her arms. A man was watering what looked like tomato plants in pots along the front of his house. A youth on a bicycle drifted past.

It was too hot to sleep. MacShane lay awake listening to the sounds of life in the street beyond the wall. A child crying. A bicycle bell ringing. The distant hoot of a truck horn. He wondered how they would re-educate him. He remembered the stories of brain-washing from Korea when he was a kid. He remembered going with his father to see *The Manchurian Candidate* at a drive-in in Burlington. It seemed silly now, but in those days people believed that communists could turn a man's mind inside out.

He was awoken by music from a loudspeaker in a tree in the compound. It was accompanied by a commentary that appeared to be intended for exercises. He stood on the bed and peered out. In the street there were people bending and stretching in time to the music.

Around 6:30 a soldier unlocked the door. MacShane celebrated with twenty press-ups and a couple of turns round the compound. The spectacle of MacShane, clad only in shorts, jogging around the compound caused much amusement among the *bo doi* who turned out in force to watch. Later, MacShane took a stroll to the bathroom and doused himself in cold water. There was soap and a clean towel. It was his best bathroom since the Majestic.

Breakfast was a boiled egg and a cup of strong black coffee. It was MacShane's first egg in captivity. Major Mau showed up around 8:30. 'Mr MacShane,' he said. 'Please come.'

MacShane followed the Major across the compound where the *bo doi* were now playing basketball. On the far side of the compound there was a small hill covered with flowers and foliage surrounded by more trees. Beside it there was a substantial French-style house with a porch, against which there leaned a bicycle. Waiting on the porch was an elderly man in blue shorts which covered the tops of his white knees. His shirt, which hung loosely below the waist, was open about halfway down his front, revealing a white hairless chest. Over

135

his head, and tilted slightly to one side, was a French beret from which tufts of white hair protruded.

'You are Mr MacShane,' he said in halting English.

'Yes, sir.' It was the first time MacShane had called anyone 'sir' since coming to Vietnam. On reflection it seemed too grand a word. 'Uncle' would have been better.

The old man extended a pink hand. 'I am Professor Tran Ngoc Man,' he said. 'I have been asked to assist in your re-education.' His smile revealed an almost intact set of gleaming white teeth.

MacShane followed the Professor into the house. 'I was in France before the war,' the Professor said. 'The European war that is.'

'South America was my beat. I've never been to Europe.'

'Never been to Europe?' The Professor shook his head in disbelief. 'Never been to Europe,' he repeated, half to himself.

They passed through a bare hallway into what must once have been the drawing room of a house occupied by a family of colonial officials. It had high ceilings and long windows with wooden shutters. The window at the front overlooked the asphalt compound where the *bo doi* played basketball. It must once have been a green lawn tended by gardeners.

In front of the window there was a stout mahogany dining table, its surface stained and worn. Around the table stood four chairs covered in leather which was held in place at the edges by brass studs. The leather had worn in places and tufts of stuffing showed through.

The Professor sat down in a chair with his back to the window. MacShane sat opposite. Of Major Mau there was no sign.

On the table there was a black plastic briefcase from which the Professor took a sheaf of papers, on one of which MacShane could make out his name. They sat in silence while the Professor leafed through the papers as though becoming acquainted with the contents for the first time. Sometimes he would nod. Sometimes his brow would furrow. Sometimes he would make a tut-tut noise with his tongue. Overhead a fan turned languidly, barely disturbing the heavy air.

136

After about three minutes the Professor put down the papers and looked MacShane carefully up and down. Then he smiled benignly. 'Tell me,' he said, 'how did a nice young man like you come to get mixed up with these gangsters?'

So MacShane explained that it hadn't been like that in the beginning. Not when he was growing up.

In those days to be an American was the greatest gift God could bestow upon a human being. What could be more natural than to want to make everyone else American too?

In those days there had been no good commmunists. The world had not been divided into countries, rich and poor, big and small. It was not made up of towns and villages and families. Good and bad people were not all jumbled together. There had just been communists and non-communists. The saved and the unsaved. The free and the unfree.

When MacShane was a kid, the television showed every night the Communist advance in Korea. Diagrams depicted the remorseless spread of communism, like desert sands. Nowadays they would have done it in colour. Red for the Reds, blue for the good guys. In those days it was just a grey shadow coming out of China and creeping down the Korean peninsula. Every night he would come home from school and the grey shadow would have crept a little further south.

Sometimes they showed arrows sweeping out of Korea, through Japan. Later the arrows came out of Vietnam and down the Malay peninsula, through Indonesia and into Australia. There were even moments when communism seemed to be lapping at the shores of California.

At school there had been a history teacher called Robert L. Grainger. He had been a captain in the marines, and everyone looked up to him. Even the other teachers. Captain G. they used to call him. He had been at Normandy in '44. 'Looking back, of course,' said MacShane, 'we should have realised that he was fighting the Germans, but somehow word got round that Captain G. had helped to save us from communism, and so people took him very seriously when he talked about the Red menace.'

One day Captain G. had brought a map of the world and hung it on the classroom wall. It was a big map, printed on canvas, and it had a piece of wood threaded through the bottom which made it hang straight.

It was also a simple map. The Soviet Union, China and the Eastern Bloc countries in Europe were painted red; the rest of the world was left blank. The red countries had no borders between them. They were just one big red mass overshadowing Europe, the rest of Asia and even the United States.

Around the red area there was a thick black line. 'This line,' Captain G. used to say, 'marks the boundary between freedom and tyranny.' The Freedom Frontier; that's what he called it.

The captain used to explain that communism was a world conspiracy that had started in the Soviet Union in 1917 and had been spreading like cancer ever since. We'd lost China in '49 and that was the biggest blow to the Free World since the Russian Revolution. Now we had to draw the line in Korea. Only America could stop communism, said Captain G., because European countries like Britain and France were too lily-livered.

The Professor listened without interrupting. Sometimes he nodded. Sometimes he smiled: a gentle smile, with no hint of mockery. A smile that seemed to say, 'I understand perfectly. In your place, I might have felt the same myself.'

Overhead the fan turned slowly. A man came and served tea from a porcelain teapot decorated with a pattern of flowers. The cups had a matching pattern. Probably they came with the house.

They sipped the tea. Still MacShane talked, his forehead bathed in sweat. Still the Professor listened, his black beret clamped firmly on his head. The gentle smile. The tufts of white hair.

It was not just Captain G. Everyone believed in the world conspiracy. No one considered the possibility that the Chinese were anything other than puppets of Moscow. Or that North Korea and North Vietnam were anything other than puppets

138

of China. Only traitors expressed doubts. And there was no shortage of traitors. Senator McCarthy was hunting them everywhere. In the Pentagon. In the State Department. Even in Congress.

The Professor was still nodding, but he no longer smiled. He had seen a lot of purges in his time, too.

Then there was patriotism. Being a Vietnamese the Professor would know all about patriotism. Every American child was brought up to believe that God was an American. Every morning of his school life MacShane had stood in line in that draughty school hall in Burlington and, hand on heart, pledged allegiance to the flag. Every American kid knows the words by heart: 'I pledge allegiance to the flag of the United States of America and to the republic for which it stands. One nation indivisible under God for all.'

In those days the President never made a speech without referring to God. God was in the Pentagon. God was in the State Department. God was everywhere the American flag flew. God was flying with General Curtis Lemay's bombers when they were pounding Korean rice farmers back into the stone age. There were times when God would have nuked China in return for a few Hail Marys.

By the time MacShane got to college, of course, things had cooled down a bit. The Reds had been stopped at Korea and the Taiwan Straits, for the time being at any rate. McCarthy had been discredited. The Vietnam war was still a twinkle in John F. Kennedy's eye.

But students in those days weren't like they were now. They didn't read books that weren't on the syllabus. There were no anti-war marches. No dope. Just good clean rock-and-roll, baseball and religion.

'Think not what your country can do for you, but what you can do for your country.' That's what Kennedy had told American youth. The speech had made a big impression on MacShane's generation. Everyone wanted to work for a big corporation or get into the high-tech industries to help NASA get a man on the moon ahead of the Russians. There were no problems that Coca-Cola or the Chase Manhattan Bank could not solve.

No one was cynical in those days. People believed what their President told them. They believed what they saw on the television or read in the newspapers. In MacShane's day most kids were patriotic. They believed in America. They wanted to see America grow stronger and they wanted to play a part in making it strong.

Or else, like MacShane, they wanted to help America defend what was hers by divine right. In that case they joined the Pentagon or the CIA.

MacShane told the Professor about his first week as a Junior Officer Trainee at Bolling Airbase. Allen Dulles and Colonel Baird had made fine speeches. You are the elite, they said. There were a hundred, maybe two hundred applicants for each of your places. We have chosen you because you are the best and in this job we want only the best. Your lives will not be like those of other Americans. Your battles will take place under cover of darkness. Your sacrifice will be unacknowledged in public. Your victories will be celebrated in secret.

They never mentioned the defeats.

Chapter Seventeen

Next day the Professor did not turn up. Minh came instead.

'We go sightseeing,' he said.

Minh wanted to take the jeep but MacShane said he would prefer to walk. They consulted Major Mau. The Major made a telephone call. 'Okay,' he said as he replaced the receiver, 'you can walk.'

It was good to be walking city streets again. Not that Hanoi was like any other city. It was more like a big village. The only cars were a handful of aged Volgas and the occasional Citroën. Mostly they contained foreigners and some had diplomatic plates.

For the rest, the traffic was bicycles, cyclos and the occasional Honda which had drifted up from the South.

Hanoi life revolved around the bicycle. There were bicycle parks demarcated by bits of string and watched over by vigilant old ladies. Bicycle repair men squatted on every street corner with little puncture kits in wooden boxes and ancient pumps with double-handles which plunged up and down like detonators.

It was a city of innocence. Even the youths who loitered on the sidewalks looked naive compared to the spivs who haunted the Saigon coffee houses. Young girls in conical hats and shapeless trousers held hands and laughed. '*Lien Xo,*' one called after MacShane, and then dissolved into a fit of giggles.

They started at the history museum, a mock-Oriental building with pagoda-like towers and pavilions, located in a shaded garden between the Opera House and the dyke. It reminded

MacShane of one of those mansions built by eccentric Californian millionaires.

The museum was designed to prove that Vietnamese civilisation was the oldest on earth. It consisted of halls of ancient pots and pans, prehistoric coffins hollowed out of tree trunks and a dozen or so large bronze drums said to be four thousand years old. The only light relief was provided by the handles on the drum which appeared to show a couple copulating. This Minh would neither confirm nor deny. Instead he moved hastily on to the next exhibit.

MacShane said ancient history wasn't his scene and Minh eventually admitted that it wasn't his either. He suggested the Museum of the Revolution might be more MacShane's cup of tea and, by a complete coincidence, it was only over the road.

The Museum of the Revolution was a veritable chamber of horrors. There were pictures of hangings, beheadings, disembowellings, and live burials. By comparison to what the French had got up to in Vietnam, Operation Phoenix looked like a social welfare programme.

Souvenirs of the French included a well-used guillotine, complete with wicker basket for catching heads. The curator laid on a demonstration. MacShane's stomach turned as the blade dropped with a clang that ricocheted off the wall.

On the way back to Plantation Gardens they detoured round the lake. Minh pointed out the main hotel for foreigners, the post office, and the Catholic cathedral. MacShane asked where he could buy a pith helmet, but Minh said ration coupons were required. He would see what could be done.

They stopped at a tea house near the cathedral and sat for half-an-hour drinking lemon juice on a terrace overlooking the lake. They talked about the skyscrapers in New York; about which bridge was longer, the Golden Gate in San Francisco or the Long Bien in Hanoi; about fall in New England; about whether American or Vietnamese girls made better wives.

'The luckiest man alive,' said Minh, 'lives in a European house, eats French food, and has a Japanese wife.'

*   *   *

The Professor came back the following day. MacShane watched him dismount his bicycle and lean it carefully against the porch of the house on the far side of the compound.

They sat in the same room and the same man served tea from the same porcelain cups. Overhead the same fan turned languidly.

'What do you believe in, Mr MacShane?'

The Professor was wearing the same black beret and the same gentle smile.

'I am a technician. It is not my job to believe.'

'But you used to?'

'I have already told you, I believe in America, in love, truth and justice – even in God and Father Christmas.'

'Father Who?'

'Never mind.' What was the point of all this? They had already milked him of all the secrets he had ever known.

'When did you stop believing?'

'I didn't stop. I just lapsed.' The Professor had taken a fountain pen from his breast pocket. In front of him on the table there was a single sheet of paper. On it he wrote the word 'lapsed' in English. Maybe he meant to look it up later in a dictionary.

'What made you, er – ' he hesitated – 'lapse?'

'I found out too much.'

'What did you find out?'

'I've already told them about Bolivia, about Brazil, about Chile.' MacShane's voice was raised. What was the point of going through all this again.

'Be patient, Mr MacShane. We have a lot of time. We must be thorough.' Still the old man was smiling that same gentle, deceptive smile. 'Was there not a moment', the Professor went on, 'when your doubts crystallised? When you knew you were on the wrong side?'

It was then that MacShane told him about the boy in Brazil. About watching while the sergeant dosed him with electricity. About hearing the screams. About the smell of piss and singed flesh. About the evil little sergeant laughing and offering to let MacShane flick the switch. About throwing up afterwards in the car park.

143

The Professor did not react. He just listened with the air of a man who had seen too much human wickedness to be shocked.

'But you carried on,' he said.

'Because the other side was just as bad.'

'Is that what they told you?'

'It's true.'

'How do you know?'

'The POWs were tortured. They went home and wrote books about it.'

For the first time, the Professor was not looking at MacShane. He looked down at the table. He fidgeted with his pen and then he sighed deeply. 'Regrettably,' he said, 'you are right. It was wrong and it was stopped.'

MacShane was on the offensive now. 'Was it stopped because it was wrong or because you were afraid of what they would say when they got home? Why, I bet there's some poor bastard being strung up by his elbows in the Hanoi Hilton right now.'

'Mr MacShane,' said the Professor quietly, 'every security force has its villains and we have ours.'

'Exactly. So now you know why I stayed.'

Round Two had gone to MacShane.

The Professor came almost every day. Sometimes he stayed all day. Sometimes he would leave before lunch. He always shook hands on arrival and, when he left, he never said when or if he would be back. The conversation followed no pattern. Sometimes he would ask questions. Sometimes he would provoke an argument. Sometimes he would let MacShane question him. He encouraged argument, tolerated insolence, and never showed anger. Not even when MacShane scored points.

Sometimes the Professor spoke frankly.

'Mr MacShane, I worry. I worry that our Party will become corrupt like those in China and the Soviet Union.

'In the war, we attracted the best people. Then it was not easy to be a Party member. Many sacrificed their lives. Now we are starting to attract time-servers, opportunists who see Party membership as a ticket to the best jobs, the best housing, the best education for their children.'

He would shake his head. 'It is a big problem. I do not know the answer.'

Once he said, *à propos* of nothing in particular, 'In our system we lack a mechanism for correcting mistakes until they become disasters.' He did not elaborate, but MacShane was left wondering whether at some time in his life the Professor had had first-hand experience of a disaster.

Sometimes they argued.

MacShane would say, 'At least in my country we can say what we like about our President and our government without fear of being clapped in jail. Look at the anti-war protests in Washington. What would happen if people had tried that in Hanoi?'

The Professor considered the question seriously. 'What you say is correct,' he said eventually. 'America is a very open society. That is an attractive feature of your system. When your government does something wrong, you can criticise it on the television and in the newspapers. You can demonstrate against it. Your Congress will set up a committee of enquiry. Every detail will be picked over and exposed.'

He paused. There was a mischievous glint in his eye. 'There is only one problem: five years later your government will do the same thing again.

'You Americans do not learn from history.'

The Professor enjoyed his little jokes.

'Mr MacShane,' he asked on one particularly humid morning, 'why does your government make such a fuss about Americans missing in action? They keep sending us lists and demand that we trace them.'

'To an American every life is important.'

'But these are dead Americans.'

'Everyone has a right to know what happened to their loved ones.'

145

The Professor smiled. 'Maybe we should send the American government a list of our Missing In Action.'

Minh came back on the fourth day. He was carrying a brand-new pith helmet. 'For you,' he said, 'special price – 18 dong.' MacShane had only dollars. Not to worry, said Minh. He would accept three dollars, but please do not tell Major Mau or the Professor.

One morning the Professor arrived with a canvas shopping bag slung from the handlebars of his bicycle. It contained two heavy objects wrapped in newspaper. They were about the size of baseballs.

'What are they?'

'Something every American should see.' He took the objects out of his bag and placed them on the table next to the teapot.

'Example A,' he said, removing the newspaper from one of the objects. It was a small yellow bomb with metal tail fins about four inches long and a screw-on top. 'Don't worry, it's quite harmless.'

The Professor unscrewed the top and passed the two halves to MacShane. The inside was empty. The explosive had been scraped out.

'Look carefully at the inside wall.'

MacShane tilted it towards the window.

'Can you see what it is made of?'

The bomb consisted of hundreds of tiny steel ballbearings embedded in molten metal.

'It is called a Cluster Bomb Unit,' said the Professor. 'Quite ineffective against strategic targets. Designed for use only against human beings. They poured millions of these on to my country. Many did not explode. They are still lying in the rice paddies, waiting for our farmers to tread on them.'

'What do you expect me to say?'

'You could say that the people who dropped these were not soldiers doing their duty. At worst they were criminals. At best, moral cretins.'

'It was a war.'

146

The old man shook his head. He seemed genuinely sorry for MacShane. 'A war?' he said quietly. 'We were not bombing Washington. We were not even bombing Saigon.'

They sat in silence for a moment. Above them the fan turned so slowly that each revolution of the single blade seemed to suggest it might be the last. Behind them the windows were open. A butterfly floated in. For a while it was the only thing that moved.

The Professor unwrapped the second object. 'Example B,' he said with a weak smile. It was another bomb, much like the first except that the screw-top was missing and the wall had splintered around the rim.

'Given to me by the Swedish ambassador. He found it in his garden after the bombing three years ago.' The Professor passed the bomb to MacShane. 'You see what this one is made of?'

MacShane peered at the part where the wall had been chipped away. 'It looks like plastic,' he said.

'Exactly. It is made of plastic splinters. And do you know why?'

MacShane did not.

'Because plastic cannot be X-rayed, which means that a person hit by these splinters cannot respond to treatment.' The butterfly fluttered between them and came to rest on the ballbearing bomb.

'Technically,' said the Professor, 'the United States is at least one thousand years in advance of Vietnam. But morally . . .' He did not complete the sentence. As though he lacked the qualifications to offer even an estimate.

Next day there was no sign of the Professor. Minh showed up around ten. 'Today,' he said, 'we go to see Uncle Ho.'

'I thought he was dead.'

Minh was not amused. One did not make jokes about Uncle Ho. 'We are going to his grave. He has a grave, like Lenin's, how do you say . . . ?'

'Mausoleum?'

'Exactly.'

MacShane wore his new pith helmet for the occasion. It was the subject of considerable mirth along the way.

They went on foot down Avenue Dien Bien Phu, a wide street lined with spacious villas, once inhabited by the cream of the French Raj.

Uncle Ho's mausoleum was a shock. A grey monstrosity, utterly at odds with its surroundings. It might have been imported from the Red Square in Moscow. A monument not to Ho, but to Stalin.

Visitors came by appointment only. They checked in at a reception office at the side of the mausoleum where Minh signed his name and MacShane's in the visitors' book. There was a queue for admission but it moved quickly and they were soon at the entrance, which was guarded by two immaculate *bo doi* in flat caps and white gloves.

MacShane removed his hat and went in. The air inside was chilled, a welcome change from the damp heat outside. Uncle Ho was probably the only person in Hanoi to have airconditioning. They walked side by side up a marble staircase lined with red linoleum. In front of them were a party of country people on a day trip, dressed in their Sunday best. The girls with black hair trailing down their backs in long plaits. Everyone clutching their hats.

They reached the top of the stairs and there he was, not twenty feet away, asleep in his glass coffin. Exactly as he was in the picture. A wispy beard. A few white hairs. A high forehead, lightly freckled. Dressed in a grey cotton tunic.

Even in death Uncle Ho had presence and when they got outside it was a while before anyone spoke. After they had walked for a minute in silence, MacShane said, 'If he was as humble as everyone says, surely he would not have wanted all this?'

Minh considered the proposition carefully before responding. 'It was what the people wanted.'

'You mean it was what the Party wanted?'

'Yes,' said Minh, 'the Party.'

*   *   *

'How old are you, Mr MacShane?' asked the Professor one steamy day as they sat in the front room of the house in the compound.

'It's in the file in front of you.'

'You are thirty-six?'

'Yes.'

It was their sixth or seventh session. Each now followed a similar pattern. When the Professor asked questions, MacShane answered with good or bad humour according to the humidity, according to whether the questions interested him and according to whether he felt the old man was trying to score off him.

The Professor only asked questions to which he already knew the answers. He rarely made notes. Just listened patiently, sometimes nodding, always with the appearance of great interest.

He always arrived by bicycle. Always wearing the same black beret tilted at the same angle. Always in a loose-fitting shirt and shorts which came down to his white knees.

It was at the final session that the Professor suddenly developed an interest in MacShane's age.

'So you are thirty-six years old?'

'You know I am.'

The Professor had taken off his steel-rimmed glasses and was cleaning them on a clean white handkerchief. Every day he had a new handkerchief. 'Are you happy, Mr MacShane?'

'There are other places. I would rather be.' The humidity was worse than ever. Even the Professor's brow was moist.

'I meant, are you happy with your life in general?'

'Are you happy with *your* life?'

The Professor did not take offence. He considered the question with his customary gravitas. He stopped polishing his spectacles and placed them on the table. The handkerchief he returned to his pocket, pausing only to dab his brow. At length he said, 'Mr MacShane, I am a teacher of history. The history of Vietnam. For more than half my life my country has been at war and it has been my job to teach young men and women about our history. Many of my students are dead.' He paused to let the memories pass. 'I hope that, before they died, I was able to help them understand the meaning of their sacrifice. If I have done that, I will die happy.'

'Also,' he added, 'I have lived to see my country liberated. That is something not even Ho Chi Minh achieved. What more can I ask from life?' He smiled at the thought. The spectacles lay on the table. He picked them up and placed them on the end of his nose.

'And now, Mr MacShane, what about you?'

At thirty-six years of age, MacShane was the owner of a two-bedroom apartment in one of the most desirable parts of one of the world's most desirable cities. He ran a two-tone Ford Pinto with air-conditioning and four-speed windscreen wipers. He used the same barber as Henry Kissinger and shared a tailor with William Colby. He grossed US $20,000 a year with six weeks' vacation. He spoke fluent Spanish and Portuguese and had done tours of duty in Brazil and Bolivia and two tours at headquarters in Langley. His superiors reported favourably on him, and by the age of forty he could expect to be head of station in somewhere like Uruguay or Guyana.

As to whether he had accumulated merit, he had been known to help old ladies across the road. Once he had mended a fuse for a woman who lived across the hallway. And in Bolivia, a while back, he had paid the bus fare for an Indian woman with a baby who was trying to bum a ride back to her village.

So far as anyone could tell, he had acquaintances rather than friends and most of them were in the same line of business. He played a little squash at the Company squash club and dined out occasionally with young ladies from the administrative side of the Western Hemisphere Division.

As to whether the human race had been in any way enriched by MacShane's thirty-six-year membership, that was the very question he had been pondering in the Rocky Mountains national park on the day that fateful cable from Lazarowitz had summoned him back to Langley.

*　　*　　*

'Have you ever loved anyone, Mr MacShane?'

In MacShane's book, to fall in love was a sign of weakness. For the first ten years he had been into fucking rather than loving. After that there was only Josie. He told the Professor about Josie and how she left him after Chile.

If he had been asked at the time, he would have denied flatly that he ever loved Josie, but it was getting on for two years since she had gone and not a day had passed without his thinking of her. If that was love, then MacShane pleaded guilty.

Suddenly it was dark. The sounds of Hanoi street life drifted over the wall of the compound and through the open window: the ringing of bicycle bells, the laughter of children, someone practising on a flute. The Professor was getting ready to go. He buttoned his shirt, gathered up his papers and scooped them into his plastic briefcase.

They walked together to the porch. The Professor put the briefcase in a string bag which he suspended from the handle-bars. 'Mr MacShane,' he said, extending his hand, 'yours is a difficult case.' He spoke as if he were a doctor, attempting to diagnose a rare disease. 'If you are to make a complete recovery, you will need a long period of convalescence. I will consider carefully what is to be done.'

With that the Professor got on his bicycle and rode away, his black beret clamped firmly on his head. MacShane never set eyes upon him again.

Chapter Eighteen

It was Minh who broke the news. 'They are going to send you to the countryside,' he said one evening as they sat watching the *bo doi* playing basketball.

'To the country?'

'Yes. To be a farmer.'

'Why?'

Minh shrugged. 'I don't know. In Vietnam most people are farmers. Maybe they think it is good for you to see how our farmers live.' He added: 'Please don't tell them I told you. Officially I do not know, but I heard Major Mau talking on the telephone.'

Major Mau came visiting bright and early next morning. 'It has been decided,' he said. By whom he would not say. For how long he would not say.

MacShane took the news badly. 'Major, I have been a prisoner for nearly three months. I would like to make contact with a representative of my government.'

'Unfortunately,' said the Major, 'your government is not represented in Hanoi. That,' he added with a smirk, 'is their decision, not ours.'

'The Red Cross are here.'

'Unfortunately, I have no authorisation.'

'I insist. It is my right . . .'

Major Mau's face flushed and he raised his voice. 'Mr MacShane, please do not talk to me about your rights. You are a spy, not a soldier. We can do as we wish with you. You are lucky not to have been shot.' Then, in a calmer voice, he added: 'In any case, your government has shown no interest in

152

you. We have not had any enquiries. No one has even reported you missing.' The Major turned. 'We leave in the morning at six. Please be ready.' And with that he left.

So it was true what Lazarowitz had said. 'If you get blown, MacShane, Uncle Sam's never heard of you.' As it happened, it was Lazarowitz who had blown it, but as far as Uncle Sam was concerned the distinction was academic. MacShane was on his own.

There was only one alternative. He would have to go over the wall. It was not a very high wall and so far as he could see, there were no guards. He was near the centre of Hanoi and it was at most a couple of miles to a foreign embassy. Most West European governments were represented in Hanoi. So was Canada. If he could make it to one of their embassies, he was home and dry. Uncle Sam could hardly claim not to have heard of him then.

Several times, when out walking in Hanoi with Minh, he had thought of making a run for it. A foreigner on his own in Hanoi would not arouse suspicion. In daytime at any rate.

All that had stopped him was the thought that he was probably down for release soon anyway. That, plus the fact that he hadn't a clue where the embassies were.

He remembered that Minh had once remarked that accommodation was not available for all the embassies and that many of them had to stay in the foreigners' hotel in the centre of the city. He knew roughly where that was. He had passed it several times on his walks with Minh. Presumably any mission based in the hotel would have diplomatic immunity. If all he had to do was make it to the hotel, he was laughing.

The problem was that time was short. He could have made it at almost any time in the last four weeks. On some days he could almost have strolled out of the main gate. But now there were less than twenty-four hours left. He kicked himself for not having gone earlier.

During the day it would be hard to get over the wall without being seen. At night he was locked in his cell from around eight until about six. That left only one option. The early darkness, between seven and eight, when the *bo doi* were having their supper.

MacShane spent the day as if he were preparing for a move to the countryside. He washed a couple of shirts and some underwear and hung them up to dry on the clothes line he had rigged up between his cell window and a nearby tree. He swept out the cell and spent the rest of the day sitting out in the compound browsing through the latest issue of *Vietnamese Studies*. At the suggestion of the Professor he had been supplied with the last two years' worth and they occupied pride of place on the little wooden table in his cell. He now appeared to be on the subscription list, since the latest issue had arrived with breakfast the previous day. Mostly it was articles on the Great Victory. There was also a piece about an agricultural co-operative near Haiphong which claimed a record harvest despite typhoons and floods. In other circumstances, MacShane might have read it more attentively.

Lunch came around noon. It was stewed pumpkins again. By now MacShane had learned that the menu only varied according to what was in season. And there were only so many ways you could serve pumpkin.

Minh stopped by in the afternoon. He was MacShane's only source of news from the outside world. He had heard on the BBC that the United States was planning to oppose Vietnam's admission to the United Nations. The old man in the Café Givral had been right: America was out for revenge. Minh also said there had been reports of massacres in Cambodia. Although he dismissed the reports as American propaganda, he did so without conviction.

Minh said he would be coming with MacShane to the countryside and might stay a day or two until he was settled in. After that MacShane would be on his own.

All afternoon MacShane was dying to question Minh about the location of the embassies, but he knew that to do so was to invite suspicion. It could also have compromised Minh. So he resisted the temptation.

Minh left around 17:00 hours. The darkness came suddenly as it always did. The *bo doi* started their dinner shortly after 19:00 hours. The compound was almost deserted. A solitary soldier was on duty outside the major's house, but his line of vision was obscured by trees. By 19:30 MacShane could wait no longer. He made a bundle out of his clothes and placed them in the bed, arranging the blanket so that it looked as though he had turned in early. One of the *bo doi* would come to lock the door around eight. With luck he would not check the bed, in which case MacShane would not be missed until morning. Without luck, they would be after him in thirty minutes.

MacShane dressed for the occasion in a pair of grey flannels, a pair of dull brown shoes, a white shirt open at the collar, and his lightweight tropical jacket. This was one time he would not object to being mistaken for a *Lien Xo*.

He strolled to the corner of the compound furthest from the camp commander's house. From the *bo doi* quarters he could hear the sound of laughter and the clatter of spoons on metal plates. He hoped they were enjoying their pumpkin stew. When he reached a part of the wall shaded by trees, he heaved himself up until he had a clear view of the road. Two cyclists went by, then an old man with an ox-cart full of manure. MacShane let himself down and waited. The ox-cart took an age to pass, and all the time MacShane was casting anxious glances in the direction of the *bo doi* living quarters.

More cyclists passed. Then an old woman and a child. She was taking for ever. There was no time to wait for her to move out of sight. As soon as she was far enough past not to hear him, MacShane pulled himself on to the top of the wall and dropped down into the street. He looked both ways. The road was still clear. The ox-cart was disappearing in one direction, the old lady in the other. It was only when he stood up that he realised that he was being watched. Standing on the other side of the road, almost directly opposite, was a small girl in black pyjamas. She was wearing no shoes and there was a large blue patch across her shoulder. She was aged about four and in her left arm she clutched a small, quite naked, baby boy.

The girl stood transfixed as MacShane picked himself up and swiftly dusted his knees. MacShane nearly jumped out of his skin when he saw her. She was standing not ten yards away, partly obscured by a tree. He took one look at her and then produced the biggest smile of his career. For a moment she seemed uncertain how to respond. Then, just loud enough to be audible, she uttered a small, '*Lien Xo.*' MacShane heaved a sigh of relief and walked quickly away. His disguise was effective.

He was in an unpaved lane which followed the wall around the compound for about a hundred yards. There were houses along one side. At the end he came to a paved road lined with medium-sized French-style villas. MacShane had been here with Minh. He knew that this road led to the Avenue Dien Bien Phu, emerging somewhere near the Army Museum. If he followed that north, he would come to the lake and beyond the lake was the foreigners' hotel.

MacShane walked briskly, keeping to the shadows and doing his best to look like a *Lien Xo* out for an after-dinner stroll. Boys and girls on bicycles drifted by. Now and then a black Volga passed, hooting furiously, its rear window curtained. He crossed a railway line, then a road junction where a policeman was going through the motions of directing traffic from a pedestal in the centre of the road. MacShane gave him a wide berth, but the policeman was too busy blowing his whistle at errant cyclists to spare him a second glance.

After ten minutes he reached the lake. Young couples, their bicycles parked against nearby trees, discreetly embraced on the stone benches dotted around the shore. A group of old men sat gossiping. MacShane stood still for a moment to get his bearings. On the far side he could make out the post office which Minh had pointed out on their last outing. (MacShane had tried to persuade Minh to let him send a postcard to his folks. Minh had given the proposition sympathetic consideration

156

before rejecting it. 'If they find out, I have big trouble' he said.)

Walking casually and keeping to the trees, MacShane made his way around the end of the lake until he was almost level with the post office. Beside the post office there was a narrow street leading away from the lake. It emerged into a much larger thoroughfare and there, not fifty yards away, was the hotel.

Like so much else in Hanoi, the Thong Nhat Hotel had seen better times. An edifice of peeling stucco stained by leaking drainpipes. There were half-a-dozen cars outside, mainly battered black Volgas with lounging drivers and diplomatic plates. One had a United Nations sticker on the rear bumper.

It was all MacShane could do not to run the last fifty yards. Once through the revolving door he found himself in a cavernous hallway with off-white walls and unpolished mahogany furnishings. At the far end there was a bar propped up by a couple of plump Europeans. Several more foreigners, almost invisible in the gloom, sat drinking in frayed armchairs. A television played, unwatched. The stairs were directly ahead and MacShane made straight for them.

The first floor was a dark corridor with doors along both sides. Every door was labelled. The first one said: EMBASSY OF THE PALESTINE LIBERATION ORGANISATION. He worked his way along the corridor looking at each door. There were more embassies, Gulf states mostly. The World Health Organisation, Oxfam, UNICEF . . . He was getting warm.

'*Puis-je vous aider, Monsieur?*'

MacShane wheeled round to find himself facing a Vietnamese youth in a white waiter's jacket. Room service was the last thing he needed right now. Nor did it help to be fluent in Spanish and Portuguese.

He hesitated. He could either slug the youth and run or come up with the necessary French. '*Oui, la Croix Rouge, s'il vous plaît?*'

The youth mumbled something, the gist of which MacShane took to be that the Red Cross was on the next floor up. He rattled off a quick '*merci*' and headed back towards the stairs. Sure enough the Red Cross was on the second floor, fourth door on the right.

He knocked. There was no sound. No one at home; that was all he needed. He knocked again. Then came the sound of an inside door being opened and suddenly he found himself facing a clean-cut blond man in a dinner jacket. In one hand he clasped a black bow tie which he had been in the act of placing around his elegant neck.

'Monsieur.'

'Do you speak English?'

'Of course.'

'My name is MacShane. I am an American prisoner. I have just escaped from a Vietnamese prison and I need help.'

For a moment the man looked thunderstruck and then he took a step backwards, one hand on the door handle.

'There are no American prisoners in Vietnam,' he said, making to close the door.

'You're looking at one, buddy.'

'I am sorry, Monsieur, there are *no* American prisoners in Vietnam. The last were released more than two years ago. Now, if you'll excuse me, I have an engagement . . .' He made to close the door but MacShane's foot was in the way.

'Pardon me, but there are more important things than dinner parties. After two years of thumb-twiddling you've got a real live customer.' MacShane was inside now and had closed the door behind him. He found himself in a small lobby with two doors leading off it. In its day this had been a fancy hotel. The door from which the elegant blond had just emerged was still ajar. MacShane pushed him aside. 'Is there anyone else at home?'

'No.'

'You're quite sure?' MacShane indicated the other door.

'There is no one else.'

'Good. Now, where were we?'

The Red Cross man looked panic-stricken. 'Look, I don't know who you are, but you must leave at once.'

'I've already told you. My name is MacShane. I am an

American prisoner. I am seeking asylum and the assistance of the Red Cross to leave the country.'

'That is impossible.' The man was casting about for some way of raising the alarm. 'You must leave at once. You will compromise our whole operation.'

'What operation? I thought you were in business to help prisoners. No prisoners, no operation. You should be grateful to me for keeping you in business.'

MacShane had come across this type in South America. Overpaid, under-worked, terrified of straying from the cocktail-party circuit. There was only one way to acquaint him with the realities of the tough little world outside. MacShane took one quick step towards the man and hit him. Once. Very hard.

The bow tie shot through the air and landed in a vase of scarlet dahlias on a table by the window. The man himself came to rest on the bed. There was no noise except the smack of MacShane's fist against the clean-shaven jaw and a sudden contraction of bed springs.

The window was open and looked out on to the street. From the distance came the wail of a siren. MacShane knew at once that they were after him.

For a moment the man lay where he fell, blinking rapidly and rubbing his jaw. When he had recovered sufficiently to take stock of his situation, MacShane resumed their conversation. 'Listen, friend, I haven't got time to go through the small print of the Geneva Convention with you. I need help and I need it fast.'

The man was sitting up now, still rubbing his jaw. 'You will have to get to an embassy,' he said. 'My superiors in Geneva would not sanction the use of Red Cross facilities for this purpose.'

'Okay, then find me an embassy. You have a copy of the diplomatic list?'

The man nodded sullenly. 'It is by the telephone.'

'Good, then start by telephoning wherever it was you were

159

going for dinner and tell them you've been unavoidably detained.'

The man moved towards the telephone and MacShane added: 'If you give so much as a hint that you have trouble, I will break your neck.' He spoke as though the prospect gave him pleasure.

The man picked up the telephone and spoke in French to the hotel switchboard. There was a pause while the operator connected him and the phone rang. The man then had a brief conversation in German with someone called Hans.

'Right, now ask the switchboard for the British Embassy.'

'It is too late to call the embassy. Better to try the ambassador's residence.'

'Okay, and when the number rings pass the phone to me.'

The man spoke again in French to the switchboard, then he handed the phone to MacShane. 'It is ringing . . .'

MacShane took the phone, but kept his eyes fixed on the man from the Red Cross. The phone was answered almost immediately. 'Withers here,' a voice boomed. To judge from the racket in the background there was some kind of party going on.

'My name is MacShane. I am an . . .'

'Look here, old boy, we've got a bit of a do on here at the moment. Won't it keep until tomorrow?'

'I am an American prisoner . . .'

'Terribly sorry, old chap, can't hear a word you're saying. Why don't you pop round to the embassy tomorrow. The consulate opens at 10. Make it 10.30 to be on the safe side.'

And with that the phone went dead.

'Try the Canadians.'

They went through the same procedure. When the phone was ringing, the Red Cross man handed it to MacShane. This time a Vietnamese voice answered. MacShane handed the receiver back to the Red Cross man. There followed a brief conversation in French. The Canadian ambassador was out – at a party at the Britsh ambassador's house.

They tried the French. Then the Italians. Then the Swedes

and finally the Swiss. It was the same story all round. Everyone was whooping it up with the British.

'In that case,' said MacShane, 'we'll call again when they get home.'

'Impossible,' said the Red Cross man. 'The switchboard closes down at nine and does not reopen until eight tomorrow morning.'

They tried the British again, but the bastard had taken the phone off the hook.

It was a long night. The Red Cross man, who was a Swiss by the name of Pierre, cracked open a bottle of Chivas Regal and after a couple of glasses he loosened up a little.

MacShane could stay the night, he said. In the morning he would drive him to the British Embassy. He was sure the British would take him in. MacShane said he had been intending to stay the night anyway. And just to be on the safe side he would sleep by the door.

MacShane was awake before six. The Swiss was still out cold. Amazing what a few glasses of whisky could do. Hanoi was waking up too, to judge by the clatter in the street.

MacShane took a peek out of the window. The chances were they'd be watching the hotel by now. They might even be watching the embassies, but that was a risk he had to take. From the window it was impossible to see whether there was anyone watching the main entrance of the hotel.

The Red Cross man had a kettle and a jar of Nescafé. MacShane made two cups of coffee and gave him a prod. He came to with a start.

It occurred to MacShane that the switchboard probably listened in to calls made from the hotel. Pierre thought this was possible. It was also possible that the embassies were tapped. Certainly the Western ones.

'In that case,' said MacShane, 'we'll skip the formalities and call unannounced.'

They waited until it was gone ten. MacShane shaved with Pierre's Remington. Pierre spent five minutes in front of a

161

mirror, examining the bruise where MacShane's fist had made contact with his jaw. They made themselves another cup of coffee and listened to the news on the BBC. It was the first time MacShane had heard the news in two months, and it was surprising how little the world had changed while he had been away.

Although Pierre expressed not the slightest curiosity as to how MacShane came to be in Vietnam, MacShane insisted on telling him. The poor man went pale when he heard he had spent the night with a CIA agent. MacShane then gave him a telephone number for Lazarowitz at Langley. He asked Pierre to telex the details to Geneva as soon as MacShane was safely inside an embassy. For good measure he also suggested that Pierre pass the details to any journalists he happened to come across. Just let that creep Lazarowitz try saying he had never heard of a guy named MacShane.

There was no one in the corridor when they set out. Pierre stuck his head round the door first to make sure. The man was shaking with fright. It was pathetic. They went down the stairs and into the lobby. Pierre walked two paces ahead. The lobby was crowded with Vietnamese and foreigners, but no one tried to stop them.

Outside there were more cars than there had been last night, with guides and interpreters standing round waiting for their foreign guests to show up. A few Vietnamese, mostly children and country people, stood near the entrance, watching the foreigners come and go. The street was busy with bicycles and cyclos, but there was no sign of anyone watching.

If challenged, MacShane was planning to make a run for it. The British Embassy was the best bet. Pierre had produced a map which showed that the British were only a couple of blocks away. The Swedes were directly behind. It was an easy walk, but MacShane wasn't taking any chances.

They got into Pierre's car, a little blue Renault, surprisingly modest for a Swiss bureaucrat. Hanoi seemed to have that effect on people. The car started first time. They reversed out and drove at snail's pace, threading in and out of bicycles, across Hai Ba Trung and left into Ly Thuong Kiet.

It was a wide spacious avenue lined with trees and old French villas fronted by high railings. Pierre stopped the car a few doors down.

'That's the British,' he said, pointing to a house on the left. The flag was just visible through the trees. At the gate there was a sentry box and in it a policeman. 'Usually they don't challenge foreigners.'

Apart from a few passing cyclists, there was no one about. Pierre was still shaking. 'Whatever happens,' he kept saying, 'you will keep my name out of it.'

These Red Cross types were not hero material.

MacShane got out and closed the car door. He thought he heard Pierre mumble, '*Bonne chance,*' but the car was moving away before MacShane's feet were on the ground.

He strode purposefully towards the British Embassy. The policeman, who had been slouched against the wall, saw him coming and pulled himself upright. When he reached the gate the policeman murmured something in Vietnamese. MacShane smiled, gave him the time of day, and strode past. Behind him he could hear the policeman calling something, this time in French. He quickened his pace, the gravel drive crunching under his feet.

At the steps he lunged for the doorbell and rang it long and loud. The policeman had given up calling to him now. There was no sound from inside. He glanced at the windows. They were closed and shuttered. He looked around hurriedly to see whether there was any other door, but there was none, so he rang the bell again. It was then that the notice caught his eye. It was typed in capitals on a piece of white paper with a Foreign Office seal. It said: TODAY IS THE OFFICIAL BIRTH-DAY OF HER MAJESTY THE QUEEN. THE EMBASSY IS THERE-FORE CLOSED, AND WILL RE-OPEN AGAIN ON MONDAY MORNING AT 10AM.

The Queen's bloody birthday. That's what they must have been celebrating last night, and that bastard Withers had quite forgotten to mention they'd all be sleeping off their hangovers in the morning.

163

MacShane turned and walked briskly back towards the gate. He would try the Swedes next. Surely to goodness they wouldn't be taking the day off for the Queen's birthday.

But it was too late. As he reached the gate he saw a jeep slide to a halt by the opposite kerb. The back flap lifted and out climbed four *bo doi*. One of them was clutching a pistol. He was an officer: MacShane could tell by the pens in his pocket.

'I think,' he said in perfect English, 'you are Mr MacShane. We have been expecting you.'

Chapter Nineteen

Major Mau took a very dim view of MacShane's escape. 'I am disappointed,' he kept repeating. 'Very disappointed.' But he was not disappointed. He was angry. Much face had been lost. 'How can you lose *one* American?' the colonel at the Ministry of Defence had demanded when he heard that MacShane had gone missing. 'Twenty soldiers guarding one American and you have let him escape.' The Major had forborne to mention that, far from being guarded by twenty soldiers, the American had been left pretty much to himself. Security at Plantation Gardens had gone downhill since the end of the war.

Still, disaster had been averted. MacShane was now back in custody and an enquiry could probably be headed off. Nevertheless it was an inconvenience the Major could have done without and MacShane would have to pay the price.

They did not take him back to his old room in the compound. Instead they made him change into a pair of red-striped cotton pyjamas like the ones he had worn at Son Tay. They took away his shoes and provided instead a pair of sandals made from an old automobile tyre. Then they took him to a room without windows. It had whitewashed walls and a bed made only of two wooden planks, without a mattress. Embedded in the wall at the end of the bed was a chain with a cuff which was attached to MacShane's right ankle and locked. It was a heavy chain which restricted his movements to a radius of about five feet. The room was lit by a bare light bulb which remained on for twenty-four hours a day but was only strong enough to provide a sort of permanent twilight. The walls were damp and quite bare.

It was the first room MacShane had been in that did not contain a picture of Ho Chi Minh.

'You will remain here while we consider your situation,' said Major Mau as the door clanged shut. And with that MacShane was alone.

Food came three times a day. It was more basic now than it had ever been. No fruit, no tea or coffee, no eggs. Just a dish of stewed pototoes or pumpkins, sometimes a bowl of rice, and, on one occasion, a few pieces of fatty pork.

The manacle was removed once a day, after breakfast, when a guard accompanied him to the wash house and the latrine. For the rest he had to make do with a pot kept under the bed and emptied only when he went to the latrine each morning.

As for the heat, it was beyond anything MacShane had ever experienced, so bad that even the little geckos, who came and went under the door of his cell, did not stay long. He lay all day bathed in a film of sweat, his clothes permanently damp. The damp pervaded every moment of every day. It was in the air he breathed, in the food he ate, and in the dreams he dreamed.

The noises he had heard in the far-off days when he had enjoyed the freedom of the compound still reached MacShane in his twilight world. He could hear the ringing of bicycle bells, the laughter of children, the siren on the post office at one o'clock. Each morning he awoke to laughter and shouting as the *bo doi* played their game of basketball.

Except for the twenty minutes each day when he did his ablutions and the few minutes when they opened the door to bring his meals, no daylight reached MacShane and no one so much as passed the time of day.

'They cannot keep this up for long,' he told himself on the second day of his incarceration. But he was quite wrong. The vengeance of Major Mau took a long time to assuage.

* * *

In years to come MacShane looked back upon this as the lowest point he ever reached. He recalled with nostalgia the interviews with the Professor, the walks in Hanoi with Minh and the comfortable bedroom in the Saigon villa which had been his first prison.

He wondered whether that spineless Red Cross man had got word of his existence to the outside world. He wondered if the man ever knew – or cared – what had become of MacShane after he had sped away in his little Renault, back to his world of cocktail parties, sustained by the 'hardship allowances' for which his posting to Hanoi undoubtedly qualified him.

He wondered whether Major Mau had worked out where MacShane had spent his one night of freedom. And when MacShane thought of that Swiss asshole, not a mile away in his hotel room with his Nescafé and his Chivas Regal, he was sorely tempted to shop him. He was only restrained from doing so by the thought that the Swiss would merely be shipped home to Geneva and he might even be grateful for that.

Many of MacShane's waking hours were devoted to devising ways of avenging himself on Lazarowitz if and when he ever got home. Lazarowitz had got him into this. Lazarowitz had blown his cover. And as far as he could tell, Lazarowitz had not lifted a finger to rescue him. Maybe Lazarowitz thought he was dead. Even so, he might have enquired.

After four days, Minh came visiting. 'Very unofficial,' he said as the guard closed the door behind him. 'I bring cigarettes.' MacShane never thought he would be so glad to see a packet of Liberation cigarettes.

'You must hide these,' said Minh. 'Not allowed.'

'How did you get in?' MacShane was sitting on the bed. The chain lay coiled in a heap at the end.

'I wait until Major Mau go downtown. Then I give the guard some cigarettes.'

'You are a good friend, Minh.' MacShane already had a cigarette in his mouth. He offered one to Minh.

'No, no. For you. You keep.' Minh had pulled out a packet of matches and lit MacShane's cigarette. He left the box on the bed beside the cigarettes.

'How long do you think they'll keep me like this?'

Minh's forehead creased as he considered this. 'Major Mau very angry. You make a lot of trouble for him.' Minh grinned at the thought. 'You could be here for some time. Maybe until National Day, when all sins are forgiven.'

'When's that?'

'September 2.'

'Christ, Minh, that's two months away.'

As it turned out, Major Mau relented after only ten days. He came personally to announce his magnanimity. But there was a catch. 'First, you must write a letter apologising for your behaviour and asking the authorities to show leniency.' The ankle chain was unlocked and MacShane was given a paper and pen. He was also allowed to emerge into the light of day.

The first draft was returned to him as showing insufficient remorse. Major Mau also rubbed salt in the wounds by suggesting that MacShane thank the authorities for his humane treatment.

MacShane was in no condition to argue. By the end of the first week he had contracted dysentery and was losing weight fast. A large sore appeared where the manacle around his left ankle cut into the skin. It was only a matter of time before it became infected.

Underneath his ten days' growth of beard his cheeks were becoming hollow, and for the first time in years he could count his ribs. By the end he could not keep food down and was drinking only water. The guards had relented to the extent of allowing him to use the latrine twice a day, but for the rest he had to use the enamel bowl under the bed. The stench had become so bad that the guards held their noses when they came to unlock him. Major Mau, when he came to announce his amnesty, did not venture beyond the doorway.

Later, it occurred to MacShane that Major Mau's change

of heart may have been prompted less by magnanimity than by anxiety not to have a dead American on his hands.

Life looked up, however. They gave him medicine for the dysentery. The wound made by the manacle healed within a few days, although it left behind a purple scar. The food also improved; fruit reappeared on the menu and there was the occasional boiled egg at breakfast. MacShane resumed his exercises – thirty press-ups and five laps of the compound each morning. The *bo doi* even allowed him to join in their morning basketball game and, when National Day came, they invited him to eat with them.

It was MacShane's best meal in months. It was also the best meal the *bo doi* had seen for a long time, to judge by the amount they ate. They started with crispy spring rolls, pork or shrimps deep-fried in rice paper. One of the pigs which had been nosing round the compound reappeared in thin strips on a bed of lettuce and doused in spices. There was a whole carp, fished that very morning from West Lake; fried frog legs, bamboo shoots, tomatoes and bean sprouts. The meal was washed down with bottles of Saigon beer, 'liberated beer' as Major Mau called it.

At the end there was much toasting in rice wine. MacShane understood little of what was said, but the sudden outbreak of goodwill was unmistakable. Major Mau even proposed a toast of friendship between the American and Vietnamese peoples – to which MacShane drank with enthusiasm. By the end of the evening he was thinking that maybe Lazarowitz had got his finger out at last. Maybe he was down for release.

How wrong he was. Two days later Major Mau called him in. 'Mr MacShane,' he said, 'the time has come for the next stage of your re-education. Tomorrow you leave for the country-side.'

'That is,' he added, 'if you don't disappear in the night.' With that he lapsed into uncontrollable laughter.

Chapter Twenty

They set off at first light. MacShane, Minh and two *bo doi*: one to drive, the other to keep an eye on the prisoner.

From his place in the back of the jeep MacShane watched Hanoi slide by. The streets were already crowded with cyclists. At the little bus station on the dyke, near the foot of the Long Bien bridge, crowds laid siege to the ticket office. A low mist hung over the Red River.

Major Mau had seen them off. This time he had shaken MacShane's hand. 'We want you to see how our people live,' he said.

'Why?'

'You are a CIA man; you should be interested in intelligence.' Major Mau had smiled pleasantly as he warmed to the theme. 'CIA spend millions of dollars to make satellites to take pictures of our country, yet still they don't know how our people live. Now you are going to see so that when you go back to America you can take some real intelligence with you.'

With that the jeep had drawn away. The major stood at the gate waving. MacShane was his last prisoner. The last of the war.

They went out across the Long Bien bridge and turned right by acres of black, twisted steel which Minh identified as the remains of the Gia Lam locomotive works.

'Where are we going?'

'To Haiphong,' said Minh. He was sitting in front, next to the driver. They were out in the country now. The rice stood high in the fields. Abundant water flowed along the intricate network of canals and ditches. Buffalo ambled along the dykes. Women and girls in conical hats were weeding fields of cabbages and lettuces. Some looked up and waved as the jeep passed.

It was a straight road, broad enough for two vehicles to pass and lined with acacia trees. MacShane had seen pictures of such roads in France.

The houses were built in clumps of bamboo and banana trees. The more substantial were made of whitewashed brick and red tiles. Most houses, however, had been thrown hastily together with mud and bamboo matting. 'Bombing very heavy here,' said Minh.

It occurred to MacShane that an American might not be welcome in this neck of the woods. 'What have they been told about me?'

'That you are a friend of Vietnam and that you have come to find out how Vietnamese farmers live.'

'They know I am American?'

'Of course.'

'They will not be too keen on Americans.'

'Don't worry. Our government has always taught us that the American people are good people. That they opposed the war and that the war was made by their government.'

'Supposing they find out the truth?'

Minh smiled. 'About you or about the American people?'

'About me.'

'Don't worry, Mr MacShane, the Vietnamese farmers are good people but simple. If our government tells them you are a friend, then you are a friend.'

They drove for nearly two hours along the road to Haiphong, but somewhere before they reached the city, they turned off to the right and bumped for several miles along a road that was little more that a cart track. It was hard to see where they were going because the road twisted and turned and was enclosed on both sides by thick foliage. They passed through farm yards, scattering chickens and ducks, and once they had to wait while a peasant prodded a fat pig out of the way.

As they went, they gathered in their wake a long trail of children, barefoot boys and girls and naked babies delirious with joy at the arrival in their village of an automobile containing what they took to be a *Lien Xo*.

In due course, the jeep with its trail of admirers came to a stone archway across the top of which was emblazoned *Dai Thang*, Great Victory, the words MacShane had seen written in stone on the side of the bomb crater at Hanoi Airport. Beyond the arch was a small paved courtyard, one side of which was flanked by a long brick building with a tiled roof. A reception committee awaited: half-a-dozen men and a woman all in black pyjamàs and rubber sandals. The jeep came to a halt in the courtyard and was immediately mobbed by children. Members of the reception committee attempted in vain to shoo them away. Eventually they fell back to let MacShane and his *bo doi* escort clamber from the back of the vehicle. Minh was already shaking hands with a large, thick-set man who appeared to be in charge. 'This is Mr Ding,' said Minh.

Mr Ding was the biggest Vietnamese upon whom MacShane had ever set eyes. He had a thick bull-neck, a square jaw and small black eyes which, to judge from their expression, were not in the least bit delighted to see MacShane.

MacShane extended his hand and received a curt handshake in response. 'Mr Ding is president of the Dai Thang people's co-operative. You will stay in his house during your visit.'

The rest of the reception committee was introduced. They seemed rather better disposed towards MacShane. Their handshakes were firm and their smiles warm.

'How many of them know?' MacShane asked Minh as they were ushered towards the large brick building.

'Only Mr Ding.'

'You said no one would be told.'

'That's what I thought.'

'Was this village bombed?'

'I think so, yes.'

'Christ, Minh, they'll cut me into little pieces when they find out.'

'Don't worry, everything will be okay,' said Minh, but he

couldn't bring himself to look MacShane in the eye.

The village meeting hall was a large bare room which smelled of fresh paint. In the centre was a stout unvarnished table flanked on each side by crude wooden benches. There were chairs at each end which matched neither with each other nor with the table. One of these had a cushion and it was upon this that Mr Ding took his seat. The other members of the reception committee sat along one of the benches. MacShane, Minh and the two *bo doi* who had come with them sat along the other. There was a tea bowl in each place and in the centre of the table two packets of Liberation cigarettes. A girl with her hair in a long plait served tea from a flask.

Mr Ding spoke first. Minh translated. 'He is pleased to welcome our American friend to the Great Victory people's co-operative.' Mr Ding showed no sign of looking pleased, but the others smiled and nodded.

The cigarettes were passed round. MacShane took one and the girl who had served tea produced a box of matches. Mr Ding spoke again.

'He says that Mrs Nam, who is secretary of Great Victory co-operative, will now give a short account of its history.' Minh indicated the woman who was seated directly opposite MacShane.

Mrs Nam was in her fifties, a small neat woman with hair tied in a bun at the back of her head. When she smiled, as she often did, she revealed a row of teeth stained brown by betel nut.

Mrs Nam spoke for about thirty minutes. She might have spoken for a lot longer had Mr Ding not interrupted. She started with the famine in 1945. That had wiped out one quarter of the population, including ten entire families. She talked of the French war. The French, she said, had burned down two villages in the area in retaliation for an ambush on the road to Haiphong. Then she talked of land reform. Some landlords who had collaborated with the French had been killed, she said. There had been some mistakes at this time, but the Party had since rectified these.

By now, dozens of little faces had appeared at the windows,

all anxious to catch a glimpse of the *Lien Xo*. Children also crammed the doorway until the crush became so great that some of them spilled inside, causing Mrs Nam to suspend her oration while order was restored, and the door firmly closed.

Mrs Nam resumed. She talked of the American war and how most of the men had gone south to fight leaving the women to manage the farming. Many men, she said, had not come back and now the village had a surplus of women.

At this point Mr Ding urged her to wind up her remarks. Mrs Nam did so in her own good time. She had lost two sons in the American war, she said. But she bore the American people no malice. Her hatred she reserved for the American government and its servants. And on that ominous note, she concluded.

Minh translated, and when he had finished everyone looked at MacShane. 'I think,' said Minh quietly, 'you must say a few words.'

MacShane took a sip of tea and cleared his throat. He was, he said, very happy that he had been allowed to stay at the Great Victory people's co-operative. He was sure that he would learn a great deal from living and working with them so that when he returned to America he could tell the American people about the life of a Vietnamese farmer.

Minh translated with a straight face. MacShane glanced around the table and saw that his message had been well received. Everyone was smiling – with the exception of Mr Ding.

After the introductions they went sightseeing. Mr Ding led the way and Mrs Nam took charge of clearing a path through the children. Word had spread that the visitor was not *Lien Xo* but a *My* and this only intensified the excitement. Everywhere he went MacShane could hear the children whispering '*My, My,*' but no one seemed hostile.

They started with the electric threshing machine. It was, they said, the most modern this side of Haiphong. To prove it they turned it on specially. A handful of rice straw was fed in at one end and threshed grain came out the other. MacShane joined in the expressions of amazement. Did American farmers have electric threshing machines, someone wanted to know. MacShane said he thought so, but not as modern as this.

They moved on to the electric pumping station. It was three years old, the first thing they had built after the bombing had stopped. It irrigated more than a hundred hectares of paddy fields. Before that the farmers had watered the land by hand or with the aid of a few diesel pumps.

The conducted tour took more than an hour. They showed him fishponds, duckponds, the brickworks and a small factory full of laughing girls who were making mosquito nets. One of them tied a piece of red thread around his wrist. 'For good luck,' she said. MacShane thanked her profusely. He needed all the luck he could get.

Mr Ding, it seemed, was a big wheel. The Great Victory co-operative consisted not of one but four villages linked by a net-work of mud tracks, and Mr Ding was in charge of the lot. Not only was he president of the co-op, but also Party Secretary. He was big in more ways than one. He was head and shoulders taller than just about everyone else around. Taller than MacShane and a damn sight broader too. He even had the beginnings of a double chin, and looked more like a mid-West farmer than a Vietnamese peasant. MacShane nicknamed him Redneck.

Redneck's house was the biggest in the village, a solid red-brick affair which had somehow survived the bombing. It had four bedrooms, a tiled roof and a considerable private vege-table garden. At the back, housed in a lean-to with a corrugated iron roof, were four fat pigs and a dozen piglets. MacShane's room was adjacent to the pig-sty. The furnishings consisted of a plain wooden bed without mattress, a quilt and a mosquito net. Beside the bed was a stool and on it an enamel washing bowl. 'He says he hopes you will be comfortable,' said Minh glumly.

'I'll get by.'

There followed a short exchange between Minh and

Redneck, after which Redneck disappeared and returned a minute later with a moth-eaten pillow and an oil lamp made from a fragmentation bomb similar to the one the Professor had produced at Plantation Gardens.

'He says, a gift from the Americans,' said Minh as Redneck held up the bomb. Redneck was smiling maliciously. It was his first smile since MacShane's arrival and there were not many more where that came from.

They ate in Redneck's living room: MacShane, Minh, Redneck and the two *bo doi*. It wasn't a bad meal – rice, chunks of pork, and plump, white radishes. Mrs Redneck served the meal, but she did not eat with them. Nor was she introduced. She was a tiny woman who bustled about nervously. Once, when Redneck wasn't looking, she threw a sidelong smile in MacShane's direction.

After lunch they fetched MacShane's suitcase from the jeep. He had been allowed to bring everything, including the typewriter and the Chomsky book. His tiny room was scarcely big enough for the suitcase. Eventually he squeezed it between the end of the bed and the wall. The typewriter fitted underneath the bed.

Minh said that if MacShane was going to be a peasant, he would need new clothes. There was a tailor in the village and Minh took MacShane to be measured for two pairs of black pyjamas. A crowd of children followed and the event was the cause of much mirth.

At first the tailor demanded ration cards for the cloth, but after a lengthy discussion Minh persuaded him that foreigners were the subject of special arrangements. Later, they found a man who made sandals made out of rubber tyres and he cut a pair for MacShane on the spot. He said they were the largest pair he had ever made.

MacShane's black pyjamas arrived early next morning. He paid for them in dong which Minh had changed for him at the bank before they left Hanoi. The pyjamas fitted perfectly. The hems were neatly sewn back. There was even a pocket on the shirt.

176

Minh nearly died laughing when he saw MacShane for the first time in pyjamas and sandals. 'Now you will be the best-dressed peasant in the Red River delta,' he said. Even old Redneck raised a smile. And outside Redneck's house a large crowd had gathered to bear witness to the spectacle. Not just children, adults as well. There was a burst of spontaneous applause when MacShane appeared. 'You are famous,' said Minh. 'Some of these people have walked five kilometres to see the American in black pyjamas. Soon they will be running day trips from Haiphong.'

But it was no laughing matter. MacShane was about to be abandoned in an isolated part of one of the world's most isolated countries. He spoke no more than twenty words of the language. There was not the slightest hope of escape and no prospect of release in the near future. The natives – Redneck excepted – were friendly, but could be expected to turn nasty when they discovered they had an American spy in their midst. And that was only a question of time.

Chapter Twenty-One

There was one stroke of luck. Minh discovered a school teacher who spoke some English. Her name was Ha. She had been evacuated from Hanoi during the final round of bombing and had not returned. She worked in an infant school at one of the other villages that made up the co-operative. It was about a mile away, and on the morning before he departed Minh took MacShane to see her.

They walked in single file along the dyke, Minh first, then MacShane in his black pyjamas followed by a herd of children. The school was easy to find because of the singing. They could hear the singing when they were halfway there.

The school was in the centre of the village. It had crumbling brick walls and a makeshift roof of thatch and matting supported by stilts of thick bamboo. It consisted of three classrooms and a dirt playground surrounded by a low wall. Miss Ha's class was the middle one. It was from there that the singing came.

The children – there were about 60 of them – sat in rows behind desks that appeared to have been cobbled together from driftwood. They were ragged little creatures with thick black hair and large dark eyes. When they caught sight of MacShane the singing petered out into a welter of giggles.

MacShane and Minh waited by the door while Miss Ha restored order. In contrast to her surroundings, she was an elegant young woman. She wore a slim black skirt which came down to her ankles and was embroidered near the hem with a pattern of red and yellow flowers. Her blouse was white and printed lightly with flowers in pastel colours. Her long black hair was guided into a pony tail which reached down her back almost to her waist. It was held in place by a red plastic clasp in the shape of a butterfly. She waited until the children were sitting and then came to the door. First she shook hands with Minh and they exchanged a few words in Vietnamese. Then she offered her hand to MacShane. 'I am Ha,' she said.

'I am MacShane.'

'I know. You are famous. Everyone is talking about the American peasant. The children talk of nothing else.' She spoke slowly but her English was clear. When she smiled her face was radiant, but it was a smile that left something in reserve.

'You speak good English.'

'Thank you.'

'Where did you learn?' There was a thin gold ring on the third finger of her right hand.

'In Hanoi.'

The children had now abandoned their desks and were crowding round MacShane. Some were pointing to the size of his feet, others stroking the hair on his arm. Miss Ha spoke sharply to them, but it did no good.

'What was the song you were singing?'

'It was about the end of the war.'

'What did it say?'

'I will write it down for you.' A small boy was dispatched to get a piece of paper and a pen. Miss Ha rested the paper against the wall and scribbled the words of the song. She smiled as she gave it to MacShane. 'For you,' she said. Her handwriting was clear and upright, the letters well rounded, like a child's. It said:

> *'The war is gone,*
> *Planes come no more*
> *Do not weep for those just born*
> *The human being is evergreen.'*

They left Miss Ha surrounded by her small, evergreen human beings and walked back across the dyke, past fields of waist-high rice. MacShane had cheered up a little. So had Minh.

179

'Miss Ha is a very good woman,' said Minh with a glint in his eye. 'You are lucky man.'

'What makes you think she will be interested in me?'

'Why not? She comes from the city and is lonely here.'

'She is married. I saw her ring.'

'I think not,' said Minh, but he did not elaborate.

Minh stayed three days – and that was longer than he should have. His orders were to deliver MacShane and return to Hanoi. He had been expected back two days ago and it was only after a row that the *bo doi* driver had agreed to return to collect Minh. The driver and his jeep reappeared on the morning of the third day and this time there was no argument.

Minh had done his best to make MacShane's life easy. He had chatted up Redneck's neighbours and asked them to keep a friendly eye on MacShane, and before he left he handed over his English-Vietnamese phrasebook. 'Here,' he said, 'you will need this.' MacShane had hesitated before accepting it. He knew it was one of Minh's most prized possessions, and it would not be easy to replace. But Minh insisted. 'Give it back when you speak Vietnamese,' he said.

Minh was worried, though he did not say so. He kept promising to visit whenever he could find an excuse. He also promised not to let the authorities in Hanoi forget about MacShane, but he was not hopeful. 'Decisions in Vietnam are not made quickly,' he said. 'And once made, they are not easily changed.'

MacShane stood watching Minh's jeep disappear as it bounced away down the muddy track that led to the main road. Minh was his last link with the outside world and there was no telling when he would be back. He remembered what the Professor had said in the house at Plantation Gardens, 'In Vietnam we have no mechanism for correcting mistakes until they become disasters.'

After Minh had gone, MacShane was quite alone. Everyone smiled at him as he wandered round the village and occasionally someone would try to strike up a conversation. They invited him into their homes and offered him tea or soup. One old man tried addressing MacShane in French but that was no good either. In the end they just sat smiling stupidly at each other. It was hopeless.

He spent the first few days exploring. No one tried to stop him and he walked quite long distances, but children followed him everywhere so he guessed Redneck was not worried about keeping track of him.

In the fields about a mile away, there was an old Catholic church. Minh said there were many Catholics in the area, but that most of the priests had gone south in '54 and so the churches were not often used. In some of the houses he had seen pictures of saints, and in one a small statue of the Virgin.

To judge by its appearance, the church was badly in need of repair. There were holes in the guttering and the yellowing walls were stained with damp and green moss. The door was padlocked, but the lock showed signs of having been recently opened and the path to the door was well-used. By the side of the church there was a small cemetery, and some of the graves were recent. The cemetery and the church were surrounded by a thick hedge of bamboo and banana trees. The little graveyard had been well-kept and there were flowers on some of the graves.

On his second visit to the church, MacShane found an old man working there. He had a scythe and was cutting grass in the cemetery. It was hot and every few minutes he paused and wiped his forehead with his shirtsleeve. When he saw MacShane he came over and started babbling in Vietnamese. It was a while before the old man realised that MacShane did not understand, but eventually he got up and beckoned MacShane towards the church. From his pocket the old man took a key and inserted it into the padlock. Inside, the church was dark and cool. There were candlesticks on the altar and a crude wooden tabernacle, also a small pulpit and half-a-dozen rows of solid pews, in better condition than the desks in Miss Ha's classroom.

The old man stood at the back while MacShane wandered around. On a stone pillar behind the pulpit, there was a faded picture of the Pope opposite a picture of Ho Chi Minh. In a corner there was a large painted statue of Jesus, his heart exposed and bleeding. Upon examination, Jesus proved to be a white man.

MacShane did his best to give Redneck a wide berth. Redneck made no attempt to conceal his feelings. In his life he had been called upon to make sacrifices for the Party, but never in his wildest dreams had it occurred to him that the Party would one day call on him to open his house to a CIA agent. He would do it because that was what the Party ordered and his was not to reason why. But the Party had not ordered him to make MacShane's stay comfortable and he was damned if it was going to be.

Mealtimes were worst. Redneck would sit there slurping away at his noodle soup and Mrs Redneck would fuss around making sure her husband and his guest had everything they needed. She was a friendly soul, and during the day when Redneck was out she would go about her housework chattering to MacShane oblivious to the fact that he did not understand a word she was saying. He gathered that the Rednecks had two sons, both of whom were in the army, and a daughter who was a nurse in Haiphong. Mrs Redneck showed him the photographs in the living room. They were innocent, clean-cut young men in baggy uniforms, like the *bo doi* he had seen in Saigon. He couldn't be sure, but from Mrs Redneck's sign language, it seemed that the girl was dead. There was no sign of any grandchildren.

On the wall in the living room there were three scrolls in fancy red and black script which appeared to have been awarded to Redneck for his services to the Party. Mrs Redneck was very proud of these and dusted them every day.

No doubt Redneck would earn himself another certificate for taking care of a CIA agent.

After a week, Redneck indicated it was time MacShane earned his keep. Early one morning he produced a shovel with a long bamboo handle and said something like, 'It's about time you got some mud on those new pyjamas.' Whatever Redneck had said, he seemed to think it was very funny, so MacShane felt justified in assuming that the joke was on him.

Redneck then introduced him to a group of girls and youths waiting in the shade of a banyan tree on the far side of the village. The youngsters were mightily amused at the prospect of having MacShane with them. Redneck then issued a few curt instructions and, shovels in hand, the little group of labourers set off across the dykes.

As MacShane was leaving, Mrs Redneck had thrust into his hands a flask of hot water and an old *bo doi* hat to protect his head from the sun. The hat was too small to have fitted Redneck so it must have belonged to one of her sons.

They arrived at the worksite while the sun was still low in the sky, but the humidity was already intense. They were to dig out an irrigation dyke that had been washed away in flooding the previous month, taking with it several fields of good paddy rice. The aim was to dig a channel two feet by two along a distance of several hundred yards, piling the mud up on each side. It was backbreaking work, made worse because the ground was waterlogged and every shovelful of earth removed was soon replaced by water. MacShane's shirt quickly became glued to his chest and later, when he took it off, the hairs on his chest were the subject of great hilarity.

The job, he ruefully reflected, could have been done in a couple of hours by one man in a mechanical digger. There were moments when MacShane would have happily invested his entire back-pay in just such a machine, but as the hours – and days – passed he was surprised to discover that he enjoyed the work.

It was good to be doing something useful again, even if it was only digging ditches, and he liked the company. The kids worked in pairs, and MacShane was teamed up with a strong young woman who was given to fits of uncontrollable giggling at the sight of MacShane with his trousers rolled up in thick, rich, knee-deep mud. At lunch on the first day she was dismayed to find that he had no food and immediately organised

183

a whip round among the others. The result was a little pile of rice and vegetables on a banana leaf.

Despite the heat, the work was not as demanding as it had at first seemed. There weren't enough shovels to go round and so they shared, working fifteen minutes, and spending the next fifteen lying in the shade of a nearby tree. Lunch was followed by a dip in a fishpond and a snooze in the shade. Sometimes MacShane would chase one of the girls along the dyke, scooping up water with his hands and splashing her to cheers from the others. They were smashing kids without an ounce of guile. It was hard to think of them as a threat to the Free World.

About this time, MacShane began to reflect on the morality of bombing rice farmers. Each of the villages in the Great Victory co-operative had been bombed. You could see exactly where the sticks of bombs had fallen by the straight lines of deep craters. They ran through fields, gardens and houses, taking out everything in their path. There was even a crater in the corner of the playground at Miss Ha's school. So much for all that crap about strategic targets. There weren't any for miles. Just little houses of thatch, mud and brick lived in by people who had been growing rice for three thousand years before America was ever heard of.

If anyone had asked Lazarowitz how come sticks of 500-pound bombs went right through the Great Victory people's co-op he would have put it down to a computer malfunction in Honolulu. Or stronger-than-anticipated headwinds. Or maybe, just maybe, there was the teeniest bit of pilot error, in which case someone might get his pay docked a couple of hundred dollars for taking out rice farms within sight of foreign television cameras.

As far as the guys in Honolulu or Washington were concerned, Vietnam was just a series of grids on a one-in-fifty map. It sure looked different when you were on the ground looking up. What was it the Professor had said? 'Technically, Mr MacShane, your country is a thousand years ahead of us. But morally – ' he hadn't finished, but MacShane could easily complete the sentence – 'Morally you are among the world's least developed civilisations.'

As the days passed MacShane began to think Miss Ha had forgotten him, until one evening a small boy arrived at Redneck's house bearing a message addressed to 'Mister MacShane'. It was written in the unmistakable hand of Miss Ha: big, childish letters. It said: 'Welcome you my house tomorrow (Sunday). Eat some food. Learn some Vietnam language. Come at middle of day.' It was signed simply HA. There followed a simple diagram showing how to get to her house.

In sixteen years of courting there was no date that MacShane was more anxious to keep than his appointment with Miss Ha. He took his best shirt from his suitcase, borrowed Mrs Redneck's old iron, and eliminated every crease. He put on his best blue corduroys and even dabbed his chin with after-shave.

Miss Ha lived with a peasant family a short distance from her school. The family had two daughters and two sons. The sons were away at war and Miss Ha lived in their room. Unlike MacShane's it was large and airy. At the back it looked out over the family vegetable garden and at the front on to a small enclosed yard. Along one side of the yard, on the wall that caught the sun, were Miss Ha's tomato plants and above them, on a trellis, a purple bougainvillaea.

What struck MacShane immediately was how few possessions she had. The bed was a couple of planks raised from the ground by mud bricks at each end. It was covered by bamboo mat and doubled as a seat during the day. In one corner there was a pillow and a folded patchwork quilt. Beside the bed there was an upturned wooden box which served as a cupboard. It was covered by a cotton cloth embroidered with a pattern of flowers like the skirt she had been wearing the first time he had seen her. That skirt, together with a couple of cotton blouses, was now to be seen on a makeshift wire hanger attached to a hook on the back of the door. There was no sign of any other clothes.

The walls were bare except for some coloured pictures

185

from a 1967 copy of *Paris Match* showing elegant young French women in clothes that would have cost years of Miss Ha's salary. A single light bulb was suspended from a wire in the centre of the ceiling. It hung so low that MacShane's head bumped against it. More bricks and a narrow plank had been used to construct a low shelf against the wall opposite the bed. On this was arrayed Miss Ha's modest library. A ten-years-old copy of *Reader's Digest, Conversational American English* by Edwin Cornelius, Jnr, half-a-dozen paperbacks and some magazines in Vietnamese and a book of children's drawings, also in Vietnamese.

'Welcome my home,' she said when MacShane showed up on the dot of noon with the usual posse of children in tow. There were some formalities to be gone through. First MacShane had to pay his respects to Miss Ha's landlords and half-a-dozen of their relatives. Then the children had to be shooed away, and that took some doing. Finally, when they were alone, Miss Ha produced two steaming bowls of rice noodles with shredded beef and shallots which, she said, had been grown in her garden.

'My English very poor,' she said as they drank the soup. 'No time to practice.'

MacShane said her English was beautiful. He said that the soup was beautiful too and, in due course, he said the same of her.

After the soup, there was a dish of fried pork and a fish liberally smeared with chilli paste. She even produced a bottle of weak Hanoi beer which she poured for him into a tea bowl, apologising because she did not have a glass. As she sat, nervously watching MacShane devour everything she put in front of him and eating very little herself, it began to dawn on MacShane that his coming was a very big deal for Miss Ha.

Later, when they sat cross-legged on a bamboo mat sipping tea, he asked about her family. She hesitated a long time before replying. A butterfly seeking shelter from the heat floated in through the window and fluttered about in ragged circles. MacShane watched it rise and fall but she did not seem to notice.

'My family beaucoup die,' she said.

The butterfly had come to rest on Miss Ha's copy of *Conversational American English*.

'My father was a teacher in a village outside Nam Dinh, about 70 kilometres south of Hanoi. He died in the land reform. He was a Party member. A good man. He fought the Japanese and the French, but during land reform he spoke against the killing. Many people die in land reform. He was against this. So they kill him. The Party killed my father.'

It was only then MacShane realised he was in a room without a picture of Ho Chi Minh.

'Later, after one or two years, they say it is mistake. They make rectification. But how can you be rectified when you are dead?'

After the father's death the family had moved to Hanoi to live with an uncle. A mother and three small children. They were paid a modest pension by the state in lieu of father. The mother had taken a job in a state department store, one of those which overlooked the lake in the centre of Hanoi. Ha, then only seven years old, had spent much of the time looking after two younger brothers. When eventually she got to school she had a lot of time to make up, but had studied hard and went to secondary school, which not all girls did in those days. It was a Catholic school near the cathedral, run by French nuns. French was the main foreign language, of course, but one nun had lived in London and she taught English: at first just one lesson a week, but later she gave extra lessons after school. The nun received newspapers and magazines from London and they would practise reading them. Sometimes, when the electricity failed, which it often did, they would read by candlelight. On summer evenings, when it was very hot, Ha and her friends would go down to the lake and read aloud to each other. That was how she learned English.

Ha was fourteen when the American war began. Her first brother was a year younger. He was lucky. Because they had no father he was exempt from military service. Instead he passed the exam to the medical school at Hanoi University. He was going to be a doctor.

Number two son was not so lucky. He had been drafted on his seventeenth birthday and went south just before the '72

187

offensive. He died in Quang Tri city. At least, that was where he was last seen alive. There were so many dead at Quang Tri that no one knew.

Six months after the telegram announcing the presumed death of number two son the family – or what remained of it – had a long overdue stroke of luck. Or so it seemed at the time. In retrospect it turned out to be the greatest disaster of all.

For years they'd had their names down with the city authorities for an apartment bigger than the two rooms they rented. Then Ha's mother heard, through a friend, that a three-room apartment had become vacant in Kham Thien street, near the railway station. It had been rented by an older couple who were moving out to live with a daughter in Lang Son on the Chinese border. Ha and her family moved in October '72, the month that Kissinger had announced that peace was at hand. It was the best place they had ever lived in. Three good rooms, a bathroom and kitchen shared with only one other family. Even a small garden where they could grow tomatoes and marrows.

In November, Nixon was re-elected by a record majority. In December, Kissinger had declared that peace was not at hand, after all. Back came the bombers. For eleven days and nights they had pounded away at Hanoi and Haiphong, pausing only on Christmas Day to allow the Free World to down its turkey and mince pies. Ha was not at home on the day that a B–52 put a stick of bombs right down the middle of Kham Thien street.

'It was during a break in the bombing. I had gone to the Dong Xuan market. I heard the siren on the post office. It meant that the bombers were coming back so I climbed into the nearest shelter. One of the small shelters that only takes two people. There was just me and another girl. We pulled the cover over us and waited in darkness. We could hear the engines of the aeroplanes. Then the sound of bombs falling. Then the explosions. The earth was shaking. Sometimes it seemed they were on top of us.'

The butterfly had gone now. Neither of them saw it depart.

They sat cross legged on the floor. Once her leg brushed against his and she made no effort to move. At least, that was how it seemed to MacShane.

'After the bombing stopped there was a silence. We sat there holding each other tight, this girl and I. I did not know her name. We talked in whispers. Waiting, waiting, waiting for the bombers to return. After more than two hours, it seemed much longer, the siren on the post office went again and we lifted the cover and climbed out. The girl went off. I never saw her again.

'I did not go home. Not immediately. Someone said they had hit the locomotive works on the other side of the river. There was no damage where we were. The market was working again and I remember exactly what I bought. Fish sauce, half a kilo of chicken, salt and soap. Then I started walking home. Halfway I met a man who said that Kham Thien street had been hit. Then I ran.

'Until I got there I still believed they would be safe. There was a shelter just outside our house. My mother was sure to have been in it. But when I reached Kham Thien I saw that the street had gone. It took some time even to recognise where my house had been. There was nothing left. Just a deep hole in the ground. And my family was gone. All gone.'

Ha did not cry. The tone of her voice hardly changed. She spoke quietly, but in a matter-of-fact way. She was not seeking sympathy. Only telling her story for the record.

'All gone,' she repeated. 'My mother, my brother and my fiancé.'

'Fiancé?'

'Yes. I was engaged on that day.' She indicated the ring on her finger. 'That is why I had gone to the market. We were going to have a big meal. To celebrate our engagement. He was a soldier. He had been home one week. We had to do it then because we did not know when he would come back again.'

They sat again in silence. In the background they could hear the clatter of pots and pans as the landlord's family prepared their evening meal. On the floor beside them the two bowls of tea were stone cold.

Ha stood up and went to the bed. She rolled back the bamboo matting to reveal an envelope lying flat against the wooden plank. It was a medium-size brown envelope which had been reused several times. There were addresses crossed out and heavily franked stamps. She walked back to where MacShane was and sat down beside him, leaving the bamboo matting on the bed rolled back. From inside the envelope she took out what seemed to be a photograph wrapped in thin rice paper. She unwrapped it carefully and held it up for MacShane to see.

'My family.'

It was an old photograph, taken maybe twenty years ago in a studio with a backdrop of jagged mountains and wispy clouds. A man, woman and their three small children.

The man was older than the woman. He looked about 40 and a bit of an intellectual. He wore little wire glasses and his hair was long enough to cover his ears. He was wearing a shirt and tie, and a western-style suit with thin lapels and trouser legs an inch too short. The suit looked as though it had been hired for the occasion from the photographer.

The woman was aged about twenty-five. She was dressed in a white *ao dai* and black silk trousers. Her thick hair had been trimmed to shoulder length and was combed forward in a fringe that covered her forehead.

The oldest child was a girl. 'That's me,' said Ha, pointing to the radiant child with long dark hair clutching her father's hand.

'Taken at Tet in 1955. One year before the Party took my father away.' She was as perfect then as she was now. Dark eyes that sparkled. A tiny nose. High cheek-bones that made smiling so easy.

'This is my oldest brother. The one who was going to be a doctor.' The little boy was standing stiffly to attention. 'At that age we all wanted to be soldiers, but that was before we knew about war. My father would not let us play with wooden guns, unlike other children. "There has been enough killing in our country already," he used to say.

'This is my brother, the one who became a soldier.' She

touched the child who was sitting on the woman's knee. 'His name was Dinh Chieu, after a famous poet. He was clever. He learned to talk very quickly. My father said he would become a great scholar.'

Very gently she placed the picture on the bed and reached again inside the envelope. This time she drew out a smaller photograph, also wrapped in rice paper. It was a portrait of a young man in military uniform. On his collar he had a single red star and his hair was cut very short. He looked very grave.

'My fiancé. His name was Phuong.'

She handled the photographs as though she was afraid they might suddenly dissolve in her hands. As though the curse which had stolen her family and her fiancé might suddenly return and take away her only memory of them.

'Phuong said the war would soon be over and then we would marry. He said he was sure it would be the last war and that our children would grow up in peace.'

She placed the photographs side by side on the bed and MacShane pondered them in silence. The picture of the family was singed along one side and at the bottom there was a deep yellow stain creeping upwards. They were a very serious little family. Apart from one of the boys, who was trying hard to suppress a grin, no one was smiling. Perhaps they had a premonition of the disasters which lay ahead.

There they were, all dressed up in their Sunday best. A father about to become a victim of the cause to which he had devoted his live. And his family, who were destined to be annihilated by a computer error in Honolulu.

Chapter Twenty-Two

Next day, while MacShane was digging ditches, Ha came to visit Redneck. How long was the American staying, she asked. None of her business, said Redneck. (The truth was he had no idea.) She had asked, she said humbly, because if the American was going to be around for some time it might be an idea for him to learn some Vietnamese. To which Redneck had responded that the American had come to work, not to take language classes. Not until Ha casually mentioned that the man from Hanoi – Mr Minh – had asked her to teach Vietnamese to the American did Redneck grudgingly assent. But only, he made clear, outside working hours.

From then on MacShane saw Ha every day. Each evening after a day digging ditches or – later – helping with the harvest, MacShane would race back to Redneck's, douse himself in water and change out of his working clothers before heading off across the dyke to Ha's house.

They met always at Ha's house for fear of falling foul of Redneck. They need not have worried. Redneck had his spies everywhere. He knew what was going on all right, but for some reason he made no trouble. Sometimes, on long summer evenings, they would take walks along the dyke, but it was hard to be discreet because MacShane was still a tourist attraction. Everywhere they went they were followed. Not just by children, but by girls and youths for most of whom MacShane was the only foreigner they had ever seen.

Occasionally they would sit with the village youths under the banyan tree or out on the dyke and MacShane would attempt to satisfy their curiosity about America. Ha would translate.

'How many rooms are there in your house?' one girl wanted to know.

'Four, including the kitchen.'

'How many people live in your house?'

'Just me.'

'What about your wife?'

'I am not married.' This news was received with incredulity followed by sympathy.

'How old are you?'

'Thirty-six.'

'And not married?'

'No.'

'Your wife is dead?'

'I have never had a wife.' MacShane found himself thinking of Josie. Afterwards he realised it was the first time in a week that he had thought of Josie.

'How do the peasants live in America?'

'Not bad.'

'How much land does one American peasant have?'

It seemed cruel to tell the truth. That the peasants in America were mostly big fat farmers who drove tractors and combine harvesters, who worked land which stretched as far as the eye could see and who were mostly very keen on bombing Asian rice farmers. So MacShane hedged.

'Our system is very different from yours.'

'America has people's co-ops?'

'Not exactly, no.'

America, he said, was a very rich country. Much richer than Vietnam. Nature had been generous to America. America had oil and fertile land in abundance. It had forests that you could not walk through in a month. It had rich deposits of gold and silver and just about every mineral you cared to name. It had eight-lane highways, 100-storey office blocks, and fifty different kinds of ice-cream.

They listened to him goggle-eyed, and when he had finished a boy at the back got to his feet. 'Sir,' he said, 'if American people are so rich as you say, why do they want to take our country too?'

*   *   *

Unlike the others, Ha asked almost no questions. She did not ask MacShane how he came to Vietnam or what he was doing at the Great Victory co-op. Or how long he would be staying or what work he did in America.

It was as though she was afraid of the answers. As if she knew that there lurked some dark secret waiting to be disinterred and did not want to hear of it.

Once, when they were sitting out on the dyke with the village youths, someone had asked what he did for a living. He was a government employee, he said. He had an office and a desk with a telephone. He shuffled paper and sometimes he travelled to foreign countries to make notes and obtain information. He was a kind of civil servant. A bureaucrat, you could say. They nodded sagely. In Vietnam they knew all about bureaucrats.

The weeks passed. Then a month. Then two months and no word came from Hanoi. Nor was there any sign of Minh. The rice crop ripened and was harvested. Every day MacShane went to the fields and helped to cut crop. Sometimes he worked with a scythe. Sometimes he followed along behind gathering up the rice into sheaves. Sometimes he helped to transport it by bicycle and bullock cart to the threshing ground, where young men fed it into an electric machine and it emerged as grains to be swept into sacks and stored. Once, when the threshing maching broke down, MacShane was able to lend a hand repairing it. It was a simple enough job, just a couple of new screws and a bit of rewiring, but they were pathetically grateful.

Gradually, very gradually, he became one of them. The children stopped following him. The girls stopped pointing to his big feet or the hairs on his chest. It was true that everyone referred to him as the American peasant, but that apart, they treated him as one of their own.

MacShane adapted too. He found himself thinking less and less of home and Josie and Lazarowitz. He abandoned all thoughts of escape. Agent MacShane, owner of a Ford Pinto and an apartment overlooking the P and O Canal in Washington, had disappeared from the face of the earth. In his place there had been born MacShane the rice farmer – or Mister Mac as Ha called him – living somewhere in the Red River delta, rising at dawn, sleeping at sunset; bathing in the fishponds and turning brown in the sun.

Only Redneck did not mellow. In two months he did not exchange more than a dozen civil words with MacShane. Even as MacShane began to pick up the language, he never succeeded in extracting more than a grunt of recognition from Redneck. But you had to hand it to the old bastard. He alone knew MacShane's secret and he never let on to a soul. Not to his wife. Not to the local Party mafia. Not to anyone.

Then one day an event occurred which caused even Redneck to change his tune.

It happened in the last week of the harvest, on a clear, crisp day. The air was so dry that people complained that it caused their skin to crack.

Most of the rice had been cut, threshed and stored in sacks in a large cool barn opposite Redneck's house. The sacks had been weighed, counted and the results duly noted in the ledger of the co-operative's book-keeper, a small bald, bespectacled man who had been a quartermaster at Dien Bien Phu.

It only remained for an official to come from Haiphong to supervise the purchase of the State's share of the harvest. The remainder would be divided out according to a complicated system of workpoints. Even MacShane had been awarded workpoints. It was a record harvest and now that it was almost over preparations were in hand for a modest celebration.

One evening, just after dark, Redneck slipped out for a stroll around his domain. He was smoking, as he always did after the evening meal. MacShane saw him go and a few minutes later slipped out to use the shit-hole at the end of the garden. He always crapped under cover of darkness because in daytime you never knew who you might run into.

On his way back he was rounding the corner of the house when he saw a shadowy figure checking the padlock on the door of the grain silo. It was Redneck, completing his tour of inspection. You could tell it was Redneck by the glow of his cigarette. The rules said no smoking near the grain store but in the Great Victory people's co-op Redneck was the rules.

MacShane waited in the shadows for Redneck to go indoors. He watched the glow of the cigarette moving through the darkness towards Redneck's front door. Suddenly it disappeared. Redneck had put out his cigarette. Or chucked it away . . .

He disappeared indoors. MacShane could hear him moving about. There was a mighty clearing of the throat followed by a stomach-turning expectoration. With that the sound of movement ceased. Redneck's bedroom was on the opposite side of the entrance hall from MacShane's, so it was an easy matter to tiptoe past without being heard. MacShane had just reached the door when something bright caught his eye. It was flame. Small at first, but growing rapidly larger. It was coming from about the place where Redneck had discarded his cigarette. The flame was spreading rapidly. It had already engulfed a pile of empty sacks and was now consuming sheaves of corn stacked against the silo in which was stored the product of six months' of hard labour. In a few minutes the lot would go up.

'Before taking action evaluate all possible alternatives with particular regard to the consequences in each case.' That was what they had drummed into the kids at Camp Peary. That was what all handbooks said. That was what Lazarowitz used to say over and over again. Evaluate. Evaluate. Evaluate.

Had MacShane stopped to evaluate, he might not have acted as he did. He might instead have reflected that he was the only witness to what had happened. That in the cold light of day a burned-out grain store might be considered the work of a CIA saboteur rather than the Party Secretary's stray cigarette butt. Particularly if there just happened to be a CIA agent on the premises and he happened to have been strolling from the back of the shit-house in pitch dark at the very moment the fire ignited. On paper MacShane's story did not look good. It would have had what Lazarowitz called 'negative impact'. Any experienced analyst would have concluded that MacShane's best course of action was to tiptoe back to bed, hope that no one had seen him, and let the fire do its worst.

But at the time none of this occurred to MacShane. If he thought of anything, it was the rice. All those weeks in the fields. All that sweat. All that rain. All that sun. All those kids who worked so hard and so long for so little. And it wasn't only their rice. It was *his* rice too.

So he did what any decent human being would have done in similar circumstances. He started hollering. Since he didn't know what fire was in Vietnamese he made do with the English. And just in case anyone hadn't got the message he grabbed a saucepan from Mrs Redneck's kitchen and banged it hard against the bedroom door and then he ran around every other house in the compound and did likewise.

Redneck was on the scene within half a minute, his trousers undone and his shirt half on. Within five minutes everyone was awake and Redneck had them organised in a line passing buckets to and from the well. Within fifteen minutes the fire was out. Losses amounted to a pile of empty sacks and about two dozen sheaves of grain. The woodwork on the grain silo was badly charred. Another few minutes and the whole lot would have gone up. And the electric grain thresher would have gone with it. As it happened, the machine escaped undamaged. It was parked not five feet from where the fire had been halted.

Old Redneck looked pale as the snows on Mount Whitney. He knew what had happened all right. And he knew that MacShane knew too. Only then did it dawn on MacShane that his situation was not good. If Redneck wanted to set him up this was his chance.

For ten minutes Redneck reflected on the possibilities. He paced up and down outside the silo, pausing now and then to poke at the ashes with a bamboo carrying-pole. Then someone slapped MacShane on the back. Someone else shook his hand. Finally Redneck came over. From his expression it was impossible to tell if the news was good or bad. But when he got there he embraced MacShane like a long-lost brother. Old Redneck was a bastard, but he wasn't that big a bastard.

From that day on MacShane was a people's hero. The Party committee presented him with a little scroll in red and black script, like the ones Redneck had on the walls of his living room. Ha translated. It said: 'The citizens of Great Victory people's co-operative record warm appreciation to their good friend MACSHEEN –' that was how they spelled his name – 'for saving rice in Number One Grain Store from destruction by fire.' It was signed by all the officers of the co-op, including Redneck. The co-op carpenter had made a frame for it and the scroll was handed over by Redneck at a little ceremony held one evening on the open space near the scene of the fire. Redneck made the presentation. He even made a little speech, which showed him to possess reserves of grace and charm that had not hitherto been visible to the naked eye. MacShane responded with a few words of Vietnamese in which he had been carefully coached by Ha. Everyone applauded and MacShane's health was toasted in rice wine. Life was looking up.

Chapter Twenty-Three

By November, blue sky had given way to thick grey cloud, and with it came a fine rain whipped up by strong gusts of wind from the east. It was a different kind of damp from the humidity of the summer: a cold, miserable damp which seeped in everywhere. The farmers began to go about wearing several layers of clothes. Some looked as though they were wearing all the clothes they possessed. They walked with their bodies arched forward against the wind, teeth chattering.

MacShane had not come prepared for winter. He had arrived in Saigon with only a lightweight sports jacket and a safari jacket. Mrs Redneck took pity on him and rummaged around in a cupboard until she found an old army pullover that belonged to one of her sons. She even darned the holes in the sleeves. Ha offered him her scarf, but it was all that she had, and in any case it was no protection from the damp.

One day Ha suggested they go into Haiphong to buy some winter clothes for MacShane. It was, she said, only about ten miles and they could catch a bus from the main road. Redneck was dubious when the proposition was put to him. Hanoi had instructed that MacShane was not to leave the co-op. Redneck was responsible and if anything went wrong there would be trouble. Ha argued, but in vain. Redneck was adamant. If it was up to him there would be no problem, but he could not risk upsetting Hanoi.

In the end, Ha went alone. She took with her fifty dollars that MacShane pressed upon her, insisting that she buy a coat for herself as well. At first she had refused to accept the money, taking it only after MacShane had pointed out that –

at the official rate of exchange – he earned in one hour what she earned in a month. Ha was taken aback by this information. At first she would not believe him, but he sat down with a pen and paper and worked it out for her. She sat shaking her head. 'My country is so poor,' she kept saying, and was only partly reassured when MacShane said that there were other things in life beside dollars.

Ha was gone all day and when she returned she had bought two Soviet-made anoraks. They were the height of luxury, with zips that did up to the chin and lined with rabbit fur. Such things were unheard of in state department stores and Ha whispered that they had fallen off the back of a visiting Russian freighter.

In their brand new anoraks Ha and MacShane were the envy of the local youth, and rumours began to circulate that she was teaching him more than Vietnamese. Actually, there was nothing in this. Not to begin with, anyway. In public they were careful. When they walked together their hands never touched. In conversation she would never tap him affectionately on the forearm as he noticed she often did with other friends.

When they were alone she would sometimes touch his hand, but lightly, almost accidentally. Once he kissed her on the cheek. She had blushed and said nothing. A few days later he put his arm around her as they sat cross-legged on the floor of her small room. She did not pull away, at least not immediately.

A week later he was walking her home along the dyke. It was dark and there was no moon. Suddenly he seized her shoulders and kissed her full on the lips. To his surprise she offered no resistance. Instead she held his embrace until they were disturbed by the sound of far-off voices. Two men on bicycles were coming towards them. When they had passed MacShane made to embrace her again, but this time she pulled away.

'Not here, it is not safe.'

'Where?'

It was clearly a matter to which she had given thought for she replied without hesitation, 'The church.'

*　*　*

Once Ha had made up her mind she went about the preparations methodically, almost clinically.

'We will need two quilts. One for the ground and one to cover us.'

'What about the key?'

'I have it.' She held up a short, flat key, the sort used for padlocks. 'I borrowed it from the old man who looks after the church. I told him I want to pray in secret.'

'You are a Catholic?'

'I was.'

'And you are not afraid of making love in a church?'

'Why should I be? God has taken everything from me. My father, mother, two brothers and my fiancé. I feel he owes me this favour.'

They made their way there separately one evening after dark. Ha went first with the quilts: her own and one she had borrowed from a teacher at her school, saying that she had spilled water on hers.

MacShane arrived five minutes later. He circled the church once to make sure they were not being followed – Company training still had its uses. The padlock was open. The door creaked as he opened it, but there was no one to hear except the frogs in the rice fields. He pulled the door closed behind him. There was a bolt and he slid it shut.

She was waiting beneath the statue of Jesus with the bleeding heart. At first he could not see her, but when his eyes adjusted to the dark he saw that she had made a bed from the quilts and was sitting upright between them. Her clothes were in a neat pile by the bed.

He leaned forward in the dark and kissed her. As he moved close the back of his hand grazed her small breast.

'You are not afraid?' he said.

'No. Are you?'

'If you are not afraid, then nor am I.'

It was only when he held her hand he realised that the ring had been moved to another finger.

They did not hurry. They lay together in silence for maybe

fifteen minutes, her small warm body half on his. Once they were disturbed by a sound in the roof, but it was only bats and the silence soon returned.

He thought it would be difficult to begin with, but he was wrong. Ha made the first move. She began by exploring his face with the tips of her fingers. She moved very gently, scarcely touching him. Ears, eyelids, nose, the stubble on his chin, the hair on his chest and so on down to the tips of his toes. She then repeated the exercise, this time with her lips.

He then did the same for her. First with his fingertips, then with his lips.

When she was ready she took his hand and guided it to the exact place. She stayed with him until she was certain he understood what she wanted and then began to move to and fro very gently on his fingertips. After a time she cried out in Vietnamese and gripped him tightly. A tear seeped out from a closed eyelid and rolled down her cheek. Whether it was for him or for her lost love, MacShane could not tell.

When his turn came he entered her carefully. She arched her back to make it easier. He did it without any of the exertion that he normally put into lovemaking and it was better than anything he could ever remember. When it was over he conceded what he had never before conceded to any woman for fear of admitting a weakness. That he loved her.

Afterwards, when they lay still again, he said: 'I am not the first.'

'No. Phuong was the first.'

'Your fiancé?'

'Yes.'

A gust of wind rattled the door and for a moment they froze. A mouse, or perhaps it was a rat, scampered along the aisle and disappeared beneath the altar.

'My mother said that we should wait until we were married. Phuong wanted to wait, too. He was sure that the war would soon be over and that we would be together. He wanted to be a music teacher. He played beautiful music. Piano, violin, flute. Sometimes in the summer he would take his flute and we would sit by the West lake and he would play for me.

They lay on their backs staring up into the gloom, not touching except that he held her hand lightly. The hand with the ring.

'I had a big argument with my mother. At first she was angry. She said I was a . . . how do you say?'

'A whore?'

'Yes. She said I was a whore. Later she apologised. She said I must do what I think is right. She even gave us her room when Phuong come home. One week later the bombers came and they were both gone.'

From then on they became regular churchgoers. Ha always chose the day. She had carefully calculated when it was safe. She kept track of her safe days in a little home-made calendar which she stored with her precious photographs in the envelope under the matting on her bed.

The routine was always the same. Ha went first with the quilts. MacShane followed five minutes later, each time circling the church to make sure he was not followed. Ha would be waiting in the darkness. Always in the same place, under the Jesus statue, her clothes neatly folded by the bed.

After making love they would lie side by side and talk. Once she asked him, 'Who was Josie?'

MacShane was surprised to hear Josie mentioned again after so long, but he knew at once what had prompted the question. He had loaned Ha the Chomsky book and had forgotten about the inscription on the inside cover.

'Josie was a girl I once knew in America.'

'Why does she say you are insensitive?'

'Because I was.'

'Did you love her?'

'Yes.'

'Did she love you?'

'I guess she did at one time.'

'Why didn't you marry her?'

'Because I was a fool.'

*   *   *

One evening as they lay together she said, 'I think that you will soon go home.' It was the first time either of them had mentioned the possibility.

MacShane went rigid. 'No.'

'They will come for you soon. I know they will.'

'This is my home now.'

'No. America is your home. Soon you will go back.' She seemed so certain. Had she overheard something? Had Redneck said something?

'How do you know?'

'I just know. Because I have been born under a bad star everything I have loved is taken away.'

He leaned over and kissed her eyelids. They were quite dry. 'I have no tears,' she said. 'It is too late for tears.'

'We could get married.'

'The Party will not allow it.'

'What's it got to do with the Party?'

'Everything has to do with the Party. They talk a lot about the people, but the Party does not trust the people.'

'You could come to America.'

'It is not allowed. Besides, Vietnam is my country.'

'I will not leave without you.'

She kissed him lightly on the cheek. 'When the time comes, you will go.'

Chapter Twenty-Four

They came for him on a grey day in January. Minh came in the same jeep driven by the same *bo doi*. MacShane was helping to repair one of the diesel pumps when he heard the engine, and he knew at once that this was the day.

The jeep bumped to a halt outside Redneck's house. Children swarmed round it, jumping for joy. MacShane was waiting, his hands stained with oil, wearing the Russian anorak that Ha had bought in Haiphong.

Minh shook his hand vigorously. 'At last, at last,' he said. 'I have good news. A man has come from America. He is in Hanoi. I must take you to see him. Maybe you go home now.' Then, seeing that MacShane was less than overjoyed, Minh took a step backwards. 'What's the matter. You don't want to go home?'

MacShane wanted to say that this was the most awful day of his life. He wanted to tell Minh about Ha. To say that he loved her and would not go anywhere without her and that, if necessary, he would remain a rice farmer in the Red River delta for the rest of his days. But Ha had forbidden him. They had been over the ground many times in the last few weeks, but she was adamant. 'Please, do not tell them about us, otherwise they will make trouble for me after you have gone. When they come, you must go with them. I will understand.' And all the while she had been shaking and murmuring, 'I have been born under a bad star.'

So MacShane swallowed hard and told Minh that he was really very happy. It would take a little time to get used to the sudden change in his fortunes but he would soon be his old self again. Inside he was sick with sorrow.

Minh said they should leave at once. MacShane should bring everything, because he would not be coming back. They went to Redneck's house. Minh and the *bo doi* driver came, too. Mrs Redneck heated a pan of water for MacShane to wash his hands, and she made tea for Minh and the *bo doi*. They sat drinking while MacShane went to his small room to gather up his possessions.

Packing was simple. Most of his clothes were still in the suitcase. He changed out of the black pyjamas and into his best trousers and a clean shirt. He took the typewriter from under the bed – the Air Vietnam baggage label was still on the handle. He looked round the room. It was bare except for the certificate they had given him for saving the grain store. At Redneck's suggestion he had banged a nail into the wall above his bed and hung it there. He took it down and put it in the suitcase, on top of the black pyjamas. He put the suitcase on the bed and closed the lid. He had to press with all his weight before he could do up the straps. He took the pullover loaned him by Mrs Redneck and went into the main room, suitcase in one hand, typewriter in the other, and pullover on his arm.

By now Redneck had arrived and was sitting talking to Minh. They were settling some kind of account. Minh had a thick wad of dong and was counting off the notes. Mrs Redneck was there too. She seemed sad to see him go. MacShane offered her the pullover but she insisted he keep it. MacShane thanked her for her hospitality. He meant every word. She had treated him as a son from the day he had arrived.

With rather less sincerity, MacShane thanked Redneck for making possible his stay at the Great Victory co-operative. He said he had learned a lot during his stay. That much, at least, was true.

Redneck looked suitably modest and said, any time, or words to that effect. He slapped MacShane on the back and shook his hand warmly. To look at Redneck as he clasped MacShane's hand, you might have thought he was saying farewell to a lifelong comrade in arms. You had to hand it to old Redneck, he had style.

*　　*　　*

MacShane said he had other farewells to make. Minh looked at his watch and said there was not much time. MacShane said it would not take long. Outside there was a light drizzle. The rain ran down his face as he jogged along the dyke, splashing through the puddles and sliding in the mud.

When he came within sight of the school he paused to catch his breath and to wipe the rain from his face with his sleeve. Then he walked to the door of Ha's classroom. Ha knew at once why he had come. She had rehearsed this moment in her mind many times. She told the children she would be away for a few minutes. They were to learn one of Uncle Ho's poems and when she came back she would test them.

MacShane waited outside until she was ready.

'They are here?' was all she said when she reached him.

'Yes, they are here.'

Without another word she crossed the school yard and hurried down the narrow track that led to her house. She was wearing the red butterfly hair clasp as she had when MacShane had first set eyes upon her.

He walked a short distance behind her, as he did when they were going to the church. When they reached her house she went inside and closed the shutters on the window overlooking her small courtyard. The flowers on the bougainvillaea had all gone.

MacShane followed her inside. She closed the door behind him. For a moment they stared at each other without speaking, then she threw her arms around him and clung desperately. He buried his head in her hair and once tried to kiss her, but she would not turn her head. 'No,' she whispered, 'it is too late for that.'

'I will write,' he said.

'No.' She relinquished her grip and stepped back almost smiling. 'It is not good for Vietnamese girl to receive letters from a CIA agent.'

'You knew.'

'Yes, I knew.'

With that she unfastened the shutter and then, reaching

down to her bookshelf, she picked up the Chomsky book and handed it to him.

'Keep it,' he said, but she insisted.

'It is yours, please take it.' He took the book and put in the pocket of his anorak.

They went outside again. The sky was as grey as ever and a light drizzle was still falling. He tried again to kiss her, but she pushed him away. She was perfectly in control. She held out her hand to him and smiled. 'Goodbye, dear Mr Mac.'

'Goodbye, dear Miss Ha.' He tried to return her smile but the corners of his mouth were quivering.

Then she turned and walked away in the direction of the school. He stood and watched her go, hoping she would look round, but she did not.

As he ran back along the dyke, he could hear the children singing.

Minh was waiting by the jeep. MacShane's suitcase and the typewriter had been loaded. A small crowd gathered to see him go. Redneck made a short speech. On behalf of the people of the Great Victory people's co-op, he wished MacShane well. He hoped that when MacShane went back to America he would tell the American people that the rice farmers of Vietnam bore them no hatred. They knew that Americans were peace-loving people and that only the American government wanted war. He said he hoped that MacShane would come back to visit them again some day. MacShane thanked them for looking after him, and hoped that there would never again be war between America and Vietnam. He also said he hoped to come back and visit them one day, but even as he spoke he knew it could never be. When he had finished, they applauded. He then shook hands with everyone and clambered into the back of the jeep.

They stood waving as the jeep bumped away down the track, and the children gave chase; but the jeep quickly outpaced them and soon they had faded back into the Vietnamese countryside. He watched until they had disappeared.

*　　*　　*

They hardly spoke on the journey back to Hanoi. Minh tried to make conversation, but MacShane replied only in monosyllables. Minh apologised for staying away for so long. He had tried to persuade the authorities in Hanoi to let him visit but they had refused. Not to worry, said MacShane. It had worked out okay.

They reached Hanoi in less than two hours. The driver hooted all the way. Several times he had to swerve, narrowly missing bullock carts piled with stones or manure. Once he stopped to swear at a cyclist.

As they were inching across the Long Bien bridge, MacShane remembered the Chomsky book in his pocket. For some reason he took it out and opened the cover. There was the inscription from Josie: *'To the most insensitive man I ever met.'* Underneath was a new message in large, childish handwriting. It said: *'THE HUMAN BEING IS EVERGREEN'* and was signed simply, 'HA'.

Chapter Twenty-Five

They came down from the bridge near the place on the dyke where Minh's sister and her friends had died. The spot where the bomb had fallen was still marked by an indentation and the stone with the three names crudely carved. The beer bottle was there too. Someone had placed a sprig of apricot blossom in its neck. Minh glanced at it as they passed, but said nothing.

As far as MacShane could tell they were heading for the city centre. They passed the central market where Ha had been shopping on that awful day three years ago when the bombers came to take away her family. Here and there you could still see the tiny air-raid shelters like the one in which she must have taken refuge. Mostly they had been filled in and small trees planted, concrete covers discarded nearby.

The *bo doi* driver was still hooting furiously, but the cyclists ignored him. The cyclists pedalled into the rain with heads down and shoulders hunched. Some covered themselves with sheets of plastic which they held in place with one hand while steering with the other.

They came to the lake with the island temple and passed round the eastern side, pausing only to let a tram pass. MacShane recognised the National Bank and the post office with its huge picture of Uncle Ho.

'Where are we going?'

'You'll see.'

At first MacShane thought they were heading for the hotel. A snapshot of Pierre, the hero from the Red Cross, flashed through his mind. It would be very satisfying to run into Pierre again.

They turned away before they reached the hotel. Down a street MacShane did not recognise. Not at first, anyway. Not until they came to the place where he had climbed over the wall on the night of his escape.

The jeep turned left into a compound. The gates were open and they drove without stopping. They came to a halt in front of a small colonial-type house with white walls and green shutters. They were back in Plantation Gardens and there, standing in the porch, waiting to greet them, was Major Mau.

Major Mau looked smarter than MacShane had ever seen him. His uniform was creased in the right places. The red stars on his collar positively gleamed. On his feet he wore, not rubber sandals, but black leather shoes. It was the first time that MacShane had seen the major in shoes.

'Ah, Mr MacShane.' The major was beaming from ear to ear.

'Major Mau.'

'*Colonel* Mau, actually. I have been, how do you say . . .?'

'Promoted?'

'Precisely.' He shook hands as warmly as if MacShane himself had been responsible for the improvement in his fortunes.

'Congratulations, *Colonel*.'

Colonel Mau made a little gesture with the palms of his hands as if to say he was quite unworthy of preferment, but he would cope. He forbore to mention that his promotion might have come six months earlier, but for MacShane's little escapade.

'You have a visitor, Mr MacShane. From America.' Colonel Mau gestured towards the doorway of the little house. From inside came the sound of coughing. A prolonged, uncontrolled fit of coughing which started in the chest and culminated in a series of fearsome noises from the back of the throat. He knew at once it was Lazarowitz.

Lazarowitz was in the room where MacShane had met the Professor. He was sitting exactly where the Professor had sat, at the same unpolished mahogany table, in front of the same window which looked out into the compound where the *bo doi* played

211

basketball. Lazarowitz looked up when MacShane came in, but he did not get to his feet.

'Sit down, MacShane.' It was just like one of those interviews in the basement office at Langley. No handshake, no smile, not so much as a 'good morning'. As though MacShane had never been away.

MacShane sat on one of the dining chairs. The stuffing still protruded through the tears in the leather.

'I've come to bail you out, MacShane.'

'Supposing I don't want to be bailed out?'

Lazarowitz looked as though he had been hit square in the face with a baseball bat. He had travelled halfway round the world to rescue this creep and it had not for one moment occurred to him that he would be received with anything less than effusive gratitude.

'What's that supposed to mean?'

'Exactly what I said.'

'Something the matter with you, MacShane? Have these gooks been brain-washing you?' For a fraction of a second there was something resembling concern in his voice.

'I may have been brain-washed, but not by the gooks.'

'Don't get smart with me, MacShane. I've come to get you out of this dump and I ain't leaving without you.'

'I didn't know you cared.' MacShane reached in his back pocket for the telex. Without a word he unfolded it and spread it out on the table. Lazarowitz read it in silence: AGENT MACSHANE STAYING CARAVELLE HOTEL UNDER JOURNALIST COVER STOP OPERATION TERMINATED STOP PLEASE EVACUATE SOONEST STOP. Lazarowitz stared blankly at the telex. He read it once. He read it twice. He read it three times. Then he took a drag on his cigarette. He was smoking a Stuyvesant, as he always did.

'Where the shit did you get this?'

'Does it matter?' MacShane reached over and recovered the telex before Lazarowitz had time to think about disposing of it. He folded the paper carefully and returned it to his back pocket.

Lazarowitz puffed on his Stuyvesant. When he spoke again

there was an air of humility in his voice. At least, it was as close as MacShane had ever heard Lazarowitz come to humility. 'Listen, MacShane, it wasn't my fault.'

'The telex has your name on the bottom.'

'But the orders came from upstairs. They wanted everyone out. Everyone. You included.'

'They didn't know I was here.'

'*Everyone*. That's what the memo said. Everyone. It was top level. From the President himself. He wanted everyone out. Those were my orders.'

'Since when have you obeyed orders, Lazarowitz?'

'It wasn't a question of obeying.' His voice had hardened now. 'It was a question of protecting our position.'

'Whose position? Yours or mine?'

'The Company's. Come off it, MacShane, there were other operations beside yours.'

There was no point in arguing. There would be time enough for that later. Right now, there was only one question to resolve, and that was whether MacShane was going or staying. He had gone over the options on his way to Hanoi. He could ask for asylum. Say that he had seen the light and that he just wanted to be a rice farmer for the rest of his days. The chances were they would kick him out anyway. They might let him stay for a few more months, but they were unlikely to let him go back to the Great Victory co-op. In which case his chances of seeing Ha again were just as slim. And what was the point of staying, if he couldn't be with Ha?

If he stayed, of course, he would be branded a traitor back home. His back pay would be confiscated. And if he ever went back, he might even have to face trial. At the very least he could never find a decent job. As things stood at the moment, he was hero material. The last prisoner of the war. Ten months in a communist jail.

The line between heroism and treachery was wafer-thin. MacShane had no desire to be a hero but he sure as hell did not want to be a traitor. He knew there was no choice. He had to go.

*   *   *

213

Lazarowitz was soon himself again. Any trace of apology in his voice disappeared. He raised his arm, drew back the cuff of his shirt and looked at his watch. 'Listen, MacShane, and listen good. There is a plane leaving for Bangkok in a little over two hours and, whether you like it or not, you and I will be on it.'

Chapter Twenty-Six

The plane was a Thai Airways DC10. It was the flight on which Lazarowitz had arrived that morning. There were not many passengers: a handful of diplomats, a couple of United Nations officials and half-a-dozen Swedish aid workers heading for the bright lights of Bangkok.

Minh and Colonel Mau came with them to the airport. Minh rode with MacShane and Lazarowitz in a battered old Volga. The Colonel bumped along behind in the jeep. 'Today,' said Minh, 'Colonel Mau is very happy. His brother is coming from Saigon. First time he has seen his brother for twenty years.'

'Colonel Mau has a brother in Saigon?'

'Colonel Mau has many brothers. His family very big. He has brothers everywhere.'

Minh was in front, next to the driver. Lazarowitz never once acknowledged Minh's existence. He just sat in the back, coughing and cursing the climate. 'Can't wait to get back to civilisation,' he kept muttering between spasms.

Noi Bai Airport was still the same collection of prefabricated huts with whited-out windows. As before there were many forms to be filled in. They were on the same glossy brown recycled paper. The same small, serious men in olive-green uniforms stood watching them complete the bureaucracy. Lazarowitz cursed loudly throughout.

An Iluyshin from Saigon landed and emitted a long crocodile of passengers laden with television sets, live chickens and Dunhill cigarettes. Two planes at once was a big deal at Noi Bai and the system was stretched to breaking point.

215

They waited while the Saigon passengers were processed. There was no waiting room, so they stood to one side of the wooden hut impartially observing the chaos. Around them a dozen small reunifications were taking place amid a welter of tears, laughter and long embraces. Lazarowitz was puffing a Stuyvesant and asking loudly, 'How in hell did we let ourselves be licked by a bunch of half-assed gooks who can't even handle two flights a day?' Dulles, he added, took two flights a minute.

MacShane's attention was caught by a commotion over by the customs desk. Colonel Mau was being reunited with his long-lost brother. There was much back-slapping and embracing. MacShane thought he glimpsed tears in the colonel's eyes. The brother had his back to MacShane. He was older than Colonel Mau and very thin. There was a girl too. About fifteen years old, with a high forehead and features as delicate as a painted egg-shell.

It was the girl he recognised first. She was from the coffee shop on Nguyen Hue. Only when the embracing and the back-slapping subsided and the man half-turned towards him did MacShane recognise Colonel Mau's brother. It was Mr Chan.

He was as thin as ever. His grey Zapata moustache had been trimmed. Instead of the Levi jeans and the technicolour shirt he wore a smart tunic buttoned to the collar, of the sort favoured by high officials. The jacket and trousers were neatly pressed. Somehow the tunic looked out of place on that spindly frame, but it was Mr Chan all right.

He recognised MacShane immediately and, if he was surprised, he did not show it. He approached through the throng. One arm was threaded through a string bag, inside of which was a bottle of Johnnie Walker whisky and a carton of American cigarettes.

'Mr, er, Jones,' he said, extending a thin hand.

'Mr Chan.'

Colonel Mau and the girl followed a pace or two behind. '*Bonjour, Monsieur*,' she said with a small curtsy.

Mr Chan's face was radiant. 'I believe you have met my brother.' He indicated Colonel Mau with a gracious sweep of his hand.

'Yes. We've met.'

'He is my Moscow brother. You remember I told you I have five brothers.'

'I remember.'

'Today is the happiest day of my life. Tonight in Hanoi I will be reunited with all my brothers for the first time in twenty years. My Paris brother, my Moscow brother, my Peking brother and my Shanghai brother. They are all here in Hanoi. Tonight there will be much feasting and, how do you say . . . ?' He indicated the bottle of Johnnie Walker in the string bag at his elbow.

'Toasting.'

'Yes, toasting.' His face was still wreathed in a gentle smile. 'We shall drink to peace, and after that, who knows? We may even drink to our friends in America,' he added, with a wary glance at Colonel Mau.

The Colonel drifted away to organise the transfer of Mr Chan's luggage to the jeep outside. When he was out of ear-shot MacShane said quietly, 'You told them about me?'

Mr Chan seemed surprised by the naivety of the question. 'Of course I told them. I waited three days and then I told them. I warned you to go, but you did not take my advice.' He shook his head sadly. The smile had temporarily deserted his face.

'And the priest?' There was no reason why Mr Chan should know about the priest but, there again, he just might.

'He is a very unlucky man, that priest. First he is jailed in the North. Then in the South and now . . .'

'Will they shoot him?'

'No. They have sent him to the Cambodian border. To dig up mine-fields. A very unlucky man.' He shook his head again.

'And you?'

'Me?' Mr Chan's face lit up again. 'I will be all right. I have my family. My daughter – ' he indicated Daughter Number

217

Six, who blushed deeply – 'she will have a good marriage. To a high cadre. I shall make arrangements in Hanoi. She is very beautiful, don't you agree?'

The girl blushed again and smiled uneasily. 'Besides – ' he leaned forward and spoke quietly so that only MacShane could hear – 'I have already taken precautions.'

'Precautions?'

'Yes,' he whispered. 'Already I have one son in America. In Boston. You may know this place. A daughter in Paris and another in Hong Kong.'

'You are very clever, Mr Chan.'

'Not clever, Mr, er, Jones: diplomatic.' He extended a thin hand. Daughter Number Six offered a shy curtsy; and with that he hobbled off, one hand resting lightly on the girl's shoulder, the bottle of Johnnie Walker swinging from the string bag on his arm.

'Who in the name of sweet Jesus was that?' asked Lazarowitz as soon as Mr Chan had hobbled out of earshot.

'That,' said MacShane, 'was one of your best agents.'

Minh walked with them to the aeroplane. 'What will you say about us?' he asked as he shook MacShane's hand at the foot of the aircraft steps.

'The truth.'

'What is the truth?'

'That you are a poor, brave, proud people. That you have suffered too much. That you deserve to be left in peace.'

Minh eyed him sceptically. 'Will they let you say that?'

'I don't know.'

Lazarowitz was already halfway up the aeroplane steps. MacShane followed him into the plane in silence. Through the porthole he could see Minh walking back alone across the empty expanse of concrete towards the prefabricated huts. There were no other planes in sight.

Future wars, Lazarowitz was saying, would be different. Americans would no longer get their hands dirty. In future, Americans would supply the technology and the training. Others would supply the lives. In Europe it would be the

Brits and the Germans. In South America the Brazilians and Argentinians; now *there* were guys who knew a thing or two about fighting communism. In Asia, well, Asia had always been a mess, but he guessed that before long the Japs would be in a position to take care of Free World interests in Asia. The trouble with the Japs was that they brought back too many bad memories, even for the good guys. In the long run, of course, there was always China. Lazarowitz had a hunch that China would turn out all right in the end.

MacShane wasn't listening. He had taken the Chomsky book from his pocket and was staring blankly at the inscription in Ha's childish handwriting. It was his only souvenir of her. He had no photograph. There would be no letters. Only a memory and six words on the inside cover of a book. 'Do not be sad,' she had said one evening when they lay together in the church. 'This is our fate and we cannot change it. We were born under a bad star. That is all.'

The plane was moving now. From the window, as it taxied along the runway, MacShane could see a peasant woman hoeing a row of cabbages. The woman looked up and waved as the plane passed.

The plane ascended rapidly, and circled once over the airport before being enveloped by thick grey cloud. As the cloud closed in, MacShane took a last look at the flooded rice paddies peppered with bomb craters and the little houses surrounded by bamboo and eucalyptus. Gradually the vision faded and soon it had disappeared completely beneath swirling cloud.

'I guess that just about wraps up Vietnam,' said Lazarowitz as the ground disappeared. 'Let's hope we have better luck in Nicaragua.'

THE END

THE FOURTH PROTOCOL
By FREDERICK FORSYTH

'A triumph of plot, construction and research. As good as any Forsyth since the Jackal'
The Times

THE FOURTH PROTOCOL is the story of a plan, dangerous beyond belief, to change the face of British society for ever.

Plan Aurora, hatched in a remote dacha in the forest outside Moscow, and initiated with relentless brilliance and skill, is a plan that in its madness – and spine-chilling ingenuity – breaches the ultra-secret Fourth Protocol and turns the fears that shaped it into a living nightmare.

A crack soviet agent, placed under cover in a quiet English country town, begins to assemble a jigsaw of devastation. Working blind against the most urgent of deadlines, and against treachery and lethal power games in his own organisation, M15 investigator John Preston leads an operation to prevent the act of murderous devastation aimed at tumbling Britain into revolution.

THE FOURTH PROTOCOL is outstanding – for sheer excitement, for marvellous storytelling – a mighty entertainment and a superlative adventure.

'Forsyth's best book so far'
Washington Post

0 552 12569 5

CORGI BOOKS

KEN FOLLETT

LIE DOWN WITH LIONS

A haunted pair flee across ice-shrouded mountains in Ken Follett's thrilling new novel about deadly intrigue and deadlier love in a small, embattled country.

A young Englishwoman, a French doctor, and a roving American each has private reasons for arriving in Afghanistan where mountain-bred natives fight a fierce guerilla war against the Russian invaders. At the centre of the battle is an elusive leader named Masud – the guerillas must protect him, the Russians must kill him.

As Masud sweeps from his hidden eyrie, bringing down death for the enemy below in the Valley of the Five Lions, treachery seeks its prey. A brave and beautiful woman finds herself trapped between two spies – one is the man she loves, the other is her husband. Follett builds the menacing tension to the breaking point, leading to a confrontation that echoes all our nightmares.

'A true master of espionage fiction'
NEW YORK TIMES

'A master of the romantic thriller'
DAILY TELEGRAPH

'A fast-moving adventure thriller'
IRISH TIMES

'Never a dull phrase'
POLICE

'Highly readable . . . rich in detail and full of surprises'
WASHINGTON POST

'Genuine excitement'
SUNDAY TIMES

'Action and throbs galore'
THE OBSERVER

0 552 12550 4

CORGI BOOKS

EDWARD TOPOL & FRIDRIKH NEZNANSKY

The ultimate Soviet thriller

'Fast moving and exciting . . . better than *Gorky Park*'
Good Book Guide

Much of this story is factually accurate – the names, the people and the places . . . the death of Brezhnev's brother-in-law was widely reported in the West. 'Death after long illness' said *Pravda* . . . although Andropov told Brezhnev it was suicide. Just *suppose* it was murder . . .

'Meaty entertainment'
Sunday Times

'Gripping and informative fiction that has an unexpected and chilling end'
Yorkshire Post

'Much more fun than *Gorky Park*'
The Spectator

0 552 12307 2

CORGI BOOKS

THE SALAMANDRA GLASS

A. W. MYKEL

Coming soon from Corgi . . .

The heart-stopping novel of international suspense and intrigue by the author of *The Windchime Legacy*.

Michael Gladieux thought he'd finished with The Group, a highly specialised unit he'd served with in Vietnam . . . until his father is murdered, his body found with a note accusing him of Nazi collaboration during the war and a glass pendant anchored to his heart with a shiny steel spike.

Who was Michael's father? Why are Washington and The Group so interested? Michael's search for answers leads him on a terrifying quest – to find his father's killer. What he uncovers is far more deadly, as he becomes the one man capable of stopping the twisted legacy of THE SALAMANDRA GLASS

Rivals Ludlum at his best!

0 552 12417 6

CORGI BOOKS

A SELECTED LIST OF FINE TITLES
AVAILABLE FROM CORGI BOOKS

The prices shown below were correct at the time of going to press. However Transworld Publishers reserve the right to show new retail prices on covers which may differ from those previously advertised in the text or elsewhere.

☐	12504 0	**THE SMOKE**	*Tom Barling*	£2.95
☐	12639 X	**ONE POLICE PLAZA (50)**	*William J. Caunitz*	£2.50
☐	12610 1	**ONE WINGS OF EAGLES**	*Ken Follett*	£3.50
☐	12180 0	**THE MAN FROM ST. PETERSBURG**	*Ken Follett*	£2.95
☐	11810 9	**THE KEY TO REBECCA**	*Ken Follett*	£2.95
☐	12550 4	**LIE DOWN WITH LIONS**	*Ken Follett*	£2.95
☐	12569 5	**THE FOURTH PROTOCOL**	*Frederick Forsyth*	£2.95
☐	12140 1	**NO COMEBACKS**	*Frederick Forsyth*	£2.95
☐	11500 2	**THE DEVIL'S ALTERNATIVE**	*Frederick Forsyth*	£2.95
☐	10244 X	**THE SHEPHERD**	*Frederick Forsyth*	£1.95
☐	10050 1	**THE DOGS OF WAR**	*Frederick Forsyth*	£2.95
☐	09436 6	**THE ODESSA FILE**	*Frederick Forsyth*	£2.50
☐	09121 9	**THE DAY OF THE JACKAL**	*Frederick Forsyth*	£2.95
☐	12417 6	**THE SALAMANDRA GLASS**	*A.W. Mykel*	£2.50
☐	11850 8	**THE WINDCHIME LEGACY**	*A.W. Mykel*	£1.75
☐	12307 2	**RED SQUARE**	*Fridrikh Neznansky & Edward Topol*	£2.50
☐	12855 4	**FAIR AT SOKOLNIKI**	*Fridrikh Nezansky*	£2.95
☐	12541 5	**DAI-SHO**	*Marc Olden*	£2.50
☐	12357 9	**GIRI**	*Marc Olden*	£2.95
☐	12662 4	**GAIJIN**	*Marck Olden*	£2.95

All Corgi/Bantam Books are available at your bookshop or newsagent, or can be ordered from the following address:

Corgi/Bantam Books,
Cash Sales Department,
P.O. Box 11, Falmouth, Cornwall TR10 9EN

Please send a cheque or postal order (no currency) and allow 60p for postage and packing for the first book plus 25p for the second book and 15p for each additional book ordered up to a maximum charge of £1.90 in UK.

B.F.P.O. customers please allow 60p for the first book, 25p for the second book plus 15p per copy for the next 7 books, thereafter 9p per book.

Overseas customers, including Eire, please allow £1.25 for postage and packing for the first book, 75p for the second book, and 28p for each subsequent title ordered.